Angel Eyes

By the same author

The Greenway
Cast the First Stone
Bird
Fade to Grey
Final Frame
The Angel Gateway
Like Angels Falling

Angel Eyes

Jane Adams

MACMILLAN

First published 2002 by Macmillan
an imprint of Pan Macmillan Ltd
Pan Macmillan, 20 New Wharf Road, London N1 9RR
Basingstoke and Oxford
Associated companies throughout the world
www.panmacmillan.com

ISBN 0 333 90676 4

9 8 7 6 5 4 3 2 1

A CIP catalogue record for this book is available from
the British Library.

Typeset by SetSystems Ltd, Saffron Walden, Essex
Printed and bound in Great Britain by
Mackays of Chatham plc, Chatham, Kent

For my son, Peter.

And for Mark, The Man in Black.
Smile, dammit!

Prologue

It was the night of Miriam's eighteenth birthday.

Her parents had thrown a big party for her, hiring a large hall on the first floor of the local leisure centre. All along one side was a row of windows slightly angled, showing off the swimming pool below and, if you looked across, another row of windows gave a view of the night sky above and the city landscape, all tall towers and lighted windows poking up at the thin cloud.

Miri had got to the DJ before her parents and he'd played drum and bass all night with a blend of hard house and Pete Tong thrown in for good measure. Family mixed with friends by then, all of them pretty far gone. Miri's mother drunk enough to try to wind to Micky Finn and everyone having a good time.

Miri looked great that night, hair freshly cut into a shining black bob that swung around her face when she danced. All the stress and worry she'd been going through those past months might have never happened for all it showed on her face. She danced with Damien, her body close to his and her hands all over him. And he was laughing, showing off, enjoying the attentions of the birthday girl.

It was pretty late when it happened. Getting on for midnight. Miri had gone to get another drink and stopped on the way to chat. She'd lost sight of Damien.

She did not see him again until she was standing beside the windows looking down into the pool hall and what she saw froze her to the spot.

Damien stood, barefoot on the high board, balanced on his toes at the very end, the strobe catching and illuminating his face with bright white light as, just for the merest instant, he lifted his head to look across at her. Then, he seemed to snatch his gaze away, lifting his arms high above his head before tipping forward in an almost graceful dive.

'Damien!' Miriam was hammering on the glass. If she could only get him to notice her perhaps she could somehow stop him in the air, reverse the image like they do in the best cartoons and make him safe.

Just before Damien hit the water, Miri was sure she saw his body twist and his hands reach out as though he'd suddenly come to his senses and was looking for a way to save himself. But it was too late and, watching through the wall of glass, there was nothing she could do.

He hit the water and sank like a stone. Damien had never learnt to swim.

Chapter One

Armitage Estate, Mallingham

There were four of them that night and the two dogs. Martin had chosen to team with Micky, a young Italian kid with a Stallone fixation. Their dog, Beck, belonged to Winter. She was a sleek, grey, German Pointer with a freckled nose and a sweet temper if she counted you as friend and something of an attitude problem if not.

It was cold, March dampness working its way inside their clothes and a sharp wind setting the clouds rolling. Martin wondered more than once just why he'd got himself into this when he could be at home and warm. The empty streets though, they had nothing to do with the weather. No one living here went out at night if they could avoid it. The buses stopped running from the city centre after six. There was a shuttle service organized by the residents' association that did the rounds for those who worked late and, thanks to Martin and his team, the taxi firms now agreed to come into the south end of the Armitage Estate. In general though, people stayed at home and out of the way.

Martin glanced around. He and Micky had moved away from the tower blocks and into the rows of Victorian terraces left behind when the developers ran out of cash. It was ironic, Martin thought. These little houses were in far better shape than the anonymous flats and tacky prefabricated houses that were supposed to replace them.

Beside him he was aware that Micky shivered then glanced sideways to see if Martin had noticed and might get the wrong idea. Micky wore a dark woolly hat pulled down over his ears and a black padded jacket and black jeans. His outfit made his face look pale in the yellow streetlights that cast odd, chequerboard patterns on the ground. The residents' association had paid someone to fit heavy cages around the lighting units. Sure enough, it had cut down on the effects of vandalism, but now the local council refused to change any failed bulbs – something about increased unit cost if engineers had to remove the cages first . . . Sometimes, Martin thought, you just couldn't win. It was yet another job left to be taken on by the residents' association.

Tonight, Micky was carrying the radio. He touched the earpiece instinctively as the voice broke through his concentration.

'They're in position,' he told Martin, keeping his voice low in a street where every sound seemed magnified by the emptiness. 'What's our ETA?'

'Three minutes,' Martin told him, watching as Micky activated the throat mike and passed the message on.

'Pete says they have a sighting. Positive ID,' he said. His eyes widened slightly. 'Our tip-off said they're preparing the drugs. And about the kids, he says there's two of them already at the warehouse.'

Martin nodded. He quickened his pace. The dog, sensing the increased tension, pulled forward against the lead and Martin noted Micky's hand move surreptitiously to the pocket of his coat. He ignored it. Micky wasn't the only member of the residents' association who carried. Martin tried not to know too much about that side of things. As a police officer, Martin knew he was walking enough of a tightrope as it was.

At the end of the street was a railway bridge, long unused. Where the tracks had once run was now a footpath of sorts, muddy and overgrown. The residents' association was campaigning to have lights rigged along its length, but cash for the project was hard to find. There had been an experiment with CCTV a few years before, but the cameras were dead easy to avoid. Anyway, the control centre was so overloaded and far away that trouble would be long gone before anyone responded to the alert.

As it was, the old railway track had become a kind of no-man's-land. A rat run between the pitches held by the various gangs that claimed to own the Armitage Estate and the surrounding projects. It marked the outer perimeter of the watch area cleared by the residents' association. The zero-tolerance zone that Martin and others like him policed every night of the week, keeping the world at bay.

Or so they pretended to believe.

Micky pulled on a black ski mask and then led the way up onto the bridge, scrambling up the bank. The dog almost dragged Martin in his wake, panting and choking against the lead. Silently, Martin pulled her back to heel and the three of them moved together across the bridge and towards their agreed position overlooking the warehouse yard.

Martin heard Micky confirm that they were now in place and ready to move down. The other team of two men and one large dog was already positioned beside the front gate leading into the warehouse yard.

Martin tried not to think how stupid this whole thing was. They had no intelligence on how many people there were in the building – estimates varied between three and six – and they had to assume that all were armed. Equally likely, they'd find themselves storming in on a group of kids using the semi-derelict place as a squat, or burst in on one of the pros entertaining a client she'd moved from her own patch. It wouldn't be the first time.

The initial tip-off they'd been given had been vague, just that a large quantity of drugs – mostly Ecstasy – was due to be moved that night and that this time there was an extra complication. Another type of merchandise to complete the order. But the details had been fuzzy and the informant not one of the residents' association's regulars, and Martin knew from bitter experience that, had they passed it to the local police, it would have been graded no higher that a code three and left at the bottom of a long list. The local force was as undermanned as any in the city. The residents' association had agreed. This one was up to them.

'Ready?' Micky's voice disturbed his thoughts. He nodded and they started off again. They crawled slowly, feet sliding on wet mud, forced to dig their fingers deep into the bank to keep some kind of purchase. Martin ticked off seconds in his mind, knowing that they weren't shifting fast enough. The thought, kept at the back of his mind until now, that this might well all be a set-up, suddenly pushed to the fore. Instinct told him this was a bad move and he could feel the time shifting beneath his feet like the wet mud.

Then he knew that it had all gone wrong. The sudden roar of a car engine in the street beyond, the splintering crash of gates smashed to matchwood as the car crashed through and a girl screaming as the warehouse doors burst open. Lights everywhere, coming on at the back of the building. Martin felt himself trapped in sudden brightness. Without thinking he let go of the dog and dived sideways, yelling at Micky to move. He rolled and came up running. Gunshots. Micky letting off three swift rounds in the direction of the warehouse door. Bloody fool, Martin thought. Wasted shots. He was aware of Pete and Ravi storming into the yard. It seemed to have taken them for ever to respond, but Martin knew that in reality it had all been less than seconds. He saw both dogs leap forward, black shapes with snarling teeth. Heard a girl screaming again. The doors of the car were open. More shots fired. Two men in the car, three more emerging from the building. One holding the limp body of a child in his arms, the other two struggling with a young girl, whose flailing limbs cutting across the men's bodies made her a natural shield that neither Micky nor Ravi could hope to aim past.

More shots. One of the men raised his arm to fire again, but Beck had him. Mouth clamped around his wrist, teeth that would almost meet before she even thought of letting go. The man was down. Ravi getting in a lucky shot as the child, taking advantage of the dog's attack, broke free. Martin shouted at Micky to get the girl, who was running in panic with no sense of where to go, likely to be caught in the crossfire. The second girl had been dumped by her captor. She lay on the ground close to the warehouse entrance, unconscious and frighteningly pale in the light that flooded through the open door. A swift glance to his right told Martin that the driver was about to cut his losses and make his getaway. Martin heard the change in engine note as the driver slammed the car into reverse. Engine screaming as his foot went down, hitting the red line. The rear passenger door hung open, ready for the others to pile inside.

Pete had realized at the same moment that the driver and his passenger were about to get away but the rear door, wrenched backwards as the car reversed, blocked his line of attack. It was up to Martin. He threw himself forward into the mêlée of dogs and wild gunfire and pulled at the driver's door, half expecting it to be locked. It wasn't. The door flung open, helped by the momentum of the reversing car. Martin made a grab for the driver, but he was strapped in and there was little hope of pulling him free. He changed tack, reaching down and grasping at the steering wheel, pulling upwards, swinging his weight against it and being dragged off his feet by the force of the moving car. His shoulder jammed painfully between the door and window strut. The driver had one hand off the wheel, tearing at Martin's wrist and squeezing at the joint. Martin could feel his hand going numb and his fingers losing their grip. Suddenly, out of the corner of his eye, he caught a movement from the passenger. Martin found himself looking down the snub-nosed barrel of a handgun, its muzzle only inches from his face.

Chapter Two

Time seemed to freeze. Martin could not breathe, only hear his own heartbeat thudding in his chest. He had woken with nightmares that something like this would happen. That the folly of his involvement with the residents' association would end with something just like this.

There was a blur of movement off to Martin's left and a shout from Micky. It happened too quickly for Martin to take in but suddenly Beck was in the car, her body crushing the driver back into his seat and her teeth sunk deep into the gunman's hand.

Martin let go of the steering wheel and dropped to the ground, ducking down behind the open door as the gunman fired, shattering the side window. Ravi had wrenched open the other door and Tyke, his dog, leapt forward, eager to join Beck. Martin felt relief pouring through his body, meeting adrenalin in a nauseating mix that clenched his stomach, turning his insides to water. He stood up and took a step back, thrusting his hands into the deep pockets of his coat in an effort to stop them shaking. He was getting too old for this game, he thought. One day, he wouldn't be so lucky.

The three men from the warehouse were lying face down on the ground, Micky in best TV-cop-stance, arms outstretched, gun hand steadied in his cupped left palm, weapon shifting restlessly, willing one of them to move, to give him an excuse to fire, while Pete dragged their arms behind them and cuffed them tightly with nylon cable ties. Nearby Ravi had control of the other two. There was blood on the ground. Two of the men had been wounded by the dogs, but their whining complaints fell on deaf ears as the dogs continued to growl warnings that they could offer still more of the same.

Martin figured that the others had the situation well under control. Himself, he felt he'd been little more than a liability this night. He shrugged and crossed to where one of the girls huddled in the warehouse doorway, arms around her unconscious companion, eyes fixed on the scene of men and dogs and blood and pain.

She looked, thought Martin, about ten years old. Black skin, deep brown eyes and hair that had been dressed in braids. The other one, her face smudged with bruises, was white and blonde, her lips almost blue with cold. He searched his memory, combing through what he remembered of the latest missing person reports. Something had come in about three days before. Two ten-year-olds, best friends.

'It's Kathy, isn't it?' he asked, dropping to one knee beside them and speaking as gently as he knew how. The girl nodded, her braids falling across her face. Behind him, he could hear Micky calling in the local police. This time, Martin thought ruefully, it might just be graded one. There were bound to have been other calls. Even in this day and age, gunfire still rated the odd bit of public attention.

It was time to go.

'Listen to me, Kathy,' Martin said softly. 'So far, you've been really brave, really brilliant and I need you to be brave for just a minute longer. I'm going to take you back inside, where it's warm, and in a few minutes the police will be here and take you home.'

Kathy began to wail, pointing at the men.

'They can't hurt you any more,' he reassured her. 'No they won't. See, my friends have tied them up really tight. The police will be here. Listen. Can you hear it?'

Kathy nodded as a distant sound of a police siren echoed in the cold air.

Martin took the girls inside, praying that the other one was not too badly hurt, knowing that he couldn't stay around long enough to find out. He heard Micky whistling Beck to heel. Told Kathy to stay where he left her, on a makeshift bed close to the only heater in the place. One of the men had left a coat hanging over the back of a chair and he took a moment more to wrap it around both girls, searching first for anything that might have been left behind.

Outside, Micky was shifting restlessly, listening to the sirens getting closer all the time. The others had already gone, fading into the dark. Martin and Micky left the way they had come in, the climb back onto the railway line just as hard going the other way. They paused, hidden by the line of trees, long enough to see the police arrive, two cars screaming into the yard and screeching to a halt only feet away from the men still lying on the ground. They heard Kathy shouting from inside the warehouse, her voice touching on the hysterical, her panic rising to breaking point in just the few minutes that she had been left alone. Then he and Micky moved quietly away along the track, down beside the bridge and back into the empty street, Micky pausing then to peel off skin gloves and black ski mask.

'I nearly made a right cock-up of things tonight,' Martin said ruefully.

His companion shrugged. 'Yeah, but we fixed it though,' he said. 'Got those bastards real good we did.'

Martin nodded. No doubt Micky and the others would meet up later to celebrate their latest success. It was an unspoken agreement that Martin never joined them. The risk was just too high, for him, for all of them, even supposing he had wished to.

'Pete said to give you the stuff,' Micky said, pulling from inside his coat a carrier bag containing a ziplock satchel. 'I left the card.' He grinned, knowing Martin didn't really approve. They had taken to leaving business cards lately. Letting the authorities know just who was helping with their clear-up rate. Small oblongs of white pasteboard bearing the legend 'Compliments of the Residents' Association' printed in bold black letters across their face.

Martin managed a faint smile, knowing it was expected of him. 'You did well,' he agreed. 'I've got reason to be grateful.'

Micky grinned again, his expression brightened by the praise Martin had given him. He clenched his fist and thumped Martin gently on the shoulder before turning down the next street. 'See you around.'

'Sure.'

Martin watched him go, worry nagging at the back of his mind that this whole thing was getting well out of hand.

Chapter Three

Martin walked back to the desert of tower blocks that occupied centre stage on the Armitage Estate. He walked, deep in thought, half listening to the pad of Beck's feet, his own quiet footsteps. The residents' association had employed two full-time security guards for the flats, using an inner-city-development grant and regular payments from residents to keep the scheme going. It kept the vandals away from the lifts most of the time, but did nothing about old machinery, long overdue for replacement.

But today the lift was working in Winter's block. Beck yawned and stretched as they got in, ready to settle down after the night's excitement. Martin knew how she felt. Winter's flat was on the eighteenth floor, crazy when you considered that he couldn't go anywhere without his chair. But Winter had chosen to live there and Martin had learnt over the years that Winter did things his own way, and if you valued his friendship then you didn't try to argue with him.

The lift stopped with a slight jerk, settling itself two inches above the level of the floor. Gita had been waiting for them. She opened the door almost as soon as Martin knocked. Smiling quickly she took the dog's lead, Beck snuffling at her hand eager to be fed, and Martin walked through to the single living room and sat down on the sofa, leaning back with his eyes closed.

'Aren't you even going to take your coat off, or aren't you planning on stopping?'

Eyes still closed, Martin smiled, then moved to shrug himself out of his outdoor clothes. Winter was sitting at his desk, a man in his late thirties with dark, shaggy hair and vivid blue eyes. Even confined to his chair, he managed to give the impression of height and strength, his upper body still well muscled. He had a stack of old CDs piled up in front of him and an emerald-green marker pen in his hand. Martin watched as he balanced one of the CDs on his finger and began to run the pen carefully around the rim.

'What have you read now?'

Winter paused long enough to smile, the operation evidently too complex for him to manage to do both things at one time.

'Gita got me another pile of old *Hi Fi* mags,' he said. 'Some of them as early as the late eighties.' He shook his head. 'Amazing what folk throw away.' He raised an eyebrow at Martin. 'These,' he said, 'were just dumped in a skip. Real collectors' stuff.'

'And the green pen?' Martin asked him.

'Supposed to stop laser scatter.' He frowned. 'Of course, it's hard to tell, you'd have to listen to two of the same recordings back to back. Same equipment and set-up, same speaker position . . .' he shrugged. 'But I thought I'd give it a try.'

'I seem to remember,' Martin said, 'that you could buy little green plastic rings to fit around the discs. You had to fight to get the damned things on, then hope they didn't jam up in the load mechanism when they sprang off again.'

Winter laughed. 'There, you see. This may not be so crazy after all.'

Gita came through from the kitchen with a tray of coffee and set it down on the low table in front of the sofa. 'He's finally going mad,' she said to Martin. 'Brain rot. Last thing was he had me down on my hands and knees fixing copper wire to just one leg of the speaker stands. Supposed to cut down on static. I hope you've got something useful for him to do.'

Martin sat up and fished the carrier bag out from inside his coat, pulling out the ziplock and tipping the contents onto the table. Winter's face lit with interest. CD and pen were deposited on the desk and he wheeled himself forward, head cocked to one side to read the documents Martin had scattered on the table.

Martin found skin gloves in his pocket and handed pairs to Winter and to Gita. 'I've had no time to look at these yet,' he said.

'We heard the sirens. Was it serious, Martin?'

He nodded. 'It wasn't just drugs this time. We'd had a tip-off about two kids, ten-year-olds. They'd been missing three, four days. It's pure luck they'd held them this long before shipping them out.'

'You know who the buyer is?' Gita asked.

Martin shook his head. 'There's a steady demand. Kids are almost a fashion accessory this season. God, you should see some of the stuff that's come into the department these last few months.'

He paused, reached out and began to sort through the stuff on the table.

A driving licence, cash, couple of credit cards. A photograph of a woman with a small child in her arms. 'Looks like one of them is a family man,' he commented. Polaroids of the two girls, stripped naked and clinging to each other, terrified.

'These the kids?' Gita asked.

'Yes, snapshots for prospective buyers, by the look of it.'

'Which means they probably snatched the kids before they had a firm buy,' Winter hazarded. 'That's why you got lucky, why they held on to them for so long.' He shook his head, the heavy mop of dark hair shaking with a life all its own. 'They're rank amateurs, Martin, that's my guess. All the pros steal to order no matter what business they're in and they've got their supply routes well laid out. These, they're amateurs trying to break into the game.'

Martin nodded slowly. 'Maybe, though our intelligence suggests a buyer was already arranged.' He shrugged. Whatever the truth of it, it was likely that tonight would yield little in real, long-term results. Times like this and Martin had great sympathy with King Canute, trying to hold back an unstoppable tide.

He assessed what they had left, fingering through the stuff on the table.

'We've credit cards in the names of John Ashton and Clive Williams,' he said. 'Could be stolen. The driver's licence in yet another name, one Colin Wilks. And then there's the picture of the woman and child. It's worth enhancing. If she's local we might get an ID. Of course,' he shrugged, 'it's not likely we'll need it. When I get in tomorrow morning they'll have spilt their souls and sold their grandmothers and, if we're lucky, plea-bargained themselves into solitary and named the buyer. Just see if you can throw up anything we don't have or they aren't likely to admit to.'

Winter nodded, gathered up the stuff from the table and wheeled himself over to the desk. For the next five minutes, Martin sat drinking his coffee while Winter scanned the documents into his computer and set up the software to decode the ID strips on the credit cards. On screen, Martin could see the data strip exploded into a hundred thousand bitmapped fragments and watched as Winter's fingers moved the pen across the draughting tablet, manipulating images that Martin could not have begun to identify. Slowly, an image began to fill the screen, a man's face, reorganized by the computer from the fragmented data on the strip. Recently a number of the banks had begun to encode the customers' pictures into the ID strip. This time they had struck lucky.

'Is this one of them, Martin?'

'Near as I can remember, yes.'

'I'll give you a call when I've put it all together, see what I can dig up.' He turned and smiled at Martin. 'Give me a little time.'

Martin crossed to the desk and gathered everything together, placed it in an evidence bag he took from his pocket. Tomorrow morning he'd slip it into the case file and the bag would just be logged in with the rest. Martin had long ago learnt to make full use of the inefficiency of the system.

Only this time, things would not work out that way.

Chapter Four

It was a cold Sunday morning, but the sun was bright and Ray was happy to be out in the garden. It was too wet to dig but Ray had been keeping himself amused, pruning the straggly buddleia and tying in the new growth of the honeysuckle.

There had been little in this garden when Sarah Gordon had moved here the previous year. The cottage itself was tiny, set back off the main street in Peatling Magna, but the garden was enormous, reaching back more than a hundred yards into the fields behind, and Ray loved it. Technically, he had a home and garden of his own, and, technically, he loved that garden too, but mostly these days he lived with Sarah and she was content to leave him in charge when it came to things horticultural.

Ray had never fancied himself as a gardener, then his aunt had left him her cottage a couple of years before. Ray had started to restore her garden largely out of love for the old woman who had given him so much during his life and in whose later years her beloved garden had been sorely neglected. He'd discovered a skill he'd never dreamt he might possess and a satisfaction which it embarrassed him even now to admit to. These days, Ray's favourite weekend dilemma was which garden centre he should visit on a Sunday afternoon – the mornings often being spent at antique fairs, a passion of Sarah's.

When Sarah had first moved into the cottage there had been little in the garden that Ray had wanted to keep. He'd let the buddleia remain in the hope that he could do something to bring it back to life. Beyond that there had only been the philadelphus, whose wonderful perfume filled the garden the previous summer, and a hawthorn, Paul's Scarlet, an intense, unaccommodating colour that went with nothing else but which Ray loved for its sheer audacity and for the way it seemed to glow even on the dullest and most overcast of days.

It was a strange transformation for Ray Flowers – he'd never thought before of his name being appropriate. A career copper whose life had been all but destroyed when someone had set him alight. His face was still badly scarred, though good medical care had improved things a great deal and his hands, which had after the accident been almost useless, had responded to surgery and physio. Although he could still be clumsy when it came to fine tasks – like tying recalcitrant honeysuckle back to the fence – he was coping well. Most of the time these days he gave his injuries very little thought until someone else's shocked reaction served as a reminder.

It had been almost two years before, while he was first recovering from his attack, that he had met Sarah, an archivist. His relationship with Sarah had done more than anything else to change his perspective on life and encourage him to look to the future. He'd taken medical retirement from the force and set up a security company with an old friend, George Mahoney. His departure from the force had not been without its drama though. In trying to find out why he had been attacked and by whom, Ray had uncovered a network of high-level corruption linked to a local drugs ring. He had found out the hard way that it was not easy becoming a whistle-blower.

But this Sunday morning, Ray had nothing more on his mind than indulging his hobby and Sarah calling to him from the house took him by surprise.

'There's someone on the phone for you,' she shouted. 'His name's Martin Galloway. He says you used to work together.'

Ray caught himself staring rather stupidly at her. 'Galloway? Are you sure?'

Sarah awarded him one of her 'looks'. 'Shall I tell him to go away?' she asked.

'No, no, I'm just surprised,' he told her, making his way towards the house. 'I haven't talked to Martin more than a couple of times in three, four years.'

He kicked off his gardening boots and went through to the living room, belatedly realizing as he picked up the receiver that his hands were caked in mud.

Sarah raised her eyebrows eloquently and left him to it.

'Martin. What can I do for you?'

'You can let me come and see you.'

'See me? I mean, of course. When?'

'How about now? I wouldn't ask, Ray, but it's important. Very important. I need someone to talk to and you're the only one who might understand.'

'You're not making much sense, Martin.'

'I've been suspended, Ray. I'm under investigation and I'm bloody lucky not to be under arrest.'

'Arrest! You're being investigated? Martin, you've always been straight as a die.'

There was silence on the other end of the phone.

'Martin,' Ray asked quietly. 'Just what is it you're telling me?'

'This time, Ray, I'm guilty as hell,' Martin told him quietly.

Chapter Five

A quick conference with Sarah and Ray was giving Martin Galloway an invitation to Sunday lunch. She was going to be out later in the afternoon which would give them plenty of time and privacy to talk over the washing-up.

After getting off the phone, Ray found it hard to settle down to anything again.

'I can't believe what he just told me,' he said to Sarah. 'Martin was always by the book, a real idealist copper. I can't see him getting into anything underhand.'

'People change,' Sarah said. 'Ray, be careful. The guy's not called you in years and suddenly he needs help. I don't like that.'

Martin Galloway arrived just before one thirty and Ray was appalled at how ill and stressed he looked. Even Sarah seemed prepared to be more sympathetic when she set eyes on him. Martin looked grey and old and tired.

He ate lunch, though it seemed like a major effort, and he tried hard to make conversation with Sarah, asking what she did and how she and Ray got together in the first place. But it was obvious he was just marking time until he could be alone with Ray. His relief as Sarah got ready to leave was palpable.

He followed Ray through to the kitchen, helping half-heartedly as he stacked the pots and ran the water, then, leaning against the edge of the kitchen table, he began to talk. He seemed to find it easier while Ray was not looking directly at him. Each time Ray turned and glanced his way, he faltered and his mouth dried. In the end, Ray looked away and listened, busying himself with the lunchtime crockery.

'I've done something truly stupid,' he began. 'I did it with the best of intentions, Ray, you have to believe that. But it was still stupid and now I've messed up big time.'

Slowly, he told Ray about the troubles of the Armitage Estate. Ray knew the place well. He'd grown up not ten streets from Armitage and many of his childhood friends had come from the high-rise blocks. It had been a troubled place since its inception, a result of sixties exuberance and design stupidity.

'I heard they were taking some of the big towers down,' he commented. 'Moving people back to street level again. Giving them gardens and a bit of air.'

'That's the plan,' Martin confirmed, 'but finding the development money is another thing. With the reputation Armitage had, there wasn't a private developer within a hundred miles would want to touch the place, and trying to get local authority funding these days is a joke. We knew the only way we could improve the place was to make it look as if the residents were trying. It's like the Saff in Leicester. Once the residents started taking things upon themselves, setting up neighbourhood-watch and community schemes, they came in for a bunch of funding. You'd hardly recognize the place now.'

Ray nodded. 'But we're not talking about that sort

of thing here, are we? Last time I looked, neighbourhood-watch schemes were legal.'

Martin sighed. 'We founded a residents' association. Imposed a regime of zero tolerance. It started to work, Ray, but it wasn't enough, not in Armitage. The police wouldn't patrol. A call on the nines was never prioritized one. That's the way it looked anyway. The truth is, we're so understaffed at the station that half the time there weren't enough officers to cover the calls. You know what it's like, Ray. We work routine overtime, even when it isn't authorized, just to get the job done. I've built up more TOIL time than I can ever use. If I took it all at once, I'd be on three months' leave, and I'm not the only one.'

Ray nodded thoughtfully. He knew the score. There were strict budgets which included limited overtime pay. If something came up requiring extra officers working extra hours and it was nearing the end of the budget allocation, then payment just didn't get authorized. TOIL, time off in lieu, always added up to more hours than anyone could possibly take and unpaid overtime was often the norm, especially in a town like Mallingham with a rising crime rate, overwhelming social problems and a young population who felt it was their right to have more than life offered. And life should offer more than anyone could get in a place like Armitage.

'The residents' association felt they should be doing more. We organized regular patrols. We clamped down on the prostitutes, the drug dealers. We targeted car crime with security-awareness campaigns, got a youth club going and imposed a curfew with the support of the local parents. Any kid under ten found on the streets after nine was taken home and if their parents weren't around we'd take them straight to the community centre and leave their folks a note. They'd have to collect their kids and answer to the residents' association. We posted names of routine offenders on the community centre door.'

'Offenders?' Ray questioned. 'Don't you think that's a heavy word, Martin?'

'It needed to be heavy on Armitage. I gave up free time, hours of it, to get the Armitage Estate turned around. We raised funds for private security on the high-rises. Key codes on the doors. Old people were beginning to feel safe again and the school – you remember Highbury Junior?'

'I should do, I went there.'

'It was put into special measures three years ago. You know, it failed its inspection. Well, it was out of special measures and commended by the Ofsted committee last autumn. Morale was raised, Ray. And we'd got developers looking to take on the estate and build proper low-rent housing.'

'So. What aren't you telling me?'

Martin fidgeted uneasily. 'Some members of the residents' committee felt we should take more decisive action. Be more proactive. The police . . .'

Ray noticed that Martin spoke of the police as though it were something he was not connected with.

'The police did nothing most of the time. We started

out reporting to them when we got a whisper. Nine times out of ten it wasn't acted on.'

'So you turned vigilante?'

'It wasn't like that.'

'Wasn't it? That's what I'm hearing.'

'It worked, Ray. We kept the dealers and the little cunts of housebreakers and joyriders out of Armitage. We were doing a good job.'

'You were delivering the warnings and the odd beatings, I suppose. The word on what would happen if they offended on your patch. How long before the kneecapping started, Martin?'

If he expected denial, none came.

'So,' Ray continued. 'What finally landed you in the shit? What invisible line did you finally cross?'

'Evidence,' Martin said. 'Withholding evidence. I mean, not permanently. Just long enough for us to check it out. Oh come on, Ray, we've all done it.'

'Have we? Not the Martin Galloway I used to know.'

Galloway laughed harshly. 'We were tipped off by an informant,' he said. 'A drugs shipment ready to be moved out, a big one, on the edge of our patch, and this time there was something more. Two kids had gone missing and the rumour was there was a buyer already lined up. They were being held just off the Armitage in an old warehouse, waiting for the pickup. It all went pear-shaped. There was shooting and . . .'

Ray turned around to look at him again. 'I saw it in the papers,' he said. 'That was your lot?'

'Yeah. The two men have been released on bail. But

there'll be no charges and it's my stupidity that'll see to that.'

'What did you do?'

'Emptied their pockets. Took everything to a friend of mine, see what he could turn up. He's a computer nerd,' he added, with a weak attempt at humour.

Ray didn't smile. 'How often have you done that?' he asked.

'A few times. Ray, it was just intelligence gathering. I always returned stuff to the locker afterwards. And there are enough sympathetic to what we were doing to cover for me.'

'Intelligence gathering. Which you couldn't do legitimately?'

'Which doesn't *get* done legitimately. God, Ray, do you know what it's like now? Do you know how many times I've taken an investigation right through to it being sent to the CPS only to see it thrown out? I've had to tell parents that the drunk driver that killed their kid won't be prosecuted because the CPS can't be ninety per cent sure of getting a conviction. An old woman whose house has been wrecked by a couple of young louts who've scared her half to death but who won't be prosecuted, even though she's picked them out in the line-up, because the CPS won't put her on the witness stand. They say she's potentially unreliable. An old lady who's lived right, been independent and self-reliant all this time, but who's suddenly told she's not good enough to give the queen's evidence.'

'And so you try and convict off your own bat. You bypass the law.'

'I thought you'd understand.'

'I do understand. I've been there. But that doesn't make it right. There has to be some measure of overall control, Martin, some guideline. And I agree it's not perfect, probably not even good. But if we stop working with it, if, as officers of the law, we choose to ignore it, we're just heading for anarchy.'

He took a deep breath, wishing Martin would leave but guessing that there was more to come. Feeling like a coward because he didn't want to hear it. Knowing how many times he himself had been tempted to bend the rules because he *knew* someone was guilty, just lacked the final pieces to make a watertight case.

And the rulings of the CPS did leave a lot to be desired, though he could hardly blame the individuals involved. He knew what their caseload was like and how little time a lawyer might have to be briefed on any given case. Half an hour before it got into court sometimes, and that was if they were lucky. And those were just the cases that got through the initial processing. He had come to realize that the entire system was flawed end to end. He knew in truth that the interview transcripts that the brief might see were merely edited versions typed up by civilian workers, whose job it was to create a synopsis that often had more in common with a student book-report than it did with what actually went on in the interview room. He didn't blame them either. Faced with the same situation, Ray would have been at a loss. What to leave in, what to leave out, how to give the best rendition of events without overburdening an already overworked junior council with detail that was probably irrelevant. But it begged the question of accuracy when a dozen hours of interviews could sometimes be condensed into less than a dozen pages of typescript.

'It still doesn't make it right, Martin,' he said quietly. 'You interfered with the due process. Because of that two paedophiles are likely to walk away scot-free. I know that wasn't what you intended, Martin, but it's what happened.'

'And if they had been arrested, *had* been charged and their case had made it to the courts? What would the bastards have got? Three years? Four years? They'd have been out in eighteen months with good behaviour and time served on remand. You know, Ray, one of them had a picture of his wife and kid in his wallet.'

Ray was silent for a moment. He filled the kettle and emptied the teapot then sat down at the kitchen table. 'What about this Winter?' he said.

'I don't want him involved.'

'He's already involved. Who is he?'

Martin shook his head. 'Used to be a copper,' he said. 'Retired through ill-health. He needs his pension. I'll not implicate him. You never knew him.' He sighed deeply. 'This couldn't have come at a worse time, Ray. That's why I've come to you. I'm right outside, but you must still have contacts.'

'Me!' Ray laughed. 'They see me coming, they bolt the doors. Surely you know what happened when I left.'

'The Pierce thing. Yes, I know. But you're still respected in certain circles. Could still pull in the odd favour.'

'I doubt it. Some very senior people went down when

I found out they were on the take from Pierce's mob. One committed suicide and a couple more took early retirement. I'm regarded as some kind of Jonah by most of what's left of the police department.'

'But you were called in last year as a consultant. That Eyes of God fiasco . . .'

'I was called in by DI Beckett. Off the record and totally unofficial. My involvement as a so-called consultant was very much after the fact and only because the local media had me written up as some kind of hero and it looked good for the department. If things'd gone the other way – and my God, Martin, they damn near did – Beckett would've been joining the unemployment queue and I think I'd've given in and left the bloody country. Look, Martin, even if I could help out, what would you want?'

'It's complicated,' Martin hedged. 'And I'm not even certain of my facts.'

'I didn't think that was an issue with you these days.'

Martin ignored the dig. 'Look, Ray, three years ago a boy was seriously injured. I headed the investigation, but it went down as an accident. His name was Damien Pinsent and he took a dive into a swimming pool at his girlfriend's eighteenth birthday party. Ring any bells?'

'Um, vaguely.'

'He was on some designer shit. Thought he was Superman. He's been in a coma ever since.'

'And?'

'The drug he'd taken was never properly identified. His girlfriend denied all knowledge and we never got the supplier. The papers reported it as LSD. That's what we told them. The truth was, we didn't, still don't, know what it was. There were rumours, but never anything concrete. For a while it seemed to disappear off the streets and consensus was that he'd been mixing it and that accounted for the weird tox reports. But it surfaced again, slightly modified, but recognizably the same stuff that had made Damien behave like a lunatic. It left two dead and another three in the loony bin. Untreatable. We had one lead. We got the dealer last time around. Said he'd scored through a friend of a friend – we never did catch up with any of them – but the contact was made through a personal ad. The supplier went by the name of Angel Eyes.'

He reached into his jacket pocket and took out two slips of paper. 'This is from three years ago,' he said, handing them to Ray. 'This second is from just last week. The wording is practically the same.'

Angel Eyes says,
Meet me at 42nd and Vine.

'What the hell does that mean? Where does he think we are? New York?'

'It has to be code for a location in Mallingham. 42, Vine Street . . . I don't know.'

'Is there a Vine Street in Mallingham? No, didn't think so. And you want me to do what?'

'Help me, Ray. My hands are tied now, but you still have the contacts. You're still a good copper, retired or not.'

'Martin. What you should be doing is going to your

superiors and coming clean about the entire thing. If this is as serious as you say it is, then it needs resources behind it—'

'Resources! What bloody resources? Have you been listening to anything I've been telling you this last hour?'

'If it's that important, it will be dealt with, Martin. I'm not the bloody cavalry. I'm one man.'

'I'll get you the manpower you need and I'll give you everything I know.'

'What? The residents' association? No way, Martin. Look, I'm retired. I've built a good life outside the force, something I never thought I'd be able to do. You're in enough shit already without adding me to your troubles or adding you to mine. I don't want this, Martin, and I'm not going to play.'

Martin said nothing at first. Then he muttered, 'I expected more from you.'

'You had no right to expect anything.'

'I thought . . . Ray, you were always one to stand up for the underdog.'

'This isn't about the underdog. It's about throwing yourself off a cliff. Martin, you must see that. You must know you've crossed the line and there's nothing on God's earth I can do for you. Come clean, tell what you have and what you suspect and get a proper investigation going. Your record's been picture perfect until now and that has to count for something.'

Again, Martin fell silent and Ray knew this was not what he wanted to hear. Then Martin looked up and stared at him.

'I see him, you know. Damien.'

'It happens.'

'No. Not like that. I know . . . I know we've all got faces that come back to haunt us. Names, places, people, usually dead people, we see in our dreams and sometimes even when we're waking if they catch us unaware. I know it's part of the job we do and it's part of being human, but this isn't like that. I've started seeing him again and I see him clear as day. Clearer than I ever saw him early on when I was all mixed up in his accident and poking about in his life. This is real. It's more real sometimes than people I know are actually there. I see him and I hear his voice. He's warning me, Ray. Telling me I'm getting in too deep and that I'm just like him. That I'm about to drown.'

Ray shook his head and then said gently, 'I doubt that's Damien, Martin. More likely it's your good sense talking. You should listen to it.'

'Sometimes I think I'm losing my mind.'

'No. No you're not. But you're going to if you don't back off now. Take a rest, Martin. They won't want to disgrace you, not after a career like yours. Plead stress, diminished responsibility. Take retirement, you know they'll offer it, and if you go to . . . who's your DCI?'

'Whissendine. Roger Whissendine.'

'Don't know him myself, but I've heard he's straight. Tell him what you told me and then take off somewhere and get yourself a holiday.'

'I can't do that.'

Ray sighed, not knowing what else to say.

'Check the Internet,' Martin said suddenly. 'Look for Angel Eyes. It's not easy to find. I had to—' He broke off, the sound of Sarah's key in the front door halting him in his tracks.

Ray tried not to be too obvious in his relief.

'I'd better be going,' Martin said as Sarah came through to the kitchen.

He stood up and followed Ray obediently through to the living room, taking his coat from Sarah who was examining both men keenly, trying to work out what had been going on.

As he reached the door, Martin turned abruptly, this time appealing directly to Sarah.

'Tell him he has to help me,' he said. 'If he has any compassion left at all. Tell him, if he doesn't, there'll be more Damiens on his conscience for the rest of his life.'

Chapter Six

DCI Whissendine looked over the statements made by the men from the warehouse. They were of varied interest. Emlyn Gardner, the driver, was already well known to the local constabulary. A car thief and inveterate joyrider from the age of fifteen, he was in it for the short-term glory rather than the long-term profits. The man riding shotgun in the passenger seat was from out of town, but likewise had form and was just a paid hand. And of the men in the warehouse, it had become clear that one had simply been drafted in at the last minute. An extra body to shift and carry and take a smaller cut of the profits, not having been in on the set-up. But the other two had caught his interest. John Ashton and Clive Williams were small-time dealers hoping to break into the mainstream. They'd been offered an opening. An in on something *big*. The opportunity, so they claimed, to work for a new outfit moving in on the Armitage, intent on pushing back the walls that the residents' association had built around their home patch. Ironically, the Armitage, now empty of all competition, was seen as a desirable piece of real estate ready for the claim jumpers to stake out.

'Who was your contact?' Whissendine wanted to know. 'Who set this up?'

But after twenty-four hours of questioning it had

become obvious that they didn't know names. They'd been drawn in by a contact of a contact who knew Eldon Firth, a feature player in the scene from way back, though Eldon's speciality was crack cocaine, not the Ecstasy and other party drugs this lot hoped to deal. But it was vague beyond belief and the man they'd met in a local pub who'd acted as go-between was unknown to them. His description, five eight, wiry, dark-haired and blue-eyed with a couple of days' stubble, was hardly detailed.

'The pub was dark,' John Ashton had protested. 'He said his name was Mack or Max or something.'

'Which was it? Mack or Max?'

'I don't remember.'

And Whissendine knew the pub. The Wyatt Arms. A local watering hole recently converted into a so-called Fun Pub complete with blaring music and what he supposed was meant to be mood lighting. It was hard enough recognizing someone you *did* know, never mind recollecting the details of a stranger's face. No doubt this Mack or whatever he was called had chosen the meeting place for that very reason.

Clive Williams had been the first to explain the presence of the two little girls, something Ashton had refused even to discuss.

'We were meant to show good faith, see. Show we understood what we were getting into. They trusted us with the shipment, but a rider on the deal was that we should get two kids, about nine, ten years old, for a special customer.'

'And you thought that was acceptable, did you? You

must have known what kind of pervert would want a couple of kids. Family man, are you? Happy to let your kids go to some pervert for his bit of fun?'

'You don't *know* that,' Clive Williams protested. 'It might have been—'

'Might have been what? A trip to Disneyland?'

'My client does not have to speculate, chief inspector,' McGilligan, Williams's solicitor, had protested mildly. 'He has merely to reply to your questions and that he is doing adequately.'

Whissendine winced now at the thought of the solicitor's supercilious expression. He'd have given a lot for the means to wipe that faint, superior smile from his face . . . He frowned down at the statements lying on the table in front of him. Whissendine had applied for, and been granted, an extension and the interrogation had continued for several hours after the initial twenty-four before charges had eventually been brought. Whissendine had every faith that they would be remanded in custody. All five men were due to appear in court the following morning.

He glanced up as McGilligan wandered into his office carrying two cups of machine-brewed coffee.

'Two sugars, wasn't it?' he asked. 'I seem to remember you liked it sweet.'

'You want something?'

McGilligan sat down and passed Whissendine's coffee across the table. 'We're both tired,' he said, 'and we both want our beds, so I'll come straight to the point. You'll not be opposing bail tomorrow, will you?'

'I won't be what?' Whissendine glared at the duty

solicitor wondering what game he was about to play. McGilligan smiled wolfishly at him, obviously quite at ease. McGilligan was one of the new breed of duty solicitors, an ex-copper who'd fast-tracked his way through the legal system and been resurrected on the other side. There were increasing numbers of McGilligan's ilk appearing, Whissendine thought. The buggers breeding like rabbits in the warmth and safety of an overstretched system desperate for anyone qualified enough to fill the legal void. Turncoats Whissendine thought them, and he wasn't the only one. Men like McGilligan were widely reviled by their ex-colleagues as traitors now employed by the other side.

'And just *why* won't I be opposing bloody bail?'

McGilligan sipped his coffee, wincing at the bitter brew the machine coughed up. Then he set his cup aside and leaned confidentially across the table.

'Misconduct,' he said quietly. 'Gross misconduct, if I'm not mistaken, and as the officer in charge, Roger, you'll be the one carrying the can.'

'What the hell are you talking about?'

McGilligan sat back once more and steepled his fingers thoughtfully in front of him. Whissendine could remember him when he'd been plain old detective sergeant. He'd been a cocky little bastard then too. And he'd never called Whissendine anything but 'sir' or 'boss' back then. Certainly never presumed to call him Roger. Once again, Whissendine experienced that deep and desperate urge to reach out and remove that smile.

He took a deep breath and listened with narrowed eyes to what McGilligan had to say.

'Picture this,' the solicitor said slowly. 'My clients were . . . arrested by this group of vigilantes. A selection of assorted yobs carrying illegal weapons who set themselves up as judge and jury, even sidelining your lot, Roger. They tied my clients up, searched them and removed their personal belongings, depositing them, according to their statements, in a ziplock pouch which was then taken away when these so-called protectors of law and order fled and your lot moved in. My clients' possessions, their wallets, credit cards, driver's licences, keys and money were removed, for what purpose we can only speculate, but they were spirited away. And yet, when I go to your property sergeant to verify this story, as per my brief, I find said possessions tucked safely away in the locker. Itemized and signed in by none other than yourself and the custody sergeant, and you know another funny thing? The time beside the list, well, let's just say it was difficult to read. Looks like some careless soul spilled their coffee all over it . . .'

He smiled again and picked up the polystyrene cup he had put down moments before. 'We all know how this muck stains, don't we?'

Chapter Seven

Winter was concerned. He had heard through his grapevine of police contacts that Martin Galloway had taken a period of unexpected leave, but that there was more to it than that. That Martin was under investigation, unofficially for the moment, but that things did not look good.

'Why didn't he tell me he had trouble?' Winter had demanded of Gita, repeating the question so many times that she finally escaped to the shops to buy a quite unneeded loaf of bread. Alone in the flat Winter tried again to contact Martin, but his home phone rang out into emptiness and his mobile was switched off.

When Gita returned she found an impatient Winter ready to go round to Martin's home to find him.

'If he's not answering the phone then chances are he's not in,' she told him reasonably.

'I suppose. But he should have talked to me.'

'From what you've said he didn't know he was in trouble last time we saw him.'

'So? He has a bloody phone, doesn't he?' He slammed his hands down hard on the arms of his chair and glared at no one in particular. Something, he was certain, had gone badly wrong.

*

Max was not pleased at the loss of his promised play-things. He'd seen the pictures of the two little girls that John Ashton and his associates had procured and spent some happy hours imagining himself taking delivery of these special gifts. And now some damned fools had stepped in and taken his pleasant dreams and cast them into the flames.

Max was more than a little annoyed.

'So, do something about it,' his employer told him. 'See it as a little bonus.'

Max smiled at the one they labelled Angel Eyes, a man who had always made allowance for his peccadilloes even though Max knew he didn't share them. He nodded. 'I might just do that,' he said.

'OK, go on and sort it, Max. You'll feel a lot better when you've brought your grievance out into the open. But, Max, keep this one clean, will you, there's a good chap?'

Max was only a little disappointed at the request.

By the Monday evening Clive Williams and John Ashton had ceased to celebrate their release on police bail and begun to feel a little insecure. Rumour was that the organization they had let down by losing their shipment was not amused by the failure and was out for blood. It was a rumour Max had taken pleasure in spreading through the afternoon, and bad news, as they say, travels fastest of all.

Fear didn't stop them going out to their local pub though. The misplaced sense of bravado, fuelled by an afternoon spent drowning their fears in alcohol, had replaced their fear by seven o'clock and Max was rather glad to see that the macho male was still alive and well and living on the Armitage. He'd figured that they might choose to stay home that night and, though Max was unbothered by that complication, it was a nice bit of a bonus that they should save him the time and effort it would be to extract them from their beds.

It was closing time before the two men staggered out, accompanied by a couple more who walked with them to the corner of the road and then waved a drunken farewell, not noticing the slightly built shadow that followed Clive Williams and John Ashton towards their homes.

'Nice evening, Clive,' Max said softly, stepping up behind him and squeezing the muzzle of a snub-nosed automatic close against his kidneys. 'Try to run, John,' he added as the other man whirled around and looked set for flight, 'and I'll simply shoot you here. By the time the good residents of Brighton Terrace are awake enough to open their curtains and look outside, I'll be long gone.'

'What do you want from us?' Clive Williams managed to gasp.

'An explanation would do for starters,' Max told him quietly.

A half hour later both men were dead, shot neatly through the back of the neck, Max taking his order seriously when it came to keeping this one clean.

He had listened as they told him how their solicitor had assured them that if they cooperated they'd be released on bail and they had fallen over themselves to fill in the details of what went on in the warehouse that night.

And Max was glad of that. The fact that they had not been remanded had been something of a puzzle to him.

And after that, it had not taken Max long to figure out who the loose cannon might be that was causing DCI Whissendine so much grief.

Martin Galloway. A man on a mission.

Max smiled. He knew Galloway well, their relationship – if you could call it that – going back a long way. Max had even been his informant for a little while. He'd make a bet that Martin Galloway still had his number.

Sitting in his car, Max scribbled a little message.

Re. Angel Eyes
Give Max a call

A few minutes later he posted the note through Martin's door.

Chapter Eight

Ray spent several days wracked by guilt. Martin left a couple of messages but Ray did not return his calls and he was grateful that Martin did not have the number of his mobile. He knew that sometime soon he'd have to talk to Martin and tell him straight that he was not prepared to get involved, but Martin had been so distraught that he was not looking forward to the confrontation.

Sarah, of course, had demanded to know what it was all about and Ray had told her. She was not impressed by his indecision. 'Talk to George,' she advised. 'See what he can dig up and if there's really something in the Angel business then *you* go to the authorities and report what Martin told you.'

It seemed like sound reasoning, though Ray still felt as though he were betraying a confidence. Unlike Ray, George, his friend and business partner, *did* have the connections where it mattered.

George could not have come from a background much more different from Ray's. Ray's origins were solid working-class, a sixteen-year-old school-leaver who'd later taken and passed his entrance exam for the police force. George was an army officer, later seconded to the Diplomatic Protection Group and then drafted sideways into what his boss, Dignan, called the Company in cynical imitation of the CIA. Flowers-Mahoney still did the occasional job for Dignan when their interests happened to coincide and Ray knew that George still used his former contacts on Flowers-Mahoney business. They had met when Ray had investigated the death of George's only child. When he suggested to Ray that they found Flowers-Mahoney, Ray had been sceptical at first, but their combination of experience had made it work and in the last six months they had not just moved their secretary from part- to full-time hours but also persuaded Philip Marsden, another ex-Dignan employee, to join them. What Phil didn't know about computers and systems security was probably not yet thought of and having him on board expanded the Flowers-Mahoney brief.

George had listened carefully to what Ray told him, making notes, but had said nothing since then. Ray was not surprised. That was George all over. One day, Ray knew, he'd walk in and drop a cartload of information in Ray's lap and probably still say nothing about it.

Phil had been intrigued by Martin's final reference to the Internet. They ran a series of basic searches for Angel Eyes but came up with nothing that looked relevant. 'Angel Eyes is likely to be something less obvious,' Phil told him. 'Not a name or a reference but maybe an image with that title. Find the right image, click on the right part of the picture and you'll find a back door that leads you straight to where you want to be.'

'Can we search for it?' Ray wanted to know.

'Do you have any idea how many images that might apply to?' Phil asked. 'You'll get results by the million and still not be any the wiser.'

The quick search they had done showed Ray the truth of that and he was forced to leave it.

On the Wednesday morning, he finally gave in to his conscience and telephoned Martin. Martin wasn't there. Instead a police officer who identified himself as Sergeant Field asked politely who he was and what he wanted with DI Galloway. He still gave him rank, Ray noted, so obviously Martin's disgrace was not public knowledge, nor did they want it to be. But Field's presence at his house begged a whole cartload of questions.

'Ray Flowers,' Ray told him. 'Martin is a friend and was a colleague not so long ago.'

'Oh? And how's that then, sir?'

'I was DI Flowers until I retired.'

'Ah.'

Evidently, Ray surmised, his fame preceded him.

They spent several minutes more in conversation. Sergeant Field wanted to know the last time he had seen or heard from Martin Galloway and if he'd mentioned going away. Ray replied as honestly as he felt able, knowing that Martin's visit to him would be easy to check and that phone records would show his several calls.

'When did Martin go away?' he asked.

'We still aren't certain.'

'Who reported him missing, then? I know he lives alone.'

'He failed to keep an appointment, Mr Flowers. We became concerned. We know that DI Galloway has been under considerable strain.' The gentle emphasis on the *Mr* was not lost on Ray.

'Yes, so I understood,' he said.

'Oh. I take it when he came to see you he seemed depressed, perhaps?'

'Anxious and stressed,' Ray told him. 'I know that he was under investigation. It must have been a strain.'

Field missed a beat, and then another. Ray could hear him scribbling on a pad and then the background noise dropped out as he covered the mouthpiece, evidently wanting to talk to someone else in the room. When he came back on his tone had changed.

'Someone will want to come out and talk to you,' he said. 'We'll want a detailed statement. I'm sure you'll understand. I'm sure you'll understand too that we don't want this spread. DI Galloway is still one of ours.'

'You think he might have killed himself,' Ray said flatly. There was another moment's silence.

'I wouldn't like to speculate,' Field said and cut Ray off before he could ask more.

The evening papers filled in the missing pieces. The warehouse incident was reprised at length together with the news that the police had made two arrests at the warehouse and that the men had been released on police bail. The men that Martin Galloway had told him about.

The trouble was, someone else had got to them. They'd been found on wasteland close to the warehouse. Both bound, both shot through the head execution-style.

Martin, Ray guessed, was now suspect number one.

*

Ray had spent an hour phoning round to ex-colleagues hoping but not expecting to get a whiff of what was going on, but no one knew very much, or if they did they weren't saying. Superintendent Whissendine had taken charge himself apparently, and was working with a hand-picked team.

Ray arrived home just after six to find Sarah making tea for the DCI himself. Whissendine stood up immediately, introduced himself and extended his hand. 'I'm pleased to meet you,' he said, taking Ray completely by surprise. 'I've heard a lot about you.'

So that was the approach they were going to play, Ray thought. He smiled, feeling as he always did the way his scars pulled at the skin and twisted the corner of his mouth, aware of the way Whissendine glanced away, finding it difficult to look Ray squarely in the face.

Sarah poured more tea. 'DCI Whissendine arrived an hour ago,' she said. 'I've let him wait.'

Ray nodded, taking the hint that she was none too pleased about it. He wondered what Whissendine had done to raise her hackles, beyond the simple fact of his being there.

'I understand that DI Galloway came to see you on Sunday,' Whissendine was saying. 'Can you tell me what it was all about?'

Ray frowned. 'I wish I could,' he said. 'But I never did get a proper handle on what he wanted. He called out of the blue on Sunday morning, said that he wanted to come and see me and made it sound urgent. I must say I was surprised. I've spoken to Martin, what, once, twice maybe in the last couple of years and only then when our paths happened to cross.'

'You were close at one time?'

'Not so you'd notice. I knew him for a number of years. We entered the force at about the same time. Took our sergeants' exam the same year. Had the odd pint after work but I wouldn't say we were ever that close.'

'But even so, you invited him over that afternoon.'

'I may have retired,' Ray said seriously, 'I've not stopped being a nosy bugger.'

Whissendine almost cracked a smile. 'And when he got here, he told you that he was under investigation?'

Ray shook his head. 'No, that was on the phone. I admit, I was taken aback. I thought at the time that he was blowing things out of proportion. Martin had always played it dead straight as far as I knew. I said as much.'

'And his response was?'

'That he was guilty as hell.' Ray paused then he added, 'But I don't think he's a killer. Someone else did for those two men.'

Whissendine's eyes narrowed. 'You know about that?'

'The shootings are all over the papers. About Martin's part in the warehouse incident? He told me. Told me about the warehouse and that he was caught withholding evidence. Told me that because of his stupidity they'd walk free. Looks like someone else reached the same conclusion.'

Whissendine was silent for a moment. 'Martin Galloway changed since you knew him?' he said.

'Not enough to kill. Not in cold blood like that.'

'And what did you advise him to do, after this confession?'

'I advised him to go to you, talk the whole thing through and then take a holiday somewhere as far away from the stress as he could get. I didn't think he'd take my advice though.'

Whissendine snorted. 'We don't know that he has.'

'You think something happened to him, don't you?'

'What I think hardly matters. But for your information, Mr Flowers, I think he's right. He is guilty as hell. I think he killed those two men when he realized what an almighty balls-up he'd made of everything and then I think he took off and that he had help. He's probably not even in the country by now. I mean, what is there to keep him here? He's no family, no real friends from what we know of him.'

'He had the job,' Ray said softly. 'He gave it all to the job and, Inspector Whissendine, he won't have gone far. He believed he still had things to do in Mallingham.'

'Things, things like what?'

Ray hesitated. He glanced across at Sarah but she was giving him no help. She really *didn't* like Whissendine, Ray realized. Sarah's lack of response caused him to modify his first intended reply. 'He said how hard he'd worked on the Armitage Estate,' Ray said. 'And though I didn't like his methods, I don't doubt the effort he put in. He seemed to think the drug dealers he and the residents' association had driven off the Armitage wanted back in. He was convinced they were out to discredit him in some way, undermine what he'd achieved on the Armitage.' Even as he told this half truth, it occurred to Ray that there might be something in it. 'He came asking for my help. You probably know I work for a security company. We deal mainly with corporate stuff, but we take on the odd investigation.'

He paused, and Whissendine nodded. 'Flowers-Mahoney,' he said. 'You're doing pretty well by all accounts.'

'Martin wanted us to help. To poke around, see what we turned up. He seemed to think I might still have old friends on the force who would feed me the info even if Martin was out of action.'

Again, Whissendine snorted. It was, Ray thought, an unbecoming habit.

'You don't have to say it,' Ray commented. 'I told Martin that I didn't have that many friends on the inside any more. I told him also that I didn't want to get involved. I was out of all that now and wanted to stay that way.'

'What happened to the famous curiosity?'

The attempts at ingratiation had worn thin very quickly Ray noted, amused by the observation. 'Oh, he'd satisfied my curiosity by then,' Ray told him. 'Satisfied it enough for me to think that the stress had got to him so far I wouldn't know what I could or couldn't believe. Martin, in my view, was becoming paranoid and with good reason. Just about everyone was now out to get him. I told him I couldn't help and he went on his way.'

'But you called him today.'

'I returned the calls he had been making to me. I felt I owed him that much and I knew I couldn't dodge him for ever. Instead, I had the pleasure of conversation with your Sergeant Field.'

Whissendine narrowed his eyes again. This was a man created out of annoying mannerisms, Ray commented to himself.

'And you declined to help him in any way?' Whissendine asked him again.

'That's what I just told you. I'm sorry, but I can't help you any more than that.'

Ray got up and took his cup across to the sink, signalling to all but the most socially inept that the interview was at an end and the DCI was, after all, on Ray's turf and not his own.

Whissendine hesitated for a moment and then stood up. He did not extend his hand to shake Ray's this time. Instead he announced portentously that someone would no doubt be in touch again. He took his card from his jacket pocket and laid it squarely on the table top, pushing it towards Sarah who said nothing and refrained from taking it. Then he took his leave.

'Was that an official visit?' Sarah questioned once Ray had seen him out. 'I expected to have to make a statement or something.'

Ray shook his head. 'No, that was *them* trying to figure out what Martin might have told *us*,' he told her.

'Them and us is it now? I'll have to remember that. And now Mr Ex-detective, you can take me out to dinner. The local pub will do. See it as punishment for that unpleasant supercilious man taking up an unaccountable amount of space at my kitchen table.'

'What didn't you like about him?' Ray was curious. Sarah's judgement was generally sound.

'He's no gentleman,' Sarah told him promptly, 'and no, Ray, that's not being a snob. I mean, he manages a veneer when he thinks it might serve him, but he hasn't got a clue. Someone told him, be nice to Ray Flowers, he might know something. What he really wanted to know was, where was Ray Flowers when those two men were being shot last night.'

Chapter Nine

Martin Galloway was in deep trouble and he didn't know what to do about it. He wasn't even sure of where he was any more.

He was driving his car. That much he *was* kind of sure of. He could feel the wheel beneath his clenched fingers and the pedals pressed beneath his feet, though it was some subliminal instinct that told him which one to press and even then . . . how could he be sure he'd got it right?

The disorientation had started about an hour before. Or was it longer? Martin didn't know that either. He remembered Max leaving a message for him and the next thing he knew was that someone was tying his hands so tightly that his fingers lost all feeling. When was that? How long ago? Martin had lost all sense of time.

At some point they had come to him and Martin could recall that moment of certainty that he was going to die. Instead, they had forced his mouth open and he could dimly recall water being poured down his throat.

He remembered choking, unable to breathe. Unable to swallow, though they still forced the bitter water between his lips and, hard as he tried, he could not help but swallow and then they had taken him outside, still choking, still trying to draw the air back into his lungs.

He soon understood that there had been more than

water in the glass. Something else, that gave the liquid a bitter taste and which, within a very short amount of time, had confused his brain and all but destroyed his coordination. But that was his last cohesive realization.

And now he was here. Driving his car along a road that looked familiar but which he could not have named.

The radio played but something was wrong with the signal and the music distorted as it came out of the speakers. It bounced around inside his head, wave upon wave of it, the phrases overlapping, layer and layer until he could no longer distinguish the tune, and then the news bulletin began and he heard his name mentioned, sandwiched somewhere between the overlapping sounds.

Martin pressed his foot down hard upon the accelerator knowing vaguely that he should be doing something with his other foot. He heard the engine scream, but the sound of it just became confused with the music and the voice of the newsreader and now the sound of horns wailing at him from somewhere outside.

Martin found that if he concentrated hard he could make out all the sounds. Music–voices–engine–car horn. Flashing lights on the dashboard firing off small explosions in his head. Tick, tick, tick of something that sounded like a bomb about to go off inside his brain.

Martin took off his watch and threw it out of the window, or thought he did. It bounced loudly off the glass and landed somewhere near his feet. He felt it crunch and groan in protest as he pressed the pedal down again, catching the watch beneath his tread.

And through it all, the voices, too far away for him

to make out the words and distorted as if he heard them through deep water.

I am like Damien, Martin thought in panic, a moment of blinding clarity breaking through the rest of the noise. And just like Damien, he was going to drown.

Martin wiped at the window trying to see out but the car was filling up with water and he couldn't see. He wiped again, frantically, and between the waves of cloudy water caught sight of trees – *Keep the pedal pressed right down. Keep going at all costs before they catch you.* Some tiny portion of his brain recognized the misted landscape and as a train screamed by so painfully – Martin cried out as it ripped right through his head – that other quieter portion of his brain told him that he was on the Welford Road, close to the cemetery and on the bridge beside the railway line – *and the car was filling up with water faster than he could wipe it away.*

Martin thumped down again upon a pedal and this time his other foot did something as well. He felt the car swerve and lurch and then an impact drive him sideways – *and still the car was filling up with water.*

Urgently, Martin tugged at the door and somehow got it open wide though something still held him in his seat – *they'd got him, they'd come and found him.*

Faces surrounded him, leering down as he struggled to reach out and shut the door again – *the water was still rising even though he'd opened the door to let it out.*

Someone reached in and touched Martin's side, their hand close beside his thigh. There was a click which resonated fiercely inside his head, adding another layer to the music–voices–car horn–train screaming – *and the rising water lapping up to his neck.*

Martin screamed and the faces drew back. He screamed again and they drew back some more. He screamed some more but this time the echoes of it just joined the waves of sound in his head. But he struggled from his seat all the same, fighting his way past the faces and the wall of sound issuing from their open mouths.

And then another layer of harmonics compounded all the rest, spun it into a leaden web that enfolded the screaming-wailing pressure inside his head.

Martin cried out. So much pain issuing from inside his head that he could feel it being taken apart cell by cell, neuron by neuron – *and the water was still rising, up to his neck now and still rising. I am like Damien, Martin thought, and I'm going to drown.*

Sarah Gordon arrived home to find her neighbour in a state of agitation.

'A man was here,' she said. 'That man who came to see you on Sunday, driving the blue Mondeo.'

'Oh? Did he say what he wanted?'

The neighbour shook her head. 'No, but he was acting very strangely, Sarah. I think he was drunk or something. He kept banging on the door and when I came out to tell him you certainly weren't home and that taking it out on the knocker wouldn't help, he just sort of looked at me as though he couldn't understand a word I said and stumbled off. I almost called the police.'

'The police?'

'Well yes, he got back into his car and, Sarah, I'm sure that he was drunk. It was only that I didn't want you embarrassed that made me hesitate.'

Sarah thanked her, wondering how long she had waited with the net curtains twitching for Sarah to get home so that she could relay her exciting piece of news. It was worrying though, Sarah admitted. What was Martin Galloway doing turning up here and what was he doing driving while he was drunk?

She turned the key in the lock and went inside. It was only about half an hour later, while taking a pile of washing upstairs, that she happened to glance down and see something bright blue lying on the floor beside the front door.

Setting the washing basket down, Sarah picked it up. It was a crumpled piece of paper, screwed tightly into a little ball, as though to make it as invisible as possible, and wrapped with bits of fluff and hair as though it had spent time tucked up in someone's pocket.

Carefully, Sarah unrolled it, flattening it against the wall. It was a scrap torn from a larger picture, a painting, part of a face with feathers behind. The hair was blond and the face pale. But what Sarah immediately noticed was the pair of bright blue eyes.

'Angel Eyes,' Sarah whispered.

Ray reached Peatling Magna just after six o'clock. The nights were beginning to pull out, he noted. It wasn't quite dark when he reached home these days, just a kind of thick twilight settling over the fields either side of the winding road that led back to the cottage. Even with a year of practice, Ray was not keen on driving that road at night, the double, almost right-angle bends and blind corners were not his idea of fun.

He'd been home only a few minutes when Whissendine knocked at the door, and brought news of Martin's crash.

'Was he hurt?'

'Physically no. Mentally he's off in la-la land. Drunk or otherwise under the influence, witnesses tell us.'

'Drunk? Martin? I don't believe that. And this happened in Leicester?'

'On the Welford Road. He was lucky, missed the rush-hour traffic by maybe twenty minutes, though the clean-up held things back. I don't suppose your friend's a popular man with the daily commuters.'

Sarah had come through from the kitchen and was leaning against the door. 'He was looking for you, Ray,' she said. She glanced in his direction. 'I tried to call you, but I knew you'd be driving home by the time I heard, so I waited.' She looked across at the DCI. 'I don't like to call him on the mobile if I know he's driving.'

He nodded, his eyes narrowing to slits again. Ray was filled with the sudden urge to force his eyelids apart and tell him to stop pretending to be cool.

'How do you know he was here? You saw him?'

Sarah shook her head. 'No, I wasn't here. He came about half past three this afternoon, started banging on the door and shouting through the letterbox. Our neighbour, Mrs Evans, came out to talk to him. She said he seemed distressed, or ill.'

'Ill? Or drunk?'

'I wouldn't know,' Sarah told him coldly. 'Maybe you'd be better served by asking *her*.'

Whissendine's head jerked back as though she'd physically assaulted him. He should learn to take better control of his emotions, Ray thought. If Whissendine thought *that* was Sarah being prickly, he should feel her when she really got started.

'I'm sure she's in,' Ray told him. 'Do you know where they've taken Martin?'

'To the infirmary, initially. We have someone with him in case he comes to his senses. Did you invite him here today?' he asked.

'Not likely, is it?' Sarah told him. 'I work until half past four on a Thursday and Ray doesn't finish until well after five, even on a quiet day.'

'Would he not have known that?'

Sarah shrugged. 'I don't know that he ever asked,' she said. She retreated to the kitchen.

'I'm sorry we can't be of further help,' Ray said.

Whissendine nodded briefly. 'What would he have come to see you about this time?'

'As I didn't speak to him, I can't really know.'

'No, I suppose not.' Whissendine sighed heavily. 'We still don't know where he's been these past few days.'

'And I can't help you. I'm sorry.'

Whissendine opened the front door. He didn't seem satisfied with Ray's answers. 'You think of anything, you'll be in touch, of course.'

'Of course.'

He watched Whissendine go and then closed the front door and followed Sarah through to the kitchen.

'What aren't you saying?'

She glanced up from the potatoes she was peeling and wiped her hands on a cloth before replying. Then she opened the kitchen drawer and delved among the junk – plastic bags and kitchen foil and clothes pegs – that filled it.

'Martin left this,' she told Ray. 'He pushed it through the letterbox. Only I didn't see it first of all because he screwed it up as small as he could.'

Ray noted the mass of creases which turned the image into a mosaic web.

'An angel,' he said. '*The* angel? You think this could be the kind of image Phil was talking about?'

Sarah nodded. 'I'd say so. You realize what I've done, don't you? I held back evidence, just like Martin did. Only I don't intend to give it to that idiot any time. Martin at least only planned to delay things.'

'No,' Ray said. 'It's nothing like that.'

He reached out for Sarah and pulled her to him, holding her close to his body and working his fingers into the weight of her dark red hair. 'Nothing like that,' he said. He felt her shake her head. 'When we first met,' she told him, 'you said I should have been a police officer, but we never did decide whether I should be good cop or bad cop.' She laughed nervously. 'Back then, Ray, I thought I knew the difference.'

Chapter Ten

It was Saturday, forty-eight hours after Martin's admission to hospital, before Ray was able to see him. He had been transferred twice in that space. Initially to the Bradgate Unit, a psychiatric ward at one of the local hospitals, where he had been assessed, then to a second, private clinic where his peace and invisibility could be assured. Redfern was an old house out at Woodhouse Eaves, set among woodland and grassy lawns.

There had been much media speculation about the man who had spun his car a full three sixty degrees on one of the narrower sections of the Welford Road, frighteningly close to one of the busier and more complicated junctions. The general description of a man in his mid-forties, with greying hair cut short and brown eyes, was sufficiently general for there to be no official confirmation that it was Martin Galloway, but it was a well-known fact all the same. One of the paramedics at the scene had asked him his name. Martin had been unable to reply but a quick search of his pockets revealed a driving licence and other personal documents and there had been several people close enough to hear when the paramedic had again asked for Martin's name and then suggested to this bewildered, terrified man just what it might be.

News reports varied. Some were concerned – what

had pushed him over the edge? It was clear that he'd gone over some way or another. There was speculation that either he had experienced a nervous breakdown – this from the more sympathetic of the media – or taken to drink big time – from the less inclined towards compassion.

When Ray was taken to Martin's room he was lying in bed staring at the ceiling. Even when Ray approached he did not move.

'He's heavily sedated,' the nurse told Ray. 'I don't know if he'll recognize you or if he'll respond even if he does. The other men who came here spent a long time trying to get him to answer their questions.' She shrugged. 'I told them they were wasting their time. I think they were policemen.'

'Has he said *anything*?' Ray asked her.

'Oh a lot of stuff, none of it really makes sense. He woke up screaming about someone called Damien. The one sensible thing he's come out with is, "Tell Ray, tell Ray" over and over again. Your name and number were written in his wallet when his personal effects were sent from the hospital. The police took them away when they came but I think Dr Dattani found your business card. She asked the policemen about you and one of them said you were an old friend. She decided it would be a good idea to send for you.'

Ray thanked her. 'I'm glad she did.'

She smiled at him. 'Dr Dattani would like a word when you've finished,' she said. 'Just ask at the desk and they'll tell you where to go.'

There was no door on Martin's room and a CCTV

camera was trained down on the bed. Ray had noted a whole bank of them at the nurses' station when he came in. A wooden chair stood beside the door and Ray took it over to the bed and sat down. Martin still did not move and Ray was suddenly at a loss. How do you talk to someone who seems as remote and abstracted as this? Not even Martin's eyes moved, though as Ray came close and watched he realized that his lips never stopped. He whispered very, very softly, the movements of his mouth almost imperceptible. For quite some time Ray just sat there, trying to find some words that might get through into Martin's injured brain, while all the time Martin whispered to himself.

'I tried to use a tape player,' someone said. 'Thought I might be able to amplify the sound.'

Ray turned. A male nurse dressed in blue scrubs stood in the doorway. He smiled at Ray and advanced into the room holding out a hand for Ray to shake. 'I'm Steve,' he said. 'Marina said you were a friend come to visit. I was on my break when you arrived.'

He went around to the other side of the bed and took Martin's hand, holding it with a naturalness that Ray envied, and chatting to the man in the bed as though he could hear and understand.

'You've had a bad time, haven't you, my friend?' he said. 'But we'll soon have you right again, don't you worry about that. And someone's come to see you.' He turned to Ray and smiled again. 'Ray, isn't it?'

Ray nodded. 'You say you taped him? Did he say anything that made sense?'

Steve slid his free hand into the drawer of the bedside

table. 'Here,' he said. 'See what you make of it. I gave a copy to the police but they didn't seem impressed,' he laughed. 'I guess they think we amateurs should leave the investigating to them.'

'I used to be a policeman,' Ray told him. 'They feel the same about me now, I think.'

'No kidding?' He gestured towards Ray's face. 'How did that happen?'

'A small case of mistaken identity. Someone with a grudge made very efficient use of an aerosol and a lighter.'

Steve winced. 'Nasty,' he said.

'Easier to fix than this.'

'Than our friend Martin? Probably. But we'll do what we can. This is a good place, not like some I've worked in.'

'The other nurse said he was sedated. Was he violent?'

Steve shook his head. 'Not intentionally,' he said. 'But he was in a great deal of distress. Didn't know where he was or what was happening to him. For Martin everyone seemed like the enemy.'

'He isn't sleeping though,' Ray observed. 'I mean, how long has he spent like this, just staring at the ceiling?'

'A long time,' Steve confirmed. 'We put drops in his eyes to stop them drying out and he has fallen asleep for short periods. The problem is, Ray, I think his dreams are even worse than whatever is happening to him while he's awake.' He shook his blond head. 'I can't imagine what it must be like,' he said softly. 'Not ever being able to escape your nightmares.'

'Can he hear us?' Ray asked Steve. Steve told him that he probably could, but that he wasn't certain that Martin could process the information. The words would be there, sounds entering the ear canal, neurons firing in the brain, but whether or not the connections were working he really couldn't say.

Steve was as helpful as he could be, answering Ray's questions as fully as possible, but when Ray asked him if they knew yet how Martin had come to be this way he hedged for the first time and refused to commit himself.

'You should talk to Dr Dattani,' he said.

Dr Sonia Dattani was a surprise. The name had told Ray to expect an Asian woman but even so he was a little taken aback to be greeted by someone who looked as though she should still be in school. Sonia Dattani was young and pretty and small.

Her black hair reached her shoulders and she was dressed in a dark blue salwar kameez, embroidered at the neck with white and yellow thread. Her ID card hung around her neck and the picture on it showed that not so long ago her hair had been much longer. She was married, he noted. Her wedding band was made of bright Asian gold. Ray liked the colour of it. It always looked so much more brilliant, more assertive than the usual jewellery-shop selection.

Her manner was friendly but very business-like.

'Do you know what your friend was taking?' she asked him once the formalities were over.

'Taking? No, you must be mistaken, Martin doesn't do drugs.'

She gave him a long sceptical look. 'He's suffering from some kind of withdrawal,' she said seriously. 'And he's suffering badly, Mr Flowers. We're not here to judge your friend, but we could help a great deal more if we knew what he was on and how long he'd been using.'

Ray shook his head, not sure that he was hearing right. 'Martin smoked the odd cigar. Drank with the lads after work but he didn't do drugs. I mean not the way you mean.'

'Not the way *I* mean?'

'Tobacco, alcohol, nothing illegal. Nothing stupid.'

'Tobacco and alcohol can be abused substances the same way that heroin can.'

'I bloody know that!' Ray took a deep breath. 'I'm sorry,' he apologized. 'That was rude and unnecessary. I'm just shocked. I've never seen anyone look the way Martin does.'

Sonia Dattani wasn't fazed. She'd seen it all before and heard much worse. 'The more reason for you to want to help me,' she told him.

'I do. I just don't know how.' Ray frowned. 'Can't you find out what he's taken? You must have done tests.'

'Oh yes, we've done tests. Every test we can think of. That's just the problem.'

'I don't understand. What did the tox results say?'

She raised an eyebrow at the terminology, then shook her head. 'We thought we had all the latest designer stuff profiled,' she said. 'And believe me, not a week goes by without someone coming up with a variation. This has us stumped. It's nothing we've seen here before and I've accessed every information exchange we're signed up to and believe me they're pretty comprehensive. Nothing. That's why it's so important you help me, Mr Flowers. He kept asking for you, wanting to tell you something. Is there anything you know? Anything he might have said, even in passing?'

Ray sighed, weighing up what he could tell her. 'What's it doing to him?' he said.

She steepled her fingers and sat back in the rather worn leather chair. 'It's psychotropic in its actions,' she said, 'directly affecting the brain chemistry in a similar way to LSD. If you think of a trip as a brief, semi-controlled psychotic episode you get pretty close to the truth of it. This substance, whatever it is, has induced a series of psychotic episodes, bad trips if you like. Every now and again he'll break out of it for long enough to attempt to take a hold on reality. These lucid interludes last for anything between thirty minutes and an hour, though it's not predictable. Then the drug kicks in again and we lose him.'

Ray was puzzled. 'That's not normal, is it,' he said. 'That's like getting drunk on, what's it called, Pernod. Then drinking water the following morning and reactivating the alcohol.'

She nodded. 'It's quite a good analogue,' she said.

'So, how long before it gets out of his system? It's been two days already.'

She pursed her lips. 'That's the other problem,' she

said. 'It has a polycrest action the like of which we're unfamiliar with. You know, maybe, that heroin will be metabolized out in a couple of days, cannabis in about a week, which is why heroin use has now taken over from cannabis in our prisons.'

Ray nodded acknowledgement. Regular drug testing had a negative effect in one way. If you knew you were going to be tested on a Monday morning and one drug would have cleared from your body if you stopped using on a Friday night and another would still be present, then it didn't take a genius to work out which would be the substance of preference, despite the problems of addiction and withdrawal.

'And this?' he said. 'It's not clearing out.'

Dr Dattani shook her head. 'Most things we take into our bodies act only once. You take aspirin for your headache, it begins to act, its action peaks, it dissipates. There are drugs that peak several times, of course, that have a built-in time release element. Most people will meet up with that kind if they buy time-release vitamins or painkillers. You can buy over-the-counter capsules that are full of mini pills, designed to break down at different, controlled rates so you get a roughly level dose throughout the day.'

'And this? It will take days? A week? Longer?'

She shook her head. 'We just don't know. So far there's been no decrease, no sign of let-up at all and that's very frightening. We still don't have all the tox results in but what we have so far points to something very strange. Unique in my experience.'

'You said frightening. In what way particularly?'

'It seems,' she said, 'to have flicked . . . if you like . . . a chemical switch in the brain that the brain seems unable to switch back. We see this kind of thing all the time, of course. It's characteristic of certain types of depression, of schizophrenia, of many types of mental illness. I tend to think of it as something like the points on a railway line. The chemicals that get unbalanced in the brain switch the points one way. The drugs we use attempt to close them back onto the main track instead of diverting everything into a siding.' She smiled shyly at him. 'I know it sounds a little strange put like that, but it usually gets the message across to anxious relatives. Without knowing what the original chemical change was puts us at a disadvantage when it comes to trying to correct it. This substance, Mr Flowers. This drug has caused what I'm afraid might be a permanent change unless we can intervene quickly and in the correct way. It's causing major storms inside his brain that plunge him into this nightmare world and we don't have a clue as yet how to block those signals. The points have been switched over, but right now we don't even know what line they're on.'

Ray thought about it for a moment and then he began to tell her about Martin's visit the previous Sunday, about the trouble he had found himself in and about Damien.

'Why would he take a drug he knew had almost killed this boy?' she asked.

He was a little surprised by her conclusion. 'We don't know that he did.'

'No. You're right. It just seems so much of a coincidence though. This boy, Martin's interest, what happened to him? And you obviously see a connection or you would not have mentioned it.'

'I think there's a connection, yes. And if you think it'll help I'll find out all I can about Damien Pinsent. But I don't even know where he was treated, I'm afraid.'

'I'll try to track him down,' she said. 'I'll start with Mallingham General and work out from there. I think I might be able to find out more than you.'

'Probably,' he agreed. 'But I'd be obliged . . .'

'If I let you know?' She thought about it. 'I can't breach patient confidentiality,' she said. 'But anything I *can* tell you, I will.' She frowned anxiously. 'Mr Flowers,' she asked, 'you seem very certain that your friend would not have taken the drug of his own volition.'

'That's because I am very certain. Martin was stupid in many ways. Full of good intentions and sometimes impulsive in his actions, but he wasn't stupid in *that* way. There's no way Martin would willingly have taken anything like that.'

She stared at him, then shook her head. 'You're saying someone deliberately administered this, knowing what it would do.'

'I'm saying that he found Angel Eyes,' Ray said.

Chapter Eleven

Ray drove back to the office in thoughtful mood. Flowers-Mahoney staff did not as a rule work on Saturdays but they had moved recently from their initial premises in Clarendon Park to a more substantial and more central location on the London Road and the extra work involved meant that Saturday mornings had been work-time for the past few weeks. The building had a lot of history to it, being the location of the first detective agency set up in Leicester. Busts of Hanky Smith in his various disguises decorated the window sconces and a blue plaque recorded him for posterity.

Ray missed the tree-lined, peaceful road that had been their earlier home, but this place had a car park to the rear – accessible unless you were driving one of the larger luxury models – and room for expansion now that they had Phil and his equipment on their team.

If Martin had come looking for him then he'd been on the wrong road, though from what Ray had seen, Martin probably wasn't thinking his way through the A to Z at the time.

George looked up as Ray came in. 'How is he?'

'Not good.' He helped himself to coffee from the jug on the hotplate that Phil insisted was kept topped up. Phil rarely seemed to eat, but he needed a constant supply of caffeine to help him through the day. Ray slumped down on the other side of George's desk and filled him in on Martin's condition and what Dr Dattani had been able to tell him.

Phil came in halfway through and Ray automatically handed him the tape that Steve had made. He disappeared and returned a minute or two later with a tape player and a pair of headphones. He hooked one side over an ear and listened with the other one as Ray continued with his account.

'Anything?' Ray asked as he came to an end and Phil switched the player to rewind.

'Odd words. It'll need work to make out any more. You say the police have a copy?'

'Apparently.'

'Then they'll have to send it away to get it enhanced. I don't think they've got anything locally that'll filter this properly and increase the gain sufficiently. That might take them a few days.'

'And do *we* have what's needed?' Ray asked him.

Phil just smiled. 'I'll take this down to Peckham,' he said to George. 'Get Mason onto it. All right if I go this afternoon?'

'Soon as you like,' George told him. 'Buy him a drink for me.'

'Peckham?' Ray wanted to know.

'An old friend,' George told him. 'Used to work at GCHQ. Listening post, you know.'

'And they let him take his toys with him?'

George smiled. 'Mason designed most of them,' he said. 'He's a nice old man. You'll have to meet him some time.'

Phil grinned again. Ray decided not to ask any more. 'Before you clear off,' he said, 'there's something else.' He withdrew the tattered bit of paper that Sarah had found from inside an envelope in his jacket pocket.

'Sarah found this,' he said. 'It was crumpled into a ball and had been shoved through her letterbox. She's certain Martin must have left it.'

'You've told the police?' George asked.

'Have I hell! Sarah didn't let on until Whissendine had left last night.'

Phil picked it up and examined it carefully, rubbing the paper between his fingers and finally sniffing at it and touching an edge lightly onto his tongue. Ray winced. Phil *did* have some funny habits.

'Torn from a magazine rather than a book,' he said.

'That's what we thought. The finish on the paper's glossier than you'd find in an art book and the paper stock seems thinner.'

Phil turned it over to examine the back. Much of it was blank white but there were fragments of red lettering along the bottom edge. 'An advert,' Phil guessed. 'One of those pretentious ones where you still don't know what they're selling even when you've read the text.'

'Sarah thinks it might be from a woman's magazine,' he said. 'I don't know why. A case of Sarah intuition, I think.'

'Nothing wrong with Sarah intuition,' George commented. 'I'm inclined to agree. Whether or not that will help us find the full image, I don't know, and until we can find the full image and what it's called our chances of turning it up in a search are pretty remote.'

'But it's a start?' Ray said.

Phil had taken the picture back. 'It might not be *that* hard,' he said. 'I can scan it, put it out on a few of the art forums. Someone out there will know.'

'You can do that?' Ray was still slightly mystified by cyberspace. He'd only just learnt to send his own email.

'Easily. I'll get on to it now, then I'll be off to Peckham.' He refilled his coffee mug and wandered back into the inner office.

Ray laughed. Then he shook his head. 'I still need to find Winter,' he said. 'From what Martin told me, Winter knows everything that Martin knew.'

'A retired police officer,' George mused. 'Did he give any idea of when he'd retired?'

'No, and Martin's been a copper for a long time. They could go back a fair way.'

'He's still in Mallingham though, almost certainly.'

'Why do you say that?'

'Think, Ray. The time factor. Martin did his little act at the warehouse, took the stuff to Winter and then got home to find Whissendine and company waiting for him. That was when, just past midnight? The reports of shooting came in from the warehouse at half past nine. That gives around two, two and a half hours for Martin and company to get away. Martin to see this Winter person and discuss what they had. Then get home. He won't have travelled far.'

It was sound enough reasoning. 'Martin's been careful to protect Winter so far,' he said. 'I wonder if the tenants' association knew about him.'

'You don't have any clue who was with Martin that night?'

'Three names. Micky, Peter or Pete and Ravi. I remember that one because of the musician. Martin mentioned them when we talked about the warehouse, but only the names, nothing else.'

'Not much to go on,' George agreed. 'You'll have to go down there, I think. Put in some old-fashioned detective work. And as far as this Winter is concerned, there must be records of who took early retirement and why. I'll get on to it.'

'I'd rather you didn't.'

'Oh?'

'Martin went to lengths to protect this man, said he needed to keep his pension. If you start poking around, someone somewhere is bound to notice.'

'Give me some credit, Ray. I used to earn my living doing this sort of thing.'

'True,' Ray conceded. 'Anyway, tomorrow, I'll go to the Armitage and see what I can stir up.'

'Tomorrow? Not today?'

'It's four already. Time I get there it'll be dark or close to, even if I leave now. I don't care how much Martin and his friends've improved the place, I'm not going there at night without back-up.'

Chapter Twelve

Sunday morning. Ray drove out to Mallingham and parked in a side road a few streets from the Armitage Estate. It was some time since he'd been on the Armitage though he'd grown up in the area and knew it well. The redevelopment that had begun in the sixties was still going on, as far as he could see. Mallingham had been bombed in the Second World War. It used to be a standing joke that the bombers offloaded anything they had left after Coventry on the place, using the big chimneys of the smelting mills to line up their targets. It had never been a pretty town – Ray had seen old photographs and it had always had that half-finished, confused air about it that it had now. Ray had been born eleven years after the war ended and grown up among the dereliction left by both the bombing and the subsequent waves of demolition as Mallingham tried to rediscover itself and take bold steps into an unknown future.

None of it had worked, Ray mused. As he drove in today he noticed that the empty places awaiting the attention of the contractors and developers were still those that had become playgrounds for Ray and his friends when they had all been kids.

The Armitage had been one of the biggest casualties of this lack of planning. The rows and rows of terraced houses such as had been Ray's home had been bought by the council under compulsory purchase. Few of the tenants had owned them back then and those few that had mostly moved into the adjacent streets and carried on as always.

This was the decade of the high-rise and the council that had built the Armitage had not wanted to seem behind the times. Three had been built, another three planned before the money ran out, and even by the time the first three had been completed the problems had already begun.

Families had nowhere for their kids to play, so the kids hung around the communal balconies and the lift entrances and the community laundry rooms and made nuisances of themselves. When they were old enough to be turned loose, they played among the rubble that had been their parents' old homes and the empty, gaping spaces that had been originally allocated for the other blocks.

A new school had been planned but never built and the kids were arbitrarily divided into two groups, one lot going to Millfield – Ray's old primary school – the other to Grove Park, a few streets away on the opposite side of Armitage.

A community centre had also been planned and eventually arrived in the mid-eighties in the form of two giant portacabins donated by a construction company building new factories nearby. They'd written the gift off as a charitable donation to the newly founded residents' association and having to move them only half a mile down the road using voluntary labour from the estate saved them a packet since they did not have to fully dismantle and remove and then dispose of the now redundant, shabby and well-used structures.

Ray remembered their arrival. The residents had painted them up, turfed the ground around them and even planted trees. The mayor had come down to cut the tape and a playgroup started three days a week. So far as Ray knew that was still the only community structure on the estate and last time he saw it was getting shabbier by the minute.

Ray got out of his car and began to walk the short distance to the estate. He passed the end of his old street and paused to glance down the length of it, noting how little it had changed since he'd been a boy. There were more parked cars, but the kids still played kerbie where space allowed, kicking a football back and forth across the street, bouncing it off the kerbstones. His dad's old house still had hanging baskets suspended from the hooks his dad had put up outside the front door and Ray was glad about that. His dad would have been pleased, he thought, and then realized how little he thought of his childhood in terms of what his mother had said and done. Odd that. It wasn't that he hadn't, didn't, love his mother, who long ago remarried and moved abroad. It was merely that she was always such a background presence in his life, rarely participating or even commenting upon it, whereas his father had always been there, right at its centre.

Ray's childhood had, he felt, generally been a happy one though. The improvised playgrounds he and his friends had made for themselves on the derelict land had been perfect for all their objective unsuitability and he found himself smiling at memories of the games they had played. The dens they had built. The time Bill Hughes had got himself stuck in a disused drain when they'd been playing hide and seek and the fire brigade had been called to dismantle the thing and get him out. It had always been a mystery to Ray and his contemporaries just how Bill had got himself in there in the first place. He was a plump little lad, as round as he was tall. He'd done well for himself in the end though. Gone on to become an accountant and now living out on the Nottingham Road, an exclusive area not four miles geographically from where he'd grown up but a million miles away in spirit.

Ray had only the germ of a plan in his mind as he walked onto Armitage turf for the first time in – he calculated quickly – maybe eleven years. His early police career had been in Mallingham, but much of the later years had been spent ten miles away in Middleton and after his father had died he'd rarely found a reason to return at all.

The events of the previous year came back to him. Ray had been dragged into an investigation concerning a cult called the Eyes of God. Just prior to his move from Mallingham CID to Middleton there had been a series of murders involving the original leader of the Eyes of God, a man called Harrison Lee. Ray had been on the team that had worked the investigation and when, fifteen months ago, there had been a series of what appeared to be copycat killings, following Lee's death in prison, Ray had been called in as an advisor. It was not something Ray liked to think about and he had not been back to the town since.

The Armitage was, at first glance, pretty much as he remembered it. Neater though, he had to admit as he looked more closely. New turf covered the banks and hollows around the tower blocks and kids ran up and down with their arms spread wide. Play equipment – *unvandalized* – filled two or three sites that Ray could see between the buildings, and saplings had been planted and left untouched long enough to have an established look, with long grass and the remains of spring daffodils growing among their roots.

Despite himself, Ray was impressed. There was a relaxed air to the Armitage Estate that Ray would not have associated with it. That, and an absence of burnt-out cars.

A couple of young mothers sat on seats atop the grass banks, taking advantage of a rare bright day, watching their children play, wrapped up warm against the chill March wind. They glanced in Ray's direction as he passed but their look was certainly not unfriendly. On every lamp post was a little notice advertising the fact that he had now entered a neighbourhood-watch area.

Ray made his way to the community centre. The portacabins were still there, but they had been painted and a chainlink fence created a compound around them. As he came round, Ray noticed a hard court had been laid in the rear and kids were playing an improvised game of basketball. Next to that and divided by a low wall was an area for the little ones covered in safety flooring and filled with brightly coloured plastic slides and rocking horses, equipment that wouldn't have been safe for five minutes together on the Armitage Ray had known. Inside, one side of the joined cabins was now designated 'Youth Club', and Ray could see a pool table and table tennis as he glanced through the door. Through the other door was an empty room with tables stacked against the walls and a stereo positioned close to a block stage. The whole was painted and cleaned and cared for and Ray could hardly believe what he was seeing. Silently, he congratulated Martin on what he had achieved, then, half heartedly, cancelled the congratulations when he remembered at what price. Martin had broken the law as clearly as those he and his friends had evicted forcibly from their streets.

The space between the two cabins, which in Ray's time had been separate, had now been filled in. This new 'room' was a drop-in centre with tea and coffee being served by a young woman standing behind an improvised counter. Martin had mentioned this and it had seemed to Ray like a good place to begin.

He stood just inside the doorway, looking at the people chatting around the tiny round plastic tables. Mothers mostly with small children. A handful of men, a few teens wandering through to buy sweets from the counter. He had, he figured, an audience of about thirty-five, and unless the Armitage had changed beyond all comprehension that was enough to give his plan a damned good start.

He waited until he knew he had been noted. A stranger to the area and a stranger with a distinctive face.

A stranger that shrieked 'police' to anyone as used to recognizing the species as you would be if you'd grown up here.

Ray didn't wait until he was challenged. He noticed one of the men pushing back his chair and starting to get up, another turning to look at him, eyes resting on the scarred face and the bulk of a body as though assessing how fast Ray might be able to run. Ray knew that old frisson of fear shiver up his spine, familiar from earlier times, and he knew that the veneer cast over Armitage was merely a veneer for all that it impressed.

He stood his ground, facing the man down, and then began to speak. He was aware of the sudden hush that spread through the place and that every eye turned towards him, ears straining for every word.

'I'm a friend of Martin Galloway's,' he said. 'Right now, Martin's lying in a hospital bed. He doesn't see anything, know anyone. He can't speak and the doctor who's treating him tells me he's in a lot of pain. I know from what Martin told me that he's done a lot of work here. That he's helped you clean the place up and make it somewhere you want your kids to grow up in and I can't believe that you'll want what happened to Martin to go unpunished.'

He paused. The media still had not confirmed that Martin was the man who'd crashed out on the Welford Road and Ray wasn't sure he should be the one who broke the news.

'Martin came to me a week ago and asked for my help,' he said. 'At the time I didn't know what I could do. Martin believed that the dealers you'd pushed out of

Armitage wanted back in. That something more dangerous than any of those you'd rid yourselves of was on its way back, and it seems he was right. Martin's investigation took him too close and someone punished him for it. Right now, we don't know if he's going to recover, but it would help him, help the investigation, if someone comes out and tells what they know. Anything they know about what Martin was looking into.'

He paused, aware that the man who'd stood up had now left the room. That another stood uncertainly looking at the door. In his hand, Ray held a bunch of business cards, blank ones he'd bought at the local stationer's and filled out with his name and the number of the office phone. The night before he'd switched it to divert to his own mobile. He fanned them out and went to the tables nearest to him, dropping them down in front of the tea drinkers and young mothers. Then he pinned one to the noticeboard on the café wall.

'You don't have to leave your names,' he said. 'Just leave a message. Any time. Anything that you might know. I know the police will have come round and asked a lot of questions of a lot of people but I'm only here as Martin's friend and I just want to find out what was done to him and why. I'm sure you'll all feel the same.'

No one spoke, though he saw glances exchanged and another of the men left, brushing past him on the way to the door.

Ray left then, making his way from the community centre, a small audience of teens and curious kids in tow.

Ray walked slowly round the Armitage Estate. At each of the tower blocks he stopped to talk to the security guard and leave his card. He was aware as he left the last that the atmosphere on the estate had changed. Once in a while he glimpsed uniformed police doing house to house, no doubt asking about the dead men. On one occasion a pair turned to observe Ray but made no move to come over and ask what was going on, despite the fact that he now headed a substantial procession. It was wary now, suspicious, more like the Armitage that he had known.

His audience had increased in number to a crowd of about thirty, kids mostly, but with a few adults watching his moves. They dogged his steps and no one spoke to him, but they talked among themselves, a low, wary murmur combined with distrustful looks as they escorted him on his slow march around their territory. Ray tried to look calm but their silence was unnerving. The way they all kept pace with him, kept the same distance from him, guided his perambulations slowly but inevitably towards the edges of their territory was intimidating.

Ray paused at the road that separated Armitage from the rest of Mallingham beside a lamp post that bore a notice advertising the neighbourhood watch. He slid a final few business cards into the gap between the rivets fixing it to the post, then waved goodbye to his escort. He made his way swiftly back to his car, aware that sweat trickled down his back and his hands were clammy and his chest tight.

Whissendine was leaning against the driver's door.

'And you think you were doing *what*?' he asked heavily.

'Shaking the tree and seeing what falls out.'

Whissendine was not impressed. 'This isn't your business any more. You should butt out.'

Ray shrugged. He dug in his pocket and withdrew a final card, slipping it into Whissendine's breast pocket. 'Just in case there's anything you want me to know,' he said.

Chapter Thirteen

Ray phoned Dr Dattani to tell her that he had found some press cuttings about Damien Pinsent. He had also found mention of Damien's girlfriend, whose eighteenth birthday party he had been attending the night he fell. Her name was Miriam Taylor and Ray had made a note of it.

He had intended merely to leave a message for Sonia Dattani and call back on the Monday morning, and was surprised to find that she was working.

'There has to be someone available in case we get weekend admissions,' she explained. 'We do it on a rota. I was going to call you, actually.'

'Oh?

'Yes. I've found Damien. It was much easier than I expected. He's in a small unit attached to Mallingham General. He's now on life support, his condition has worsened over the past months, but his parents, well, his mother, won't give up hope and won't let them take him off.'

'You mean, he's clinically dead?'

'I'm afraid so. And there doesn't seem much hope. Sometimes, when you have what we call a vegetative state, then there is some hope of there being a return to consciousness on some level. That's not the case with Damien.'

'It must be very hard on the parents.'

'Oh, so hard. Impossible. Apparently they've tried everything over the years. His mother has even brought in some kind of spiritualist to try to contact him. I suppose his mother feels she has to try everything, however bizarre.'

'A spiritualist?'

'Something like that. Medium, spiritualist, fortune-teller. I don't know much about that sort of thing.' She paused. 'They must be in so much pain. Damien was their only child.'

Ray thought for a moment. 'I'd like to see him,' he said. 'And talk to his family and his friends.'

'I thought you might. I've arranged for us to visit later this afternoon if you're free.'

'Us?'

'I thought the staff might be willing to say more if I were with you and I have to admit, I'm curious about this too. Martin is a unique experience and I'm hoping he stays that way, but . . .'

'But you're afraid he won't.'

'I'm afraid he won't,' she confirmed. 'I'll meet you there at four, if that's OK. Apparently the mother visits every Sunday afternoon, so we should get to see her too.'

Ray thanked her and then Sonia Dattani said awkwardly, 'The police came back and wanted to know what we'd talked about.'

'You told them?'

'I gave them an outline. I didn't know what else to do. They seemed interested and I thought, well, we all want the same thing, don't we?'

'That's all right,' Ray said. He'd figured it would happen and, like she said, they were all supposed to want the same thing.

'They know most of it already,' he said. 'Anyway, I guess I don't qualify for patient confidentiality.'

'You should be glad of that,' Sonia Dattani told him.

It was exactly a week since Martin had come to see him. Ray met Dr Dattani at Mallingham General, running from the car park through rain pouring out of a leaden sky. The cold sunshine of the morning now a distant memory.

She was dressed in jeans today. Jeans and a bright pink sweater and standing in the reception area talking to a good-looking young man whom she introduced as her husband, Sunil.

'His brother lives not far from here,' she explained. 'I'll be joining them after, if you don't mind giving me a lift.'

'No, of course not,' Ray agreed. 'I'm truly grateful to you for organizing this.' He was aware that Sunil was assessing him, this intruder into their Sunday afternoon, but he must have passed muster because the goodbye was friendly enough and he seemed willing to trust Ray to take care of his wife.

'Have you been married long?' he asked her.

'Just over a year. I wanted to wait until I'd got my qualifications and a decent job. Sunil is a pharmacist. He runs his own shop and he wanted me to qualify as well. It's good to have support. Are you married, Ray?'

'I was. It kind of fizzled out a long time ago. She's remarried now and very happy I believe. I have someone though,' he added. 'Her name's Sarah and she's very special.'

Sonia nodded. 'That's good,' she said. 'It isn't right for people to be alone.'

'Had you known Sunil long before you married?'

She laughed. 'Is that a polite way of asking if it was arranged? Actually, we practically grew up together. Our parents were good friends and it was kind of understood. Oh, we both saw other people when we were away at university, but nothing seemed to sit right, you know what I mean. Sunil and I have been good friends for so long that it seemed easy to take that other step.' She smiled at Ray. 'I think that's the most important part of any marriage anyway, don't you, that you're good friends.'

They had reached the extension that housed the unit where Damien had been for the past two years. It was away from the main part of the hospital, attached only by a long corridor with windows down either side and Ray wondered if that were deliberate. The rain lashed at the windows and as they walked between the glass the lightning had begun and thunder made the windows tremble in their frames.

'Does Damien's mother know we're coming?' he asked, raising his voice to be heard above the storm.

Sonia nodded. 'The staff here thought that she should be warned. The doctor I spoke to described her as fragile, easily distressed. She's been told that you're a friend of Martin's.'

'Does she know what happened to him?'

'I don't think so. Play it carefully, Ray. She sounds as though she's had all that she can take.'

Damien Pinsent lay in a white room. He was so young, Ray thought. Pale skin and dark hair brushed back against the pillow. He was wired to machines that ticked and hissed in time to the artificial pattern of his life. What there was left of it.

His mother sat beside the bed fumbling through a collection of music tapes and talking to her son in a fast, low voice. She seemed to be telling him about the next-door neighbour's dog. That it had run away and nearly been hit by a car up on the main road, but she spoke so fast and so breathlessly that there seemed to be no concentration on the words. Ray guessed that she had long since abandoned the search for anything meaningful to say. Now she just sought to fill the silence, to block out the sound of the machines that pumped air into inactive lungs and infused a dead brain with oxygen.

'Mrs Pinsent.' Sonia approached her softly. At first the woman did not appear to hear. Sonia crouched down beside her and touched her hand, saying her name again. This time Emily Pinsent looked around.

'I'm Dr Sonia Dattani,' she introduced herself. 'Dr Kepple told you we'd be coming today.'

For a moment Emily Pinsent looked blankly at her, then, finally sensing Ray's presence, she glanced in his direction.

'Oh, Martin's friend,' she said. 'Yes, they told me. Is Martin here?'

'No, I'm afraid he's not, Mrs Pinsent,' Sonia told her. 'He had an accident, you see. I'm looking after him until he's better.'

'Are you another policeman?' Emily Pinsent asked Ray. 'Martin said he would try and find the one that did this to my boy. He said he'd find them. Has he found them?'

'Martin's very ill, Mrs Pinsent,' Ray explained. 'He asked me to see what I could do.'

'Ah, yes I see.' She looked back at Damien. 'He's a good man, Martin. You know, sometimes he'd just come in and sit with me. Often not saying a word, but it was so comforting just to know that someone cared.'

'I didn't know he did that,' Ray told her.

'No one did. He told no one. That was Martin's way.'

Yes, Ray thought, and that was the pity of it.

'Does anyone else visit?' Sonia asked.

Emily shrugged. 'His father couldn't bear it any more,' she says. 'He divorced me in the end because he couldn't bear it. We couldn't agree, you see. He said that we should just, you know, let him go. But I couldn't do that. Not my son. His friends used to come but after a while that tailed off. They had their own lives. I couldn't grudge them their own lives.'

'Miriam Taylor,' Ray said. 'Did she still come?'

'Miri came for the longest time. She's a good girl. They went out together, you know. Then Miriam went away to university, you know, not long after . . . not long after this happened, but she didn't finish her studies. Damien stopped her, you see. Knowing what had happened to him. It hit them all so hard.'

Ray wondered if that were the real reason that Miriam dropped out of college. He could think of a dozen reasons why she might have done so that had nothing to do with Damien but he did not say anything. It was clear that Emily's world revolved about her son and she assumed that for everyone else that must also be the case.

'Where *is* Martin?' she asked suddenly.

Ray was surprised. He thought they had explained to her. 'He's in hospital,' he told her gently. 'He crashed his car.' He looked at Sonia, hoping he was taking the best line here. She nodded at him. Emily was in no frame of mind to absorb anything more complicated.

'Was he badly hurt?' she asked, but even as she framed the question the brief concern that lit her pale grey eyes was gone and she looked back once more with full concentration at the shell of her only son.

'He'll be all right,' Ray told her, hoping that it was true.

'Yes,' Emily nodded. She reached out and took Damien by the hand. 'That's what I keep telling them.'

Startled, Ray realized that she was again talking about Damien.

Ray felt profoundly depressed as he and Sonia left the hospital.

'Could Martin end up like that?' he asked her.

She shook her head. 'What you see with Damien is the result of oxygen starvation,' she said. 'He drowned, Ray. They may have got his heart started again, but he must have been starved of air for far too long. The drug can't have helped, but it wasn't the primary cause.'

'Poor woman,' Ray said. 'Poor kid. I can understand why Martin wouldn't let it go.'

Sonia nodded. 'I've talked to the doctor in charge. They've been urging her to withdraw support and let him die but she's convinced that Damien is still in there somewhere and that one day he'll wake up.'

Ray thought about the image of Damien that Martin said he kept seeing and toyed with the idea of telling Sonia about it. But it didn't seem relevant. Martin was stressed and exhausted. It was a measure of just *how* much that he should start seeing apparitions in broad daylight.

Instead, he allowed himself to fantasize for a moment, to let himself suppose that Martin might truly have seen the boy, his spirit roaming free while his body remained chained to the life-support system that could breathe life back into lungs but not into such a seriously damaged brain.

'I think,' he told Sonia Dattani, 'that I'd just want to die.'

Chapter Fourteen

They left the hospital and Ray dropped Sonia Dattani at her brother-in-law's house, declining her invitation to come in and meet her family. He felt that he had already imposed too much upon her free time. He checked his mobile for missed calls. There were none. As yet no responses to his visit to the Armitage that morning, but Ray was not discouraged. The people he wanted to speak to would have to discuss among themselves first what best to do.

Back at Sarah's house he discovered that George had dropped a list off for him. It contained the names of all those officers who had taken early retirement from Mallingham over the previous ten years. Eagerly, Ray looked it over, wondering how George had managed to come up with it so fast, but there was no sign of anyone called Winter or any variation on the name. Disappointed, Ray put it aside. He settled down to spend the rest of the evening with Sarah and wait for the next moves to be made.

The next move was a surprising one. Just as Ray had resigned himself to a quiet night in front of the television, the telephone rang. It was DCI Whissendine.

'Meet me for a drink and we'll talk.'

At eight o'clock he met up with the DCI at the Black Horse by the Victoria Park on London Road.

Ray had been surprised when Whissendine had suggested this place, being a good way off the DCI's patch, but he agreed readily enough, curious as to what he wanted.

Whissendine was alone and that and the choice of location told Ray that this was to be an off-the-record chat. So off-the-record that not even his close colleagues would know about it.

'Do you know more than you're letting on?' Whissendine asked him as they took their places in the corner of the already crowded lounge bar. In summer it was pleasant to sit out in the gardens of the Black Horse, but at this time of year it was far too cold and everyone packed inside. 'If you do, Ray, I urge you to come clean. This is bigger than you think.'

'In what way?'

Whissendine took a thoughtful slurp of his pint. 'Ray, we've got a good officer down already, and he is, was, a good officer for all his faults, all his mistakes. I don't want to see you going the same way.'

'Is that a threat?'

'Not from me. Ray, we knew what Martin was on to. We let him run with it, just to see what he'd turn up. Not the warehouse business. That caught us off guard, but his hunch that whoever did for Damien Pinsent was on the roll again. But I couldn't put resources I didn't have into what might be a wild goose chase.'

'Turned out not to be though, didn't it? And Martin suffered the consequences.'

'I didn't see you exactly rushing to his aid. The impression we got was that you didn't want to know until Martin was hurt. Avoiding the man's calls doesn't exactly give the impression of solidarity.'

Ray sighed. 'No,' he said. 'I didn't want to know. Do you think there is a link between this warehouse business and the two dead men and what Martin was looking into on the drug side?'

'You gave me the impression *you* did. No, just a bluff, was it?'

'I'm beginning to think it was more of a lucky guess. Martin was making waves. Big waves, and his influence was spreading outward from the Armitage. I've no doubt that if the Armitage started getting the funding pumped into it that he hoped it would, other areas would, take a lesson from what he'd done – the legitimate side anyway. I saw what a difference had been made when I went there yesterday.'

'You created a few waves yourself. One of our informants phoned us, suggested we might want to rescue a big fat copper with a scarred face before someone taught him a lesson. I told my lot to keep an eye open.'

'I saw your officers doing house to house but they seemed to want to keep clear of me. Who was in this residents' group of Martin's? Do you know that?'

'Oh, we know all about the legitimate membership. Who made these little night-time forays with Martin is another matter. A connection between the would-be child pornographers and the local drug scene wouldn't surprise me though. Organized crime tends to cover all the bases.' He frowned thoughtfully. 'Martin was getting careless though,' he said. 'Withholding evidence is a serious matter. I can't understand why he did that.'

'Martin was exhausted, probably wasn't thinking straight.' So they had no idea about Winter, he thought. Or that this was not the first time.

'Probably so,' Whissendine confirmed.

'What led you to him that night though? He told me you and Field were waiting for him when he came home.'

'We had a tip-off that something was going on that night. When the shooting started we realized it was bigger than anyone had let on. I went to Martin's place to warn him off, catch him at it. The truth is, Ray, I'm not quite sure which. I hoped there'd be nothing to talk to him about but he handed me the evidence bags then. We weren't waiting to arrest him, caution him or any other damned thing. I went there as a friend. It was almost as if he wanted to be found out, wanted to end it.'

'And what did you do with the stuff then?' Ray asked curiously.

But Whissendine didn't answer directly. 'I respect him, Ray, as an officer and as a man. I'm deeply sorry for what's happened to him. We should have closed in on him before, demanded he tell us everything he'd found thus far and pulled him right out. As you say, he was exhausted, and I think he knew it.'

'He knew it was time to hand things over,' Ray mused. 'That's why he betrayed himself to you, gave you the evidence bags when he could quite easily have kept quiet. I think that was why he came to me.' Martin's visit was taking on a new complexion. 'It strikes me that Martin was making a cry for help. Trouble was, no one was listening.'

'Why didn't he just come straight out with it? If he'd found something conclusive, why didn't he just come to me? Had he given me something to work with I could have made the investigation official and put some resources into the field.'

'You're making the assumption that he knew you were shadowing him.'

'He probably suspected. But if he had or he hadn't why didn't he come to me if he knew anything that could give me a reason to open a case file, get things moving?'

Ray held back, there was only one reason he could think of for Martin's continued deception. He didn't trust someone. Whissendine? Someone else? Ray didn't know.

'As it was,' Ray said, 'he took it upon himself and obviously found the source, then got poisoned for his trouble.'

'Why do that?' Whissendine asked. 'That's what I keep coming back to. Why not just kill him?'

'To send a message to the rest of us,' Ray said grimly.

Chapter Fifteen

The residents' association action sub-committee had convened a meeting at Winter's flat. Ray's little exhibition following close on the shootings had unsettled everyone and there was a predominant feeling that perhaps their association had become too deeply embroiled. It was one thing to beat up the occasional dealer and to expect the odd brawl, but it was quite another to have two men shot execution-style not half a mile from where your kids played and your family shopped.

What Winter had to tell them did nothing to reassure.

'Martin believed that the dealers were about to make a move,' he said. 'I don't mean the small-time players who sell the occasional E and think they're the next Mafiosi. I mean the likes of Pierce and the mob that was ready to push Pierce to the wall three years ago.'

'You think this was a punishment killing?' someone asked. 'For letting down whoever owned that stuff?'

Winter nodded.

'And what about those kids? I've not let mine out of the house since. I mean, if we hadn't done something . . .'

No one spoke. There was no need.

'What happened to Martin was no accident,' Winter said. 'I don't know what happened yet, but I knew Martin for years. He didn't drink and drive and he certainly didn't do drugs. Whatever else he was, he was no hypocrite. He believed in what he was doing here.'

'Look, we know that,' Ravi said quietly. '*We* knew Martin too and we've got to know you these past couple of years. And we said from the very beginning you were one of our own. Pig or not. You were all right and like we told Martin, as long as you wanted to stay here, we'd make sure you did OK.'

'I know. And I'm grateful. We both are.'

Gita took his hand and squeezed it tight. 'We ought to talk to this Ray Flowers,' she said. He might at least be able to tell us how Martin is and what the hell is going on.'

Pete, who'd been with Ravi at the warehouse that night, nodded slowly. 'Wouldn't hurt,' he said. 'And I say we don't let ourselves be scared shitless by this. We fight back. So long as we all stick together we can keep the bastards out.'

Winter grimaced but he said nothing. A general murmur of approval rippled through the room. And so it was decided. A group of them would interview ex-Inspector Flowers and find out what he knew.

As the residents' association sub-committee filed out, Micky held back, waiting for a word with Winter. He'd been silent all evening, watching the ebb and flow of conversation but adding little to it.

'I'm scared,' he said without preamble.

Winter paused. 'Micky, I know what happened three years ago. What's happening now . . . Martin was convinced it was all connected. Watch your back. Even better, take yourself away for a while until this all blows over.'

'I can't do that. What would I tell my family? And what if . . . what if I did go and something happened to them because of me? I couldn't live with that. Pete's right. We've got to face things head on.'

He left then and Winter wheeled himself over to the window to watch him go back across the grass. A dark figure with a darker shadow, slipping from protective pool of light to protective pool of light, and a second figure close behind, though casting no answering shadow on the ground.

Chapter Sixteen

The call Ray had been waiting for came on the Monday evening while he was watching television with Sarah. Or rather, while he was trying to watch, his attention sliding repeatedly from the flickering images on the screen. It was a brief conversation, but one that forced Ray to break his self-imposed rule about not straying onto the Armitage Estate at night.

'Call George,' he told Sarah, 'and tell him where I've gone. I'll check in with you every hour and if I don't, then telephone Whissendine and George and get them to send the cavalry.'

'I want to come with you.'

'No. I need you here, just in case, and anyway if they see two people in the car it might frighten them off.'

Sarah looked mutinous and seemed as though she might argue. Instead she asked, 'Do you know who *they* are?'

'They said they represent the residents' association, that's all I know. Don't worry, Sarah, I'll be fine, but you're my back-up just in case.'

Ray drove through a miserable drizzle-filled night out to Mallingham and parked his car where he had been told to on the road separating the Armitage from the terraced streets. He wasn't happy about doing this. He could remember a time when anyone who left their vehicles there would come back to find their hubcaps missing and often their wheels as well, but the caller, a young man from the sound of his voice, had given him little option. 'We want to see you arrive,' Ray had been told. 'We want to see that you're alone. Then we might think about talking to you.'

Ray waited by his car, leaning against the door as Whissendine had done a few days earlier, and peering out through the mist of rain, straining to see across the wasteland that still lay between where he stood and the nearest of the tower blocks.

'Don't turn around, Mr Flowers,' a polite but accented voice behind him instructed. Instinctively, Ray jerked his head towards the sound.

'I asked you not to do that,' the voice told him.

Asked, Ray noted, interested that at least whoever it was went to the effort of being polite.

A hand came to rest on Ray's shoulders. The owner of the hand pressed close behind him, pushing him away from the car. 'Listen, Mr Flowers, we want to talk but we can't talk here. So we're going to have to take you somewhere else and we'd rather not risk you seeing anything, like us, or where you're going, so I'm going to put a blindfold on. You understand.'

Ray nodded. 'All right,' he said. 'But I'm warning you, I've promised someone that I'll call in every hour to let them know I'm all right. If I don't they've got instructions to call the police.'

'I told you he weren't to be trusted,' a second voice

said. 'How do we know he's not already got them down here?'

'Relax,' a third voice told the speaker. 'It's the kind of precaution Martin would have told any of us to take. He doesn't know us from Adam, does he? What was he supposed to do?'

The second speaker subsided into quiet grumbles while the first man tied a soft blindfold across Ray's eyes, knotting it tightly but carefully at the back of his head. He took Ray's arm.

'Now walk,' he said.

Ray tried to keep track of how long they had been moving. At first he counted, losing his place at about the fifth set of sixty, but he didn't think it had been much more than ten minutes before they stopped. He could see nothing, though he opened his eyes wide and tried to look through the confining cloth. Then he closed them again, blinking against the fragment of cloth that trapped beneath his lids. The man led him carefully and when they came to rough ground a second hand grasped his other arm and guided him over the mud and stones that told Ray they were probably crossing one of the building sites that surrounded the Armitage.

He heard a door open up ahead of him. A loud, echoey sound as though the door were large and a creaking of the hinges as if it were heavy or little used. Inside, his footsteps echoed against a hard floor yet the temperature change was little different from that outside, if you allowed for the chilling effects of the rain. Straining his ears he fancied that he could hear water. One of the old warehouses then, he guessed, backing on to the canal and about a quarter of a mile or less from the Armitage. They must have taken him by a longer route than was necessary just to confuse his senses all the more.

The men released him and Ray immediately put up a hand and began to remove the blindfold.

'Leave it,' the first voice said, and Ray did as he was told, but the swift glimpse he had managed told him that the man in front of him at least was wearing a ski mask. That much had been clear from the dense blackness where his face ought to be, though in the gloom of the warehouse Ray could have sworn to little else.

'You have them on fast dial?' the first man asked. 'Whoever it is you're going to ring.'

'No,' Ray said. 'Maybe I could . . .' He toyed for a moment with the idea of not calling home. Of letting Sarah call in the police and be damned with the entire thing, but the idea died almost as soon as it was born. He didn't feel threatened by these three. Not really threatened. Uneasy, maybe, but whatever they wanted he didn't think it was to do him harm.

'Tell me the number or the name if it's in your phone book.'

'Sarah,' Ray told him. 'It's in the index under Sarah.'

He listened while the man pressed buttons, getting into the call registry and then pressing to call. He felt the plastic case of the telephone pressed against the side of his face and heard the ringing on the other end. Then Sarah's anxious voice came on the line.

'I'm all right,' he assured her. 'I'll call you in an hour. No, Sarah, look I'll tell you all about it later.'

The phone was taken away.

'Now tell us about Martin,' the second voice said.

For the next fifteen minutes or so Ray told them what had happened to Martin Galloway. The drug, the car crash, the state he was now in. From time to time someone would ask a question and he was surprised at their genuine concern. Martin was evidently someone these men cared about and someone they looked up to. Ray wondered how they were going to fare now that he was gone.

'I need to find a man called Winter,' Ray said. 'Martin told me Winter knew what he was doing. I've reason to believe he lives either on the Armitage or close by,' he added.

There was silence. Ray could visualize the three exchanging glances, maybe. Considering what they should tell him. He wondered if he should tell them that Winter had once been police, but refrained from doing so. Martin they had accepted despite his profession. Ironically, because of it in some ways. Ray was not sure how they would react to Winter.

'I need to find him,' Ray reaffirmed. 'If I'm to help Martin and find out who did what they did to him then I think the only one to be able to help me will be Winter.'

'He didn't tell *you* nothing,' said voice number two.

'He told me that he thought the dealers who supplied Damien were back. That he thought they'd be pushing it on the streets again and that there were likely be more Damiens. He seemed to think that he was getting close to finding the source and it looks like he was right. He told me that other people had already died.'

There was another period of silence and then the

third voice, the young one that had spoken to him on the phone, said thoughtfully, 'One thing just don't make sense to me. A dealer don't want his muck to kill people. He wants them to go on taking it, otherwise he's going to lose profits, ain't he? So why push something like you say he gave to Martin?'

He had a good point, Ray thought. 'I don't know,' he said. 'The only thing I can think is that he gave Martin a much higher dose than would be sold on the streets. Any drug can kill outright if you give someone enough.'

'It didn't kill him though. It messed him up but it didn't kill him.'

Ray nodded slowly, remembering the conversation he had with Whissendine and the conclusion they had reached that Martin was meant to be an example. A warning of what could be done. 'When did Martin get involved with all of you?' he asked.

They thought about it for a while, then the one that had blindfolded Ray commented, 'From the sound of it about the time this Damien boy was hurt. Yeah, must have been about three years ago.'

That fitted in with Ray's own guess. Damien had not come from the Armitage but there were kids a-plenty like him on the estate. It was strange though, he reflected, that even after all these years, Martin himself still lived only streets away in the little house his parents had owned.

Finally, they led him back to his car and told him to count to twenty-five before removing the blindfold. Ray did as he was told, then pulled the binding from his eyes and glanced around, blinking in the sudden brightness of the yellowed streetlights.

He got into the car – untouched as far as he could see – and pulled the mobile from his pocket where the lead man had replaced it moments before. He fingered the blindfold thoughtfully. It was a woman's scarf, very soft to the touch. Cream in colour but with a pattern printed in pale green around the border. Silk, he guessed from the feel of it. Someone was going to be annoyed when they looked for it and found it missing. A faint floral perfume clung to it as though it had been worn recently.

The use of the blindfold might well have been a last-minute addition to their plans. Unnecessary on the one level if, as he suspected, they all wore ski masks. Unless they genuinely didn't want him to have any idea of where he had been taken. Ray was more inclined to think it had been added to increase the sense of drama and to hopefully throw him even further off balance. On that level, it had worked. He hated to have to surrender that much control to another person, even when, unlike tonight, it involved a person he felt he could trust. And he would defy anyone to have endured this experience and not found it at least unsettling.

What immediately suggested itself to Ray was that the young men of the residents' association, or one of them at least, enjoyed the game they played as much for the role play and the tang of Hollywood as they did for the more serious intent they all claimed to subscribe to. He had no doubt about their sincerity, but he guessed that this fulfilment of fantasy may be almost as important and it made him wonder just how much of an open secret the involvement of each would be in a place like the Armitage. It was, he figured, only a matter of time before someone talked and that their betrayal would be as likely the result of someone's pride in what they were doing as from any sense of malice.

He thought briefly of calling Whissendine and that reminded him that he had not reported to Sarah and his hour was up. She picked up on the second ring and it was evident that she was worried sick.

'George is here,' she said. 'I wanted to report you missing ten minutes ago, but he wouldn't let me. He said we'd have to give you a bit longer.'

'I'm fine,' Ray told her. He didn't add that he had nearly forgotten his promise to phone her. He didn't think that would go down too well. 'I'm coming home now.'

As he signed off he thought again about Whissendine, but he knew as soon as the thought entered his mind that he wouldn't follow it through. He wouldn't give the superintendent any more clues as to the identity of the residents' association action group. Not yet, anyway. He knew that he was probably being stupid but some odd sense of loyalty to Martin stopped him from involving the police in the night's little adventure.

He shook his head in disbelief. He was taking exactly the same kind of action that he had condemned in Martin only the week before.

Chapter Seventeen

George was already at the cottage when Ray returned. He recounted the night's events to them, Sarah shaking her head and telling him that she'd never get used to all this cloak and dagger stuff, though Ray knew that she'd been through far worse with him in the two years they'd been together.

George was inclined to agree that the scarf was a last-minute improvisation and with his reasoning about the members of the residents' association.

Sarah was looking at the scarf. 'Shouldn't it be bagged or something?'

'I don't think it'll be much use as evidence,' Ray told her. 'It hasn't been used in any crime. It is distinctive though. Someone will be missing it.'

Sarah picked it up and examined it closely. She held it close to her face, inhaling the slight perfume as Ray had done. 'Nice perfume,' she said, 'not cheap, I'd say, but the scarf isn't cheap either, Ray. It's hand-printed by the look of it and all the edges are hand-rolled and finished.' There was a small tag still attached to it that Ray hadn't noticed. 'Milan,' she said. 'I wonder if that's where it was made or where it was bought. And there's some kind of logo above that. A little rose within a heart.'

'Doesn't sound like an Armitage object,' George commented.

'Snob,' Sarah retorted. 'Just because you live in a lousy place doesn't mean you don't want better. The residents' association should have shown you that. What I was wondering, though, is if someone bought it themselves, either here or there. Or if it was a present, maybe from someone with family in Milan. Mallingham is like Leicester. It has quite a sizeable Italian community.'

'You have a point,' George told her. 'Any little clue to who our three men might be is better than nothing. You mentioned an accent, Ray?'

'Yes, but not Italian. I was thinking about that. Faintly Asian I would say, but regional. Like Sonia Dattani only less educated. More a rhythm than an accent, if you know what I mean.'

George nodded. 'And the other two?'

'One was definitely local. He sounded the oldest of the three. The one that objected to my using the phone. The other, the one I spoke to on the telephone, he used all the regional inflections, ain't and so on, but didn't have a strong local accent. Again, there was a rhythm there, but I couldn't tell you more than that. We're still no nearer to finding Winter,' he added, bitterly.

'No,' George agreed, 'but Phil is due back tomorrow with the tape and we might have some results on the picture.'

'Maybe, but it'll be afternoon by the time I get to know. I've got to go out to Willmotts again. They want to extend the system we installed to their second factory.'

George smiled at the look on his face. He knew that Ray found this side of their business, the supply of tailor-made security systems and the seemingly endless seminars they ran on risk assessment, very tedious. But it paid, and paid well.

It was well after midnight and Ray was yawning widely enough to be unable to conceal it behind his great paw of a hand.

'Time to call it a day,' he said. 'You want a bed for the night?'

George shook his head. 'It'll take no more than twenty minutes this time of night.' He kissed Sarah on the cheek. 'Until tomorrow then,' he said.

Chapter Eighteen

Tuesday morning had been a profitable one financially, Ray thought as he drove back to the office, but he was ready to get back to what he saw as the real problem at hand. He'd had his mobile switched off all morning, as was his habit when seeing a client. He hated what he perceived as the rudeness of taking calls from other people when he was meant to be concentrating on the particular needs of someone in front of him. In his previous incarnation as a police officer he had recognized the inevitability of this happening, but now that he had a choice in the matter he chose to do things his own way.

He'd switched all calls to divert back to the office phone for Rowena to field. He felt a little guilty though, wondering how many nuisance calls she'd have to deal with after his paper chase around the Armitage.

He arrived back at the office to find Phil and George waiting for him to join them. Rowena followed him through from their tiny reception area and dropped his messages onto the desk in front of him.

'Three potential customers,' she said. 'George dealt with another two but these asked for you specifically.

Two hang-ups. Three verging on the obscene and a young man who sounded rather anxious asking if he could please have his mother's scarf back.'

Ray apologized for the nuisance calls. 'Did he say what he wanted me to do with the scarf?' he asked.

'He suggested you dropped it off at the community centre,' she told him. 'He said you could give it to whoever was on duty at the time.'

Ray laughed.

'You should leave a message that it's been bagged and tagged and sent to Whissendine,' George suggested. 'That would shake him. Then all you'd have to do would be to wander round the Armitage looking for someone too scared to go home.'

'It's a thought,' Ray agreed. 'It'll have to wait anyway, Sarah has it. She's doing a quick tour of the big department stores in her break. See if anyone can tell her about it.'

'That's what I like to hear,' George said. 'The keen amateur, sleuthing through their lunch break.'

'I'll tell her you said that.' Ray turned to Phil. 'Anything on the tape or the angel picture?'

'Yes to both,' Phil confirmed. 'I don't know what you'll make of it though.'

The tape was already in the player. Phil played it to them and they listened closely. The words were clear enough now, though Martin's voice was weak and he was speaking quickly as though trying to pack things into too short a time.

'In deep water,' he whispered. 'Deep under water.

Drowning. The car, full up with water and I'm going to drown. Just like Damien, I'm going to drown.'

They listened to the tape until it ended but it was much the same all the way through. Ray could not hide his disappointment. He'd hoped that this might give some clue as to where Martin had been, but it was nothing, just the ramblings of an injured mind.

'What about the picture?' he asked.

'Ah, now there we've been luckier,' Phil told him. 'We know what it is and we know more or less what the picture was torn from. Sarah was right about it being a woman's magazine. The image had been used in a recent ad campaign but unless you're into reading women's glossies you'd not have seen it.'

He handed Ray a printout of the complete image. The angel in question was simply a fragment of a much larger painting. It appeared to be a nativity scene.

'It's from an altarpiece,' Phil told him. 'Unknown artist, though I don't suppose that matters. Eleventh century apparently. Italian, painted in tempera colours. It's called the Adoration of the Angels.'

'And have you found the website you were talking about?'

Phil shook his head. 'Not yet. The painting is fairly obscure, but even so we've found representations of it all over the place. The forums I did the search on came up with over two hundred instances of it being used and I'm working through them. Of course it might not be any of them and like I said it was used in the ad campaign. A couple of people on the forums mentioned the advert and I went out and bought a copy of *Cosmopolitan* just to have a look. That's not where your version came from though, Ray, the paper quality's different and so is the article on the back.'

He handed it over for Ray to see. 'Here's your angel, advertising perfume.'

'Perfume?' Ray thought of the lingering scent on the silk scarf.

'Already considered that,' George told him. 'I went out and found the stuff. I'm willing to swear it isn't the same. The perfume on the scarf is light and floral. This is heavy, sort of oriental and spicy.'

'Oh,' Ray sighed. 'It was just a thought.'

'And that's all we have right now,' George confirmed. 'A lot of thoughts and not much progress.'

Ray nodded disconsolately and wondered if Whissendine was faring any better.

Chapter Nineteen

That evening Ray collected Sarah from work at the Records Office and they drove out to Redfern to see Martin.

It turned out she had had more luck with her questions about the scarf than they had with their enquiries. Phil was still working his way painstakingly through the search results looking for hidden portals in the images. Ray was beginning to wonder if it were not just a time-consuming wild goose chase and Martin had meant something else entirely by leaving the screwed-up picture. Given Martin's mental state at the time, it could mean nothing at all.

But the scarf was more promising. It couldn't be bought locally, Sarah told him, and her hunch had been correct. It was expensive, costing upwards of eighty or ninety pounds.

'For a scarf?'

'For a hand-printed scarf, each one slightly different.'

'Make a lot of mistakes in the printing, do they?' Ray wanted to know. 'Exclusivity guaranteed because the workers are unskilled primates.'

'Behave yourself. It's a beautiful piece, even you admired it.'

'I'm going off it rapidly. No wonder that young man's in a panic though,' he said laughing. He told Sarah about the phone call.

'You'll give it back?' she asked him. Told him rather, from the tone of her voice.

'Yes, I'll give it back. Anyway, you were saying it couldn't be bought locally.'

'No. One of the assistants in Debenhams recognized the logo and asked her supervisor. I said I wanted something like it for a friend's birthday. They checked on their computer and their London and Leeds stores carry the full range.'

'Leicester not good enough for it then?'

'I told you to behave. Ours isn't such a big store. Anyway, it was either bought there or in Milan. She told me Debenhams have exclusive rights in the UK. I don't know if that helps though,' she added, catching Ray's mood. 'We don't seem to be making much progress, do we?'

'No,' he admitted. 'But we will. Something's bound to break sooner or later.'

He smiled across at her and took his hand from the steering wheel long enough to clasp her hand. He rarely allowed Sarah to drive when they were together. Aggressive barely covered it. She scared him stupid.

'It's often like this,' he told her. 'Nothing and then more nothing and then suddenly it all falls into place.'

Dr Dattani was no longer at Redfern, having left for the night. Ray wasn't surprised, but was glad to find that Steve, the male nurse who had made the tape, was on duty that evening.

He played the cleaned-up tape for him. Steve listened,

then commented cheerfully, 'It's better quality than the one the police had. Theirs was full of hiss.' He shook his head. 'Poor bugger. My guess is that the water was a part of his hallucination. A big part from the sound of this. It explains something though. I've been thinking about it since I heard the police tape earlier this afternoon. He keeps holding his breath and making a kind of waving or wiping movement with his hands like he's trying to clear something away. Then he'll take a deep breath as though suddenly he can breathe again.'

'Is that a new thing?' Ray asked.

Steve shook his head. 'No, he's done it off and on since he came in here. It happens mostly when the sedative is wearing off. We let him come to as full consciousness as we think he can bear. Dr Dattani's hoping to see an improvement. Each time we've had to sedate him again though because he starts getting so agitated. We noticed it before but until we heard the tape today we had no idea what he was doing. When he does it now I try to tell him that the water's going away and he isn't going to drown, but I don't know if it's getting through.' He frowned. 'Sometimes when a patient gets a fixation like this, it's linked to something in the real world that's playing on their mind. Do you know what it could be?'

'Damien drowned,' Sarah said.

Ray nodded. 'There was a case he worked on about three years ago,' he said. 'A young man, high on something, dived from a high board into a swimming pool. He couldn't swim.'

'He died?' Steve asked.

'No. He's been in a coma ever since. His mother won't give up on him. Neither, I think, did Martin. He still used to visit.'

Steve nodded. 'That's sad,' he said. 'And it explains some of what is going on in his head. Maybe it'll help. I don't know. Nothing else seems to.'

They left shortly afterwards, still feeling disconsolate. Ray wished he had access to Martin's home and paperwork but the police were no doubt keeping an eye on the place and he wasn't keen anyway on the idea of breaking and entering. Not unless he had to, though he kept the thought in mind for future reference, visualizing the layout of Martin's house and compensating himself with the thought that the police would probably have removed anything that looked remotely useful.

'You could talk to Whissendine again,' Sarah suggested. 'Pool resources.'

'You mean I could give them what I know and then leave well alone while they get on with it.'

'It's a thought, Ray. It's a sensible thought.'

'Then maybe I still lack sense. I don't ever remember it being one of my virtues.' He frowned, 'And I can't get out of my head that Martin came to me and not to Whissendine. That maybe he felt he couldn't trust someone. Field or Whissendine or someone higher up.'

'And maybe he was like you and just paranoid.'

'You've got to admit, I have good reason to be.'

'Maybe. But not every one of your former colleagues is corrupt, you know.'

'No, I know.'

'Martin was already sick,' Sarah pointed out, cutting through his thoughts. 'From what I saw of him, he was at the end of his tether. He admitted to you that that night at the warehouse he was slow and nearly got himself killed as a result. Maybe he wasn't thinking straight all round. That he'd spent so much time being a maverick he couldn't remember how to be a team player. And remember what Whissendine said about him handing the evidence over even before he was challenged. It strikes me he wanted to be taken out of harm's way.'

'He played team games with the residents' association,' Ray reminded her. 'And we only have Whissendine's word for what happened that night. Martin was still under investigation.'

'Was he? Then why wasn't he formally arrested, only cautioned? Why wasn't someone keeping an eye on him instead of just cutting him loose to chase this dealer all on his own? And as for the residents' association, he didn't play with the team, Ray, he played guardian angel to a bunch of well-meaning amateurs making like they're all Bruce Willis or Charles Bronson.'

Ray thought about it. 'Maybe you're right about the residents' association,' he granted, 'but the internal investigation into what he'd been up to . . .' He trailed off. He hadn't asked Whissendine about that. He'd mentioned what Martin had told him, of course, but Whissendine had made no direct comment, had merely said that they had known what Martin had been looking into and had been waiting to see if he turned up anything worth following through. Ray had considered it a little unorthodox at the time but had not really thought it through. He did now and the conclusion he reached startled him. But he shoved it aside, not liking it. There were too many implications.

He returned instead to Sarah's comments about Martin. 'I know he was stressed out,' he admitted. 'He talked to me about seeing Damien everywhere. Glimpsing the boy standing on street corners and following him around. Maybe he'd have ended up somewhere like Redfern even without the drug.' He paused. 'Look, Sarah, I'll make a deal. If I don't find Winter in the next three days I'll give what I know to Whissendine and back off.'

'And let him arrest you for impeding a police investigation?'

He looked sideways at her. 'I thought that was what you wanted me to do?'

'I only said it was the sensible thing to do and, anyway, that was before you had that new thought.'

'What new thought?'

'The one that's still stewing around in your brain. The one that just hit you with a sledgehammer.' She waited, then shrugged. 'OK, share it with me in a minute then. Anyway, I can't believe you'd bow out to Whissendine. First off, you feel you have some kind of perverted moral obligation to protect these would-be heroes of the residents' association because you know that in their shoes and given someone like Martin to organize you you'd be half inclined to behave in the same way.'

She stopped his protests with a wave of her hand. 'Don't give me that bullshit, Ray. I know you far too well. You have full respect for the law only as far as it agrees with your moral standpoint at any given moment. You, George, Martin, you're all cut from the same cloth. Flexible, if I'm being kind, though I can think of less complimentary ways of putting it. And you'll protect Winter, whoever he is, because Martin had some reason for doing so, and until you know if you agree you'll give him the benefit of the moral doubt. Am I right?'

Ray shrugged. 'Maybe just a little bit.'

'And now. What was this epiphany you had just a moment ago?'

Ray hesitated. 'It's a bit of a half-baked one,' he admitted, 'but it occurs to me that as Whissendine knew what Martin was on to, he must have known all about Damien. Martin was convinced that this dealer, this drug, was back on the streets or about to be. My guess is that Martin came very close to identifying who and what last time. That the producer knew exactly *who* was on to him and that forced him to go to ground. That this was personal. I think Whissendine knew that too. I think Whissendine, or someone equally high up, deliberately used Martin. Used him as a decoy, hoping that his presence would flush this suspect out into the open.'

He shrugged. 'Sarah, this is all guesswork. I can't be sure of any of it, even my reasoning being right, but my gut instinct is that I am. Martin was deliberately left out there in the cold, dangling like a worm, ostensibly an officer disgraced and unsupported.'

'And the bait was taken,' Sarah finished for him.

Chapter Twenty

Rowena dropped a pile of messages onto his desk and threatened to have the number changed. 'Five hang-ups this morning,' she said. 'Three obscene phone calls, two of which were physically impossible, four more that were just abusive and two with giggling children. Next time, Ray, just give them your mobile number, will you? Oh, and that young man called back again about the scarf. He's sounding pretty desperate.'

Ray grinned at the thought of the would-be Charles Bronson scared of his irate mother.

He apologized to Rowena, who just shrugged and told him she'd bought herself a loud school whistle so the Armitage Estate was going to have more than its fair share of perforated eardrums by the time she was done with them. Ray wondered vaguely if that constituted some kind of an assault, but Rowena was in no mood for him to suggest it. Not wanting to end up as her first victim, Ray left well alone.

He'd already decided to go out to Mallingham that afternoon anyway to try to see Damien again. He didn't know what good that would do, but while he was in the area he could deliver the scarf. He fervently wished he had access to the police records into Damien's accident.

Ray had spent the morning gathering more information from the newspaper archives, glad that the local papers, the *Mercury* and the *Mallingham Guardian*, were part of the same group and therefore gave him access to both sets of records. He spread the news clippings out on the desk in front of him, considering what little they revealed of Damien's life.

At first it had been reported as a tragic accident. Damien, presumably drunk, had got into the pool hall and jumped from the high board. Questions were asked. Why wasn't the pool hall locked? How had the boy gained access? How much had he drunk? And then the story that Damien had been taking drugs.

Ray was surprised at how this changed the complexion of the reporting.

Damien had been a few days' shy of his own eighteenth birthday, so it was technically not even legal for him to have been drinking. In the earlier reports this was glossed over in the general air of tragedy. Teenagers drank, was the view taken, there were adults present, it was a birthday party after all and Damien was not so far short of legal age. Three days on and the headlines screamed about the teenage junkie who'd jumped when high on heroin or crack cocaine, depending which account you read, an assessment later challenged and rectified to LSD – one paper even devoting a two-page article to the history of the drug in the story's wake.

There were several pictures of Damien. School pictures mainly and a couple of Damien with friends, one on a ski trip with his college. The other picture had, by coincidence, been in the newspaper archive from an earlier event when a filler story had featured students celebrating the end of their exams. Damien Pinsent and

Miriam Taylor together with a couple of other students, James Hogg and Michael Morrelli, standing in front of the college gates, posed in the act of throwing old exam papers into the air.

Damien had been set for university, the report said. Wanted to study Law – an irony stressed several times in the reports of how he had met his death.

Ray looked thoughtfully into the face of the young man with dark hair and laughing, gentle eyes, and tried to square it with the Damien he had seen a few days before, the prison pallor of his skin, the closed eyes.

Ray drove out to Mallingham early in the afternoon. There were few people in the community centre, being a weekday, just an elderly couple drinking tea and chatting to an equally elderly friend. He could hear children playing in the room which housed the wooden stage and the stereo and guessed it must be a playgroup day, their laughter and the thump of a couple of dozen small feet as they ran up and down echoing through the wooden building.

The same girl he had seen on the Sunday was serving behind the counter.

'Not making any speeches today then?' she asked him, eyeing him a little warily.

'No, not today. I need an audience to get the full effect.'

She started to laugh, then thought better of it and bit her lip. Ray pulled the scarf from his raincoat pocket.

'She dropped it,' he said, handing it to the girl and wondering if she'd respond. 'I said I'd bring it in here.'

He wasn't disappointed. 'Oh,' she said. 'Mrs Morrelli's. She'll be really pleased to get it back. It's her favourite.' Then she paused and gave him a puzzled look as though the oddity of him having this object suddenly struck her.

Ray awarded her one of his best lopsided clown smiles and waved goodbye before she could think any more.

Mrs Morrelli, he thought. The first link in a very tenuous chain. But he was halfway back to the car before he remembered the picture. Damien and his friends standing outside of Grange sixth-form college in the middle of Mallingham. One of the boys had been called Morrelli. Michael Morrelli. Ray walked swiftly the rest of the way back to the car, grinning inanely. It was just a little thing, but now he knew almost certainly who had called him to the Armitage Estate on Sunday night.

When Ray arrived at Damien's room Emily Pinsent was sitting at her son's side. For a moment Ray caught himself believing that she had not moved since the Sunday, so similar did the tableau seem. Then he noted that she was not alone.

Emily looked up as he came in but she showed no surprise, simply signed to him to be quiet, then patted a space at the end of Damien's bed, indicating that he should sit down. Ray did as he was told. There was an air of excitement surrounding Emily today that had been absent on the previous visit.

The cause seemed to be this other woman sitting on the opposite side of the bed and writing something on a large lined pad.

She was a youngish woman, Ray decided, late twenties, early thirties, though with a short, overpermed hairstyle that made her look older and was not the most flattering she could have chosen. She was dressed in blue trousers and a cream sweater. A warm jacket hung over the back of her chair. Her eyes – pretty eyes, Ray thought – were green grey and the touch of shadow on the lids reflected and lifted their colour. The lipstick was well chosen, too, pink with a hint of bronze that complimented her skin tone. Ray had begun to notice things like this since Sarah. The hair, he decided, was probably an expensive and much regretted mistake.

She was writing swiftly, the pencil in her hand dancing across the pad, but her eyes were not focused upon the page. Instead they were fixed firmly on Damien's face.

Ray said nothing until she had finished, catching the tension in the room and not wishing to break it. Emily leaned forward eagerly to see what the woman had written, taking the pad from her and hugging it close before even looking at the words. Her pale eyes shone and colour touched her cheeks.

'I'm so glad you're here,' she said to Ray. 'I've got someone to share this with now.'

'I'm sorry,' Ray said. 'I don't quite understand.'

'This,' Emily told him, nodding to the woman, 'is Frida Appleton. She's a specialist in contacting our lost ones. A little like a medium, isn't that right, Frida?'

The woman smiled but there was a tension at the corners of her mouth. Maybe, Ray thought, she wasn't as pleased as Emily to have him present.

'She's been trying to contact Damien for me and this is the second message we've had so far.'

Ray frowned. He recalled what Sonia Dattani had told him about the family trying something like this. 'I'm sorry,' he said, 'but I understood that mediums contacted the dead?'

'Or the displaced,' Frida told him evenly. 'Sometimes a soul can be lost but the body not die. Like in this case.'

Ray wasn't sure about the definition, but he let it pass. Emily was scrutinizing the pad. She looked upset.

'I'm sorry, dear,' Frida told her, 'but it's much the same as before.'

Emily nodded. There were tears in her eyes and the excitement had left them. 'I had hoped . . .' she began. She shook her head and wiped ineffectively at the tears that had begun to course down her cheeks. Frida took tissues from the box on the bedside table and handed them to her.

'He seems trapped in that moment,' Frida Appleton said softly. 'I thought I'd be able to guide him past it by now but I'm afraid it's going to take much more time.'

Emily nodded. She seemed unable to speak.

'Can I see?' Ray asked. Emily handed the pad to him.

Ray read the words the medium had written and felt himself grow cold.

In deep water, the words said, *deep under water. Drowning. Full up with water and I'm going to drown. Just like him, I'm going to drown.*' The words almost identical to those on Martin's tape.

Chapter Twenty-one

Ray had never considered himself to be a believer in anything until he had moved into his aunt's old cottage. Mathilda, who'd lived there most of her life, had always considered that the place was haunted by a former resident and Ray's experiences there had forced him to agree that Katherine, who had inhabited the cottage in the 1640s, was certainly still a presence in the house.

Beyond that though, he had been sceptical. The Eyes of God incident the previous year had drawn Ray deeply into the belief systems of those who lived their life according to occult forces quite incomprehensible to him in many ways. His experiences from that time had taught him that when people have a strong enough belief in something, very odd things could be induced to happen. What to make of Frida Appleton, though, was something else.

He listened quietly while the two women talked. What did the message mean? How best could Frida help Damien break free of wherever his mind or his soul had been trapped? He took the opportunity of a break in the conversation to ask Emily if she knew where Miriam Taylor would be living now. She gave him the information, writing it on the same pad and scribbling the address of both Miriam's parents and the flat Miri now rented, but her mind was clearly not on Ray's question. She was wholly concentrated on what she believed might be a message from her son.

'You've done this before?' Ray asked Frida. 'With Damien I mean?'

She nodded. 'The last message was much the same.'

'And when was that?'

'Two, no, three days ago. We'd tried before but with very little happening. It's my hope, Mr Flowers, that now Damien knows that I'm here to listen, and has learnt how to reach me, the next messages will be a lot more positive.'

'Positive? In what way?'

Frida sighed. 'I can see that you're not a believer,' she said kindly.

'I don't discount anything. But I find it hard to accept what you're doing, yes.'

'I can understand that,' she told him. Ray, who didn't actually like this woman very much, thought that was very big of her.

'I understand,' she repeated. 'But our aim is something that you can surely be sympathetic to. We want to bring Damien back. Back to his body. Back to his loved ones.'

Ray didn't feel he could add to that. He wondered what would happen if Damien did come back. What would there be for him to come back to? Was there anything left in that rather beautiful head for Damien to activate again? He remembered a ghost story he had once read about a woman who had wished her loved one back. And he had come back, except that the body had been filled with embalming fluid and chemicals that permeated the flesh. The poor man came back into a body that screamed with pain.

'Where did you learn to do this?' Ray asked her.

'It isn't something you *learn*, Mr Flowers,' she told him. 'It's a gift you're born with.'

Emily had been watching the exchange anxiously. She reached out and touched Ray's arm. 'I have to try everything,' she told him quietly. She shook her head sadly, whether at him or at the situation Ray could not tell. 'Ask Martin,' she said. 'Martin would have understood.'

Miriam Taylor ran down the steps of Wrighton House and headed towards her car. She'd had a rough day. The group of students she had been working with, under supervision of her tutor, had major learning difficulties and many were also physically disabled. Most of the time Miriam loved what she was doing. A gifted musician herself, she was keen to pass on the pleasure she gained to others and when she had been accepted on this course it had been one of the high points of her life. In reality though, working as a would-be music therapist was hard-going, for all its rewards, especially when, as today, she'd had to deal with two serious epileptic fits, one child vomiting all over her shoes and a serious temper tantrum from another child who always insisted on possession of the drum and had today been denied it.

Consequently, by the time she left for the evening, Miriam was not in the best of moods.

'Miss Taylor?' A voice called out. 'Miss Miriam Taylor?'

She turned. 'Yes.'

The man came across the car park towards her. He was in his late twenties, Miriam decided. Blond, tall, quite nice-looking. He didn't look like a student and she didn't think he could be a lecturer. She knew most of them by sight at least.

'I'm Richard Hayes,' he told her. 'I work for the *Mallingham Guardian.*'

'The what? Oh, the newspaper.' She frowned at him. 'You want to talk to me?'

'Yes, Miss Taylor, I do. You're a friend of Martin Galloway's, I believe.'

'You mean DI Galloway? I wouldn't say I was exactly a friend.'

'But you heard about his accident?'

She regarded him warily. 'Mr Hayes. Just what is it you want?'

'Just to ask you, Miss Taylor. You heard about his accident?'

Miriam turned away from him and fumbled in her pocket for her car keys. She always told herself that she should keep them handy, especially when it was getting dark – though the car park was well lit from dusk onward.

'He crashed his car last Wednesday on the Welford Road. He's in hospital, Miriam.'

'I heard the rumours.'

'Not rumours. Truth. I know the police have refused to confirm that it was him, but I've interviewed the paramedics and several of the people who were there that afternoon. There's absolutely no doubt about it. Which begs the question, why are the police not releasing his name? Why all the secrecy?'

She had found her keys now and opened the car door. 'How the hell should I know? Look, Mr Hayes, I already said I've nothing to say. Now I have to get home.'

'I interviewed DI Galloway after Damien's accident,' he said.

'Damien? What does this have to do with Damien?'

'Rumour has it Martin was still looking for Damien's supplier. Rumour also has it that Martin was as high as a kite when he crashed his car.'

'Martin? Martin Galloway? No way.' She laughed and it was evident that she could not even entertain the thought.

'He's been taken to a private clinic, Miriam. In rehab. What do you say to that?'

She stared at him, the laughter dying on her lips. Then she shook her head.

'No,' she said. 'I don't believe you. I got to know Martin Galloway pretty well after . . . after Damien. He was great with Damien's parents too, especially his mum. Martin Galloway would never do anything like that. I know how he felt about Damien.'

The journalist did not comment and Miriam carried on. 'And what's more, you start making up stories like that and I'll report you.'

'To whom?' he asked curiously.

Miriam looked confused.

He closed the notebook he had been holding in his hand and stuffed it into the pocket of his Barbour coat. 'I'm not making anything up,' he said softly. 'Martin Galloway is in Redfern Psychiatric Hospital. He was taken there after the accident and the paramedics are convinced that he was DIC.'

'DIC?'

'Drunk in Charge. Drunk, or otherwise inebriated. They use the same shorthand for drink or drugs.'

'They told you this?'

'No,' he admitted. 'They're too careful of confidentiality to do that. But there's a lot they didn't deny and, like I said, I interviewed others that were at the scene.'

Miriam shook her head again. She turned back to the car and got in, slamming the door and locking it against his presence.

Richard Hayes stood back, watching as she sped away.

Miriam arrived home. She had driven like an idiot through the centre of Mallingham, slowing only when she turned into the end of her street and home, safety, was in sight. She had moved away from her parents' house the year before, renting, with their help, a small flat on the other side of town. The flat was in a converted house and she had a share of the garden and a parking space in front on a gravelled area.

She parked her car and was fumbling with her keys again, this time for the communal front door, when she heard a voice behind her. 'Miss Taylor? Miriam Taylor?'

For an awful moment she thought that the journalist had followed her or somehow raced across town faster than she had done. She whirled around, ready to give the awful man a piece of her mind, but it wasn't Richard Hayes that stood behind her. It was a fat man with a face like a distorted mask. Tense and nervous already, Miriam squealed in shock. The man raised his hands placatingly. 'I'm sorry,' he said. 'I didn't mean to startle you. Emily Pinsent gave me your new address and said that you might talk to me.'

He slurred his words slightly, she noted abstractedly. The muscles of his mouth were tight. 'Who are you?' she demanded. He held a business card in his outstretched hand. Reluctantly, she took it from him. Ray Flowers, she read. 'Flowers-Mahoney Security and Investigations. You're what? A private investigator?'

'I'm an ex-policeman,' he said. 'I used to work with Martin Galloway.'

Galloway. Again. She was getting sick of this already. 'And you want? What?'

'Just a few minutes of your time. To talk. You might know that Martin had an accident a few days ago.'

'And I suppose you want to tell me he's in rehab too?'

'I'm sorry? In rehab?'

Miriam relaxed slightly. So the bastard had been lying after all. 'Sorry,' she said. 'Some journalist was waiting for me when I came out of class. He wanted to talk about Martin, he said. Asked if I'd heard about the accident and claimed that Martin was in some mental hospital. In rehab after taking drugs.'

'Redfern,' Ray said. 'He's in Redfern, but he's not in rehab, at least not in the way I think the journalist must have meant.'

Miriam stared at him. 'That's where he said Martin was,' she said. 'What's happened to him? What's . . .' She broke off and closed her eyes, trying to get a grip. 'You'd better come inside,' she said.

The flat was small but neat and tidy with posters on the wall in clip-frames and books stacked on wobbly flat-pack shelves. She said nothing while she made them both coffee, not trusting herself until she had her thoughts in order. When she took the mugs through from her cupboard of a kitchen the strange man was pacing the floor, examining her bookshelves and the pictures on her wall.

'What happened to him?' she wanted to know.

'He'd been given a drug. I don't believe he took it of his own volition. The doctor taking care of him thinks it's similar to what Damien had taken. He's very sick, psychotic. We don't know if he's going to recover.'

She stared at him, her fingers growing limp on the handles of the scalding mugs. Gently, Ray took them from her and set them down on the table beside the bay window. He pulled out a chair for her and she sat down.

'Did Damien know what he was taking?' he asked her. She was well off balance, Ray could see, but no doubt she'd soon recover her equilibrium and he wanted to take advantage before she did. 'Who supplied him with it?'

Miriam stared out of the window. Rain splattered against the glass and the sky had grown thickly dark, both with the rain and with the coming night. The darkness cast her reflection into sudden relief, made it look as though she were sitting in some darkened garden on the other side of the window. That was how she felt, Miriam thought. On the other side of a familiar world. 'Damien didn't do drugs,' she said. 'It was me. Me who got in too deep. Damien pulled me out. And we fell in love.'

It felt so strange to be saying this, she thought. She continued to stare out of the window. While she kept her focus on that other woman sitting in the shadowed garden, saying these things didn't seem so hard.

She took a deep breath and turned back to look at this stranger with the ravaged face. 'We were all just kids,' she said. 'Seventeen-year-old kids doing something that got out of hand.'

'And you told the police about this, this whatever it was that got out of hand?'

Miriam shook her head. 'Not all of it,' she said. 'My parents would have chucked me out if they'd known even a fraction. And nothing we didn't say would have helped Damien.'

'You can be sure of that? No. I didn't think so. But you told Martin.'

She nodded.

'When did you tell Martin?'

'It was after everything was over. When they'd decided that Damien was just another statistic. A kid on drugs that damn near killed himself, and there were a lot of high-profile deaths around that time. Kids doing E mostly. Damien just sort of blended into the background.'

'But you?' He paused, searching for the right words. 'Miriam, did you think it was *not* an accident?'

'I didn't know, Mr Flowers. I just knew that Damien didn't do drugs. Not . . . I mean it was just that one stupid time. I knew that I could have been in a lot of trouble if my parents had found out. I didn't know what to think.'

Ray considered for a moment.

'What were you taking?'

'Cocaine mostly.'

'Expensive. Had money, did you?'

'I got what I needed.'

'How? Did you steal, Miriam? What did you do to finance your habit?'

Miriam didn't reply. 'I think you should go now,' she said. 'I don't want to talk to you any more. It's all past now. It can't help Damien.'

Ray didn't move.

'I asked you to go. Please!'

'Miriam, you've carried this around with you for the last three years. Had you come clean at the time and told everything, the police might have had somewhere to look. They might even have found the supplier. Martin believed that others had been killed and maimed, you know. Not just Damien. Did he tell you that?'

She shook her head. 'No. Look. I don't know any more than I told you. Now please, please go.'

'I'll leave,' Ray told her. 'But we're going to talk

again, Miriam. You, me, and probably the police, you know that, don't you?'

Stubbornly, she shook her head.

'Miri,' Ray said. 'Miri, you were earning drug money working for the dealers, weren't you? What were you doing, Miriam? Acting as a runner, maybe? Or a courier? A pretty, respectable-looking girl. Straight-A student, good home. Not the sort anyone would suspect, eh?'

Miriam had turned back to gaze out of the window, though Ray knew she saw nothing, just their own reflections in the glass. He left quietly then, closing the door softly behind him as she watched him through the mirror into that other dark.

Chapter Twenty-two

It was already seven o'clock but Ray was on a roll now and reluctant to go home until he had done one more thing. He had paused long enough at the hospital to find a phone with a local directory. There were two families named Morrelli on the Armitage Estate. Ray took a chance and played a hunch that Michael Morrelli had been named after his father. M. Morrelli lived in Cobden Street, one of the newer streets on the Armitage, built in the eighties to take the overspill from the top floors of the towers, which were steadily becoming more and more uninhabitable.

The Morrellis were in the middle of their evening meal, the house filled with the scent of fresh bread and oregano, reminding Ray that it had been hours since he last ate.

Micky had been expecting him. He did his best to calm the anxiety of the rest of his family and led Ray through to the other room so that they could talk in peace.

'I knew you'd come. It was the scarf, wasn't it? Stupid, weren't I?'

'You improvised. You got it wrong. No big deal.'

'What are you going to do?'

'Do?' Ray asked him. 'Do I have to *do* anything, Michael?'

'I mean about the other night. And about the—'

Ray held up a hand to silence him. 'I know nothing,' he lied. 'Nothing for certain so let's keep it that way just now. No, I want to know about Damien Pinsent, about Miriam Taylor and what she and Damien had going. I want to know about Miri and her little drug habit and I want to know how you fitted into all of it.'

Micky stared at him. 'How do you know about Miri?'

'I talked to her.'

'She *told* you?'

Ray sighed. 'One thing about you lot, at least you're loyal. You all knew, didn't you?' He slipped the news clipping from his jacket pocket and handed it to Micky. 'What went on, Michael? What the hell were you all up to and why did none of you say something after what happened to Damien?'

Micky shrugged awkwardly. 'We were scared,' he said finally. 'They threatened us, Mr Flowers.'

'Who threatened you?'

'I don't know. Not names and that, but we each of us got a letter. They knew exactly who we were and where to find us. They said that what happened to Damien could happen to any of us any time. Us or our families and we'd never know until it happened. We daren't go to the police.'

'But you told Martin?'

'Every day we waited for something to happen to one or other of us and even when it didn't, even when Miri went away to uni, we couldn't settle down, neither of us. I thought it was Miri's fault. She'd been in with those people but Damien always said Miri didn't know what she was doing and we couldn't blame her. After Damien, we tried to put it behind us and try to move on.'

He shook his head. 'We couldn't do that though. Miri dropped out of uni and when she came home she spent all her time pretending life was normal. We didn't see each other and that was hard. Mr Flowers, we used to be inseparable.'

'Sweet,' Ray commented harshly. 'Michael, stop romanticizing it. You were friends, sure. But things were falling apart for all of you even before Damien's accident, weren't they?'

Micky regarded him with an expression of real pain in the soft brown eyes. 'I guess I was in love,' he said.

'Who with? Miriam?'

He laughed. 'Miriam? No way. Miri was everyone's favourite. Pretty, clever, popular. Damien and me, we'd been friends since we were little kids in junior school. Me, I was kind of on . . . outside of things at Grange. Came from here when all the rest lived on the other side of town. Even Damien after his family moved away.'

'You were the kid from the Armitage.'

Micky nodded.

'Mate, I've been there. It isn't worth the pain. Listen,' he added, trying to pull the conversation back to where he wanted it. 'Who threatened you? What was Miriam mixed up in?'

'I don't know. Truly, I don't know.' He drew a deep breath, then let it out with painful slowness. 'She was a runner for her supplier, did she tell you that?'

'Near as damn it.'

'That night Miri said she wanted to try something

new. Something she'd heard about but it hadn't hit the streets yet. She said she'd got it because it was her eighteenth. Said it had been a birthday gift.' He shook his head angrily. 'I told her. Told her I thought she'd finished with all that. She'd promised Damien that she'd finished playing those stupid fucking games. She said it was none of my business and that, anyway, this was different. She'd stopped with the hard stuff, this was just . . . just to have a good time.'

Ray was thinking hard. 'And didn't that seem a little odd to you? Something that hadn't hit the streets yet and she was being given as a gift, free, gratis and for nothing, given it by the guy she'd stopped working for?' He shrugged. 'Don't know what you think, Michael, but given that scenario I'd run a mile before I took anything someone like that was about to dole out.'

'I told her that. But she wouldn't listen to me. Miri . . . Miri is a lovely person, Mr Flowers, but she could be so pig-headed when the mood took her.'

'Lovely,' Ray echoed, unable to keep the disgust out of his voice. 'You were at this party?'

'No. I was so angry with her that in the end I didn't go. Maybe if I had . . .'

Micky glanced towards the door. His family could still be heard, moving about in the kitchen diner. He shook his head. 'Not Miriam,' he said softly. 'I wasn't in love with Miriam.'

It took a moment for Ray to catch on. 'Ah,' he said softly. 'Damien.' He half laughed, knowing it was inappropriate but unable to help himself. 'Lord but do you lot lead complicated lives! And you've lived with all this for the past three years. Lived with all the threats and . . . Did Martin know all of this?'

Micky nodded. 'Martin didn't judge,' he said. 'And when he promised to keep his mouth shut, that's exactly what he did.'

'So I've noticed. But God, Michael, I wish he'd let a little more loose when he needed to. If he'd opened up before. If *you'd* opened up before, we might be a lot further on than we are now. I'm working blind, Michael, trying to tie this together piece by piece and Martin's just lying there in that hospital bed . . .'

'Like Damien,' Micky said. 'Just like Damien.'

When Ray left it was well after eight o'clock. He realized that he had not called home and that he'd had his mobile switched to silent and had missed three calls, all of them from Sarah. He thought again about what Micky had told him. Micky said he had not kept the letter but Ray didn't know whether to believe him. He thought it more likely that Micky had either kept it hidden, where he could look at it from time to time and, perversely perhaps, keep the fear alive. Or perhaps he had given it to Martin, in which case did Whissendine have it? Did he know what it was all about?

He called Sarah and apologized profusely before she had the chance to say anything well deserved, but to his surprise she brushed his apologies aside. 'Dr Dattani tried to reach you earlier,' she said. 'She's tracked them down. The other ones. Two dead and one in a secure unit suffering from severe paranoia.'

'Tracked who down?' Ray demanded, his thoughts muddled still with Micky's revelations.

Sarah sighed. 'The other ones like Damien,' she said. 'The others given that bloody drug.'

Chapter Twenty-three

Ray arrived at the Dattanis' house about half an hour later. They lived on one of the new developments on the outskirts of Leicester, in a smallish modern detached, built in a mock-Tudor style. Inside, the house was decorated with coordinated papers and subtle paint. It looked as though an interior designer had been let loose, stylish but oddly characterless.

Sunil, who'd answered the door, saw him looking. 'This was the show house,' he said, smiling. 'We've only been here a few months.'

Sonia Dattani stuck her head around the kitchen door. 'I'm making tea,' she said. 'Would you like some?' She was boiling spiced milk on the stove. It smelt sweet. 'Or I can make you some English style if you'd like?'

'Would you mind? I'm afraid I hate sweet tea. You can blame Sarah. I used to drink it with three sugars but she weaned me off and now I can't drink it any other way.'

She laughed and asked Sunil to fill the kettle.

'Sarah said you've been trying to reach me.'

'Oh yes. I rather think I've struck gold.' She removed the pan from the stove, leaving the tea to infuse, and wiped her hands on a cloth before fetching a sheaf of faxed notes from the living room.

'Go on through,' Sunil said. 'I'll see to this. I think you'll be very interested, Mr Flowers.'

'Ray, please.'

'Ray then.'

He followed Sonia into the blue living room. The furniture was their choice, he guessed. A large cream suite dominated, with silk cushions in bright colours scattered on the sofa. A painting of an autumnal English landscape hung above the fireplace and in the corner of the room a camphorwood table served as a small shrine with a small silvered image of a child holding a snake.

'Krishna?' Ray asked.

'That's very good,' she applauded. 'Now sit down and take a look at this.' She handed him the faxes and sat back to wait for his reaction. Ray riffled through. They came, he noticed, from clinics in three different health authorities. Two postmortem reports caught his attention first: the tox results so similar they had to be the same substance and the confusion expressed by the pathologist also very similar.

'How does this compare to Martin?' he asked.

'Very close. You'll notice small variations, as though someone's been tinkering with the mix. But there's no doubt, Ray. You'll find a tox report from our third subject, too, the survivor. Again, slight variations.'

'What's the chronology?' he asked, skimming the pages and trying to work it out.

'The first death, then Damien, then our paranoid subject, the second death and now Martin. The first death was, I think, two months before Damien.'

Ray glanced up at her. 'Sonia, if two people took

this drug, would there be a different effect? Would one survive and one not? One be unaffected and one not?'

She frowned. 'What do you mean? Ray, do you have reason to believe this happened?' She sat forward. 'You have someone who took the drug and survived with no ill-effects? Ray, that would be . . .' She gestured that it would be incomprehensible.

'I don't know for sure. I was told tonight that someone procured the drug for themselves and Damien and that she intended to take it as well. I can't know for sure yet if she did or not. But would it be possible? Even remotely possible?'

Sunil had come through with a tray and heard this last part of their conversation.

'Some people can have an allergic response to a drug that in others is totally harmless,' he commented. 'Maybe you should be looking from that point of view, though, frankly, no one could take that kind of chemical cocktail and not get a reaction. It's interesting though,' he added. 'The chemical profile is similar to some drugs used to control psychosis. That got us thinking. Sonia talked to a Dr Oliver this afternoon. He's sending information over tomorrow by courier.'

'Courier? Why not fax it now?'

The Dattanis exchanged glances. 'What he had to say was a little controversial, Ray. We didn't want just anyone getting hold of it.'

'Like what?'

Sonia hesitated for the briefest moment. 'Ray, Dr Oliver is an expert in the field of psychotropics. He's a biochemist working for one of the bigger drug companies, a firm called Psycotrex. You probably won't have heard of it, they market under another name. I sent our results in to him and all the additional information I've picked up in the past few days. Mine hasn't been the only inquiry. The psychiatrist taking care of Samuel Tompkins, the paranoid patient, also approached him a few months ago and he began to speculate but he didn't know there had been others. Until now.

'Ray, Dr Oliver thinks that this didn't start out in any street lab. Its level of sophistication is just too high and the evolution is too complex. He thinks it started out in a lab like his own. A corporate institute somewhere, or a pharmaceutical company. That it got out and this is the result.'

Ray stared at her. 'How?' he asked.

'You're the detective,' Sunil pointed out. 'A disaffected employee possibly. Though they'd have to have some knowledge.'

'But why would anyone create a drug that sends people doolally?' He rubbed his eyes wearily. 'I'm tired and I get the feeling I'm being stupid here.'

'Just a little,' Sunil told him. 'This drug, whatever it was, is a lot like some standard treatments in its profile. What if that's how it started out but something went wrong. Ray, for every drug that comes onto the market there have been twenty, thirty attempts that didn't get past the computer modelling. Others that didn't make it past the animal trials. Whoever stole this would almost certainly have known something about it.'

'But why steal something that, if you're right, was

designed to treat psychosis? I can't see there being an interest in that on the street.'

Sonia shook her head. 'You're forgetting our conversation the other day,' she said. 'Tripping is controlled psychosis, put simply. Any upset in the chemical balance of the brain will have some kind of effect. Some increase endorphins and make you feel good. Some cause the body to react against the sudden flood of one chemical by overproducing something from the seratonin group and that can cause increased anxiety, even paranoia. You've heard of those cases maybe where LSD was used to treat psychiatric problems in the sixties and caused long-term depression. We know that long-term cannabis use may cause short-term memory loss. There's some evidence that Ecstasy, which makes the person feel the world is a beautiful place for a while, can cause an answering swing towards anxiety. Magic mushrooms sometimes result in flashbacks.' She held up her cup. 'If I don't have my tea, Sunil can't live with me.' She smiled. 'I'm not being flippant. I'm just trying to point out how fragile the chemistry of the brain can be and how easily we all, almost all of us, change it on a daily basis without giving it an ounce of thought until it goes wrong. It could be they thought that if they modified this drug, they'd get something that increased the high, made people feel good. That's basically what modern antidepressants are designed to do.'

Ray sipped his own tea thoughtfully. Most of this he knew, one way or another, but it was useful to have it all put into context. 'Can I ask you something that may sound totally irrelevant?' he said.

'Fire away.'

'Today, I went back to see Damien. His mother was there and so was a woman called Frida Appleton who claimed to be some kind of medium. She had this pad and was writing on it without looking. She said that she was trying to communicate with Damien.'

'Automatic writing,' Sunil said.

'Yes, that was it.'

'Did she get a message?'

Ray nodded. 'Yes, that was the strangest thing. It shook me for a moment.'

'What did it say?'

Ray reached into his pocket. In tearing the page with Miri and her family's addresses from the pad he had also purloined the message. He hoped that Emily would forgive him when she finally noticed. 'This,' he said.

Sonia frowned as she read the words that Frida Appleton had written there. 'I think your medium had a crossed line,' she said. 'This is the same, almost word for word, as Martin's tape.'

Chapter Twenty-four

Flowers-Mahoney had a visitor the following morning in the shape of Richard Hayes.

Ray regarded him with wary interest remembering how upset Miriam had been and wondering how much the young man actually knew.

'You've been out to see Martin Galloway a few times,' Hayes said without preamble, 'and you've been nosing around on the Armitage, Galloway's patch. Is there anything you'd care to share with me, Mr Flowers?'

Ray laughed at his directness. 'No, Mr Hayes. I don't think there is.'

'But you're a friend of DI Galloway,' Hayes persisted. 'He'd come to see you the day of his accident.'

'Apparently,' Ray confirmed. 'But I wasn't there.'

'Was he drunk?'

'I don't believe so.'

'So what was he on? I've witnesses who say he wasn't exactly the model of sobriety that afternoon.'

'So, talk to them.'

Richard Hayes sat back and regarded Ray with a mix of frustration and amusement. He hadn't hoped to learn much with his confrontational approach, Ray knew. He was merely sounding him out. Observing his reaction. It was the sort of thing Ray himself had done often enough.

Hayes reached down for his briefcase. It was a soft leather affair shaped like an old-fashioned satchel and so well worn it could be a survival from his schooldays. He unbuckled it and withdrew a hefty folder and laid it on the desk.

'Read,' he said. 'Then talk to me.'

'I'll read. I don't promise conversation.' Ray jerked his thumb towards the coffee-maker. 'Help yourself,' he said. 'But I hope you like it strong. I think Phil would have it intravenous if he could find a way.'

'Phil. Your computer guy.' He peered through the half-open door into the inner room that was Phil's domain.

'Sit down, Mr Hayes,' Ray instructed him. 'The deal was I read, you sit and drink coffee, not I read while you snoop.'

Richard Hayes laughed but sat back down again. Despite himself Ray found that he was warming to the younger man.

It took almost an hour and two refills of coffee – Hayes drank as much as Phil, Ray observed – for Ray to get through the wodge of notes. When he had finished, he replaced them in the folder and took a more serious look at Richard Hayes.

'Do we get to talk now?' the journalist asked.

'I'm still thinking. Why did you maintain this interest, Mr Hayes?'

'Call me Richard.'

'Calling you Richard implies that I'm going to cooperate, have a conversation with you. Right now I'm just asking the questions.'

'OK. Why did I continue to be interested? Hmm. OK, several things. I talked to a lot of Damien's schoolfriends. To his family. Anyone who'd talk to me, and at first it was actually pretty easy. They were all in shock and when people are in shock they do one of two things. I'm sure you know that, Ray— Mr Flowers. Sorry, I was forgetting. They either clam up tight or you can't shut them up. Well, the first couple of days there were a few, like his friend Miriam, wouldn't say a word to anyone. And his parents were at the hospital all the time and didn't make any statements until about a week later. Others, though, just couldn't believe it. Damien was always so sensible, so sensitive. Such a good student. He didn't even drink to excess. OK, you allow for the denial, but even so the image I got of the kid didn't fit in with him getting loaded and jumping from a great height.'

'I thought in the beginning it was assumed he was simply drunk. That's what the reports said.'

'Hmm. Yes, they did, but even from the first few hours the rumour mill was grinding. Damien's girlfriend, some said, wasn't as innocent as she made out. Her parents thought the sun shone out of her backside and so did her teachers, but there were enough dissenting voices to make me look harder and I found another side to Miss Miriam Taylor, one her parents wouldn't recognize.'

He paused and took another swig of coffee. 'Go on,' Ray told him.

'Then the talk began openly about Damien having had more than a couple of beers.'

'I read the news articles.'

'Then you know the tone changed. Public opinion could cope with a kid who drank a little too much. After all, what kid hasn't done that? How many adults have those Oh-God-did-I-really-do-that type of memories they hope their oldest friends won't talk about? But somehow the collective memory is less comfortable when it comes to illegal drugs, especially after the high-profile deaths that happened around the same time. And you know as well as I do, Ray, that telling Joe Public just how many deaths a year there are as the result of alcohol and smoking just doesn't compete with the one teenage girl who tries a drug once and dies.'

Ray nodded slowly. He wasn't sure he liked the way Hayes expressed himself but the facts, well, Ray couldn't disagree with those.

'But you dropped it,' he said. 'Publicly, I mean.'

'Pressure from above,' Hayes agreed, 'and I don't mean God. The editor is mightier than the Lord.'

'But you kept on anyway.'

Hayes nodded. 'Part of it was Martin Galloway,' he said. 'I saw some of what he was doing on the Armitage. I liked what he was trying to achieve, and then, of course, there were the rumours about him and about the so-called residents' association. You've just seen my file. The clear-up rate on the Armitage is like something out of a forged government report and if you read between the lines of the stories then you start to see it isn't the police who are making the arrests. They get called in to take over when the local association makes a citizen's arrest. They get tipped off and find a would-be burglar locked in a room he's been careless enough to break into without noticing the owner's suddenly acquired a bloody big dog. Funny, a time or two the householder didn't remember acquiring one either, but who's counting, especially when the would-be housebreaker cops to a dozen more and makes the local police look good. Then, there is the tour de force.' He slipped a hand into his pocket and produced a small pasteboard card. '"Courtesy of the Residents' Association". Cocky or what? One was left at the warehouse that night when there was all that shooting. Good thing though, wasn't it? Two little girls returned home, shaken but unharmed, and then, of course, a few days later, the men concerned found shot in the head. What I want to know is, what possessed the police to let them out on bail, knowing the strength of public opinion in cases where kids are involved.'

'The way I read it the connection between those men and the warehouse was made public only after they were shot.'

Hayes shrugged, conceding the point.

'What makes you think Martin was involved in any of this?'

'Aw, come on. These were his boys. He founded the residents' association. Martin Galloway had lived next to the Armitage all his life. It was in his blood, under his skin. You want more clichés, you think of them. You hear what I'm saying and you know I'm right.'

'I take it you disapprove?'

'What gave you that idea?'

'The fact that you believe Martin was doing drugs.'

Hayes laughed. 'I said I believed that he was high. That's all.'

Ray thought for a moment and then stood up and reached across to shake the journalist by the hand. 'Nice knowing you, Mr Hayes,' he said. 'My secretary will see you out.'

Chapter Twenty-five

Hayes would have been surprised to see where Ray went next. His walk took him across town and to the spiritualist church he had passed many times but never entered. It was in an odd location, next to a supermarket and opposite a multi-storey car park.

Ray went inside, not sure why he was there or what he was going to say to anyone. An elderly woman with thick, pale grey hair stood in the lobby arranging flowers. She looked up when he came in.

'Hello, can I help you? There isn't a circle this afternoon, I'm afraid.'

'A circle?'

'The development circle,' she smiled. 'But I see you didn't come for that. How can I be of help then?'

Ray frowned. 'I'm not sure if you can. Look, a friend of mine has become involved with a medium. Or that's what she calls herself. This friend is taking her very seriously and I'm worried about her pinning too much hope on, you know, on this medium being right.'

'I take it you're not impressed by the lady's credentials,' she said. 'Have you seen her work? Are you familiar with the way we normally do work?'

'We? Oh you mean you're a . . . No offence,' he added. 'I'm pretty ignorant about spiritualism.'

'Come on through to the office,' the woman said. 'I'll see if I can enlighten you.'

He smiled. 'That *would* be nice. I could use some enlightenment right now.'

She laughed then. 'We can but try.'

Ray told her about Damien without giving names. He described to the woman, who told him her name was Gladys, the way that Frida Appleton had used automatic writing to take down the message. She nodded, understanding.

'Automatic writing. I know of people who use it. I know nothing about your lady, by the way, but that doesn't mean a great deal. Personally I can't do it, my thoughts start chattering away and before I know where I am I'm composing a shopping list.' She laughed, as much at Ray's surprised expression as at her own joke. 'My dear, we have to see the humour in these things. Spirit doesn't want us to be gloomyboots.'

'Do you think she could be genuine?'

'Who's to say? I've never heard of automatic writing being used to contact someone in a coma before, but anything is possible I suppose. If she came here and used the development circle then we'd know how many . . . well, hits she had, if you like. We'd be able to assess how much of what she did was cold reading and how much was from spirit and, believe me, sometimes that's hard even for the individual to know.'

'Cold reading?'

'We all pick up a whole load of clues about people and the kind of lives they lead almost without knowing it. Almost invisible things, unconscious clues, which we add to the way we consciously make decisions about people we meet for the first time. We revise those conscious decisions as we go along, but the unconscious ones often stay with us and become assimilated into our . . . our inner picture if you like. Then, *we* believe, there are the things we are told about people from spirit.

'You, for instance. Looking at you on a straightforward level I see a man in his mid- to late forties who's had a nasty accident. You're fairly well dressed but not ostentatiously. You wear the same type of clothes as you wore ten years ago just because they're comfortable. You're not, I think, a manual worker, but you have calluses on your hands that might indicate a hobby which involves manual effort. You wear no wedding ring, but that in itself means nothing. I would guess, married and divorced. Most men of your age have been married at some point and a wife you still had would have made an effort to change your way of dress.' She laughed. 'I didn't say that you weren't in a relationship though. I can tell you are.'

'How?'

'The moment of outrage when I implied that a woman would have changed you and you didn't have one around to try. You felt, all of a sudden, that you had to defend yourself and were about to tell me about your current lady.' She laughed again. 'But this relationship is one of independent minds rather than bonds of convention.'

Ray shook his head. 'You're good,' he said.

'Oh I could go further but something tells me you've used similar techniques yourself. You're either police or ex-military, just from the way you're aware of your surroundings and make a point of observing. I'd go for police. No offence but you look as though you've more Colombo in you than colonel.'

Ray grinned at her. 'Ex-DI,' he said. 'But this cold reading stuff. It wouldn't tell her what to write, would it?'

Gladys looked thoughtful. 'How was your friend's son injured?' she asked.

'Ah,' Ray nodded.

'His mother would be bound to have told her. Of course she would. Look, I'm not saying that this woman isn't genuine, and if you like, I'll ask around, see if she's on any of the registers.'

'You keep registers?'

'Only of our own membership. But she might not be local, you know. Leave me your number and I can give you a call.'

She paused and gazed thoughtfully at him for a moment or two. 'Are you sure this message came from the boy?' she said.

Ray tried hard to control his reaction but the woman nodded gently. 'I thought so,' she said. 'You've told me half a story, haven't you?' She smiled at him. 'That's all right, I don't need to know. But I'll tell you one thing, my dear. You didn't tell me a complete truth either when you said you knew nothing of the spirit world. There's a young woman very close to you, who has scars upon her face, who passed over well before her time and in violent circumstances. I think she said, her name was Katherine.'

Ray froze. Katherine was the woman who had lived

in his aunt's cottage. The woman who had died so long before Ray was even born, but who had refused to leave her beloved home. There were very few people who knew anything about Kitty.

'Come with me and talk to Emily,' he said.

Chapter Twenty-six

Mid-afternoon Sonia Dattani called and told Ray that she had the information she had been expecting from Dr Oliver and, better than that, as far as Martin was concerned, he had been able to suggest some new therapies they might try. They were still at the human-testing stage but he thought that his pharmaceutical company might well be willing to include Martin in their trials.

'They're thinking what great publicity this will be once it's all over,' she said.

'Who cares so long as it helps. Will it help?'

'We won't know unless we try. I can't keep him sedated for ever, Ray. He's been talking again though and Steve seems to think this is slightly different. He's taped it for you. Want me to send it?'

Ray told her he'd be coming to see Martin soon anyway and could collect it then. 'Would it be useful for us to go and see Dr Oliver? I mean, if you could spare the time.'

'We've got three new admissions today and two more expected. I'll be working up preliminary assessments for the next few days. No way I can get away, Ray. I'm sorry.'

'Sorry for what? You've been wonderful. When you and Sunil can make it we'll have to have dinner together or something. You'd like Sarah.'

Sonia smiled, he could hear it in her voice. 'I'm sure I would. Look Ray, my beeper's going off, I've got to run. Later, OK.'

He put down the phone feeling a little guilty about involving her. A momentary rush of fear cramped the muscles of his stomach, though he couldn't totally fathom why.

Maybe it was Micky's letter, he thought. The one the young man had told him about the night before, threatening what would happen should any of them interfere.

Was he endangering Sonia and her husband? And what about Sarah? He had worried always about her being involved in dangerous situations, though he knew she would frown upon such anxiety. Sarah had been beside him throughout many disturbing experiences and he had come to rely upon her advice and clear-headedness far more than he liked to admit.

Ray shoved these negative thoughts to the back of his mind, but he had decided one thing. He would have to go to Whissendine. This was getting far too big for him to handle on his own. He wasn't looking forward to it though, knowing just how many lives were going to be dragged through the mud in the process.

Miriam had been unable to think straight since her talk with Ray the night before. She'd hardly slept, and when she had she had dreamed of Damien. Of those last seconds of his fall, stretched and distorted beyond counting, time pulled taut like a rubber band then suddenly compressed in that instant when she was certain Damien had come to his senses and reached out blindly for help.

She had gone to college but the morning had been a wasted one. Unable to concentrate on the lecture she had left at lunchtime and wandered into the local park. She had sat down on a bench beside the river and watched the world go by, trying to regain sufficient equilibrium to tackle an afternoon of study.

Four o'clock saw her still sitting there though her feet were chilled and her body was stiff with cold.

The river flowed, dull and grey and oily, reflecting the March sky, and Miriam let her thoughts flow with it, detached and grey and oily, fading with the daylight.

A soft voice spoke her name, drifting through the twilight. He spoke twice before she really heard.

'Hello, Miri. I said hello.'

She'd know the voice anywhere. Miriam closed her eyes, shutting out the view of the river and the grey day. She felt him move behind her, his hand resting lightly on the bench just beside her shoulder. She shook her head and opened her eyes again as though that might make him go away, but he moved around the side of her and came to sit down on the bench so close that she could feel the warmth of his body through the denim of her jeans.

'Damien.' She daren't look. She closed her eyes again, tears pricking painfully at her eyelids, her chest tightening with the pressure as she hardly dared breathe in case he went away . . . in case he might really be there.

'Damien?' She was alarmed by the sheer wealth of

longing in her voice. He took her hand, she could feel the warm gentle pressure of his fingers as he clasped hers.

Slowly, not daring to breathe, Miriam opened her eyes. Please be there, she whispered, the feeling of his hand upon hers so real and so strong.

She turned her head, fraction by fraction, neck stiff and shoulders rigid as though if she turned too fast . . .

But he was gone. The bench beside her was empty and the sudden cold against her thigh chilling to the bone after the warmth where Damien's body had so briefly been.

She lifted her hand to touch her face, covering her mouth with her fingers while the tears coursed down her cheeks, her hand still warm from Damien's grasp.

Chapter Twenty-seven

Miriam had felt too unsettled to want to be alone that night. Her bedroom at her parents' house was always left ready for her and it was not uncommon for Miri to return for at least one night in any week. Moving out and claiming what independence she had was not something Miriam had found easy, so when Ray went to find her at her flat, he found himself redirected by her downstairs' neighbour.

Her parents still lived not more than a couple of streets from where Damien's mother lived in the family home, just off the Nottingham Road. Curious, Ray drove past Damien's house. It was neat and well cared for, though the hedge was in want of a trim even this early in the season and the garden looked neglected. He guessed that Emily Pinsent did not place such activities high on her list of priorities. A list that had Damien at the top and Damien at every entry. The house, a semi-detached bay-windowed building the like of which could be found everywhere, was unremarkable. Not like the Taylors'.

Mr Taylor, Ray had learned from the news clipping, had been – presumably still was – a consultant at the local hospital. His wife, Joyce, did some kind of secretarial job. She was described as a PA, which was how Rowena described herself, Ray had noticed, when she was trying to impress. Between them they were more than comfortably off, a fact reflected in their house: large, detached, with an in–out gravel drive, separated from the road by a low wall and wrought-iron gates, though these stood open and looked more for show than for security.

Miri had grown up here and knew nothing else. Not like Damien's family, who had moved from streets like those around the Armitage Estate. Miri would, Ray guessed, have had plenty of available money – unless the family lived way beyond their means – enough to support a drug habit without having to do anything else. So why did she get involved beyond the act of purchasing? Did she have to account for what she spent? Or did she do it simply for the adventure?

Mrs Taylor opened the door. Ray explained that he was a friend of Martin Galloway's. It was a moment before Mrs Taylor seemed able to recollect who that might be. Ray showed her his card and she took it between her fingertips as though afraid of contamination.

'I used to work with Martin,' he told her. 'I was a DI until I retired and set up with Mr Mahoney.'

'So? What do you want with my daughter?'

Ray tried to look apologetic when in fact he was feeling rather annoyed. The way the woman looked at him was not the way anyone would regard an equal. He found it distasteful. 'I'm sorry to drag up the past, Mrs Taylor,' he told her. 'But Martin never gave up hope of finding who supplied Damien Pinsent. He turned up a few more leads and I just wanted to run some names past Miriam. She might recall something.'

Mrs Taylor regarded him coldly. 'Miriam has done her best to put all this behind her,' she said. 'To forget about Damien. What happened to that boy came close to wrecking her life, Mr Flowers. I won't have her upset again.'

'Damien Pinsent's life *was* wrecked, Mrs Taylor,' Ray pointed out. 'And he *was* your daughter's friend. Her close friend.'

'And I'm sorry for him. Sorry for his family. But what can *I* do?'

'You can let me talk to Miriam.'

Mrs Taylor took a deep breath. 'Mr Flowers, if there is new evidence then I would guess the police will investigate. Not some private investigator who happens to claim friendship with a very suspect soon-to-be-ex-policeman.'

'I'm sorry?' That last comment had thrown him.

'I've read the papers, Mr Flowers. Martin Galloway was being investigated apparently. He's a suspect in the murder of those two men killed last week and he crashed his car. Driving while drunk. You can imagine what I think of DI Galloway and his supposed friends.'

Ray felt his anger rising. 'Mrs Taylor, when I arrived, you gave me the impression that you couldn't even remember Martin Galloway. Now you come out with this . . . speculative rubbish. Where did you hear all that crap anyway?'

She looked affronted at the language. She half closed the door and Ray expected her to slam it in his face. He moved forward to stop her but she had other things in mind, reaching to grab a stack of newspapers from the hall table, Ray saw as he squinted through the gap.

The evening editions of the two local papers and one national were handed to him.

'I got my information from here, Mr Flowers,' Joyce Taylor told him triumphantly. She watched, satisfied, as Ray scanned the articles. Martin Galloway, the speculation went, had taken evidence which might have convicted these two men. Taken it for some purpose of his own that was not yet clear to his colleagues. When he'd been found out and the men released because he had effectively corrupted the chain of evidence, he had killed both men and then gone out, got drunk and crashed his car.

Ray read the mix of truth and lies with growing irritation. He looked for a by-line but it had none, merely citing a staff reporter as its author.

Ray folded and then dropped them onto the porch step. 'I want to talk to Miriam,' he repeated.

'And I want you to leave. Now, Mr Flowers, or I'll call the police and have you charged with harassment.'

'Do that,' Ray told her. He sat down on the top step. 'Call them, now.' He took his mobile phone from his pocket and held it out towards her. 'You'll find Superintendent Whissendine, probably under W. Or maybe you'd like me to phone him for you. The simple fact is, Mrs Taylor, I'm not leaving here until I talk to Miriam.'

'It's all right, Mum.'

Miriam appeared in the doorway behind her mother. Until that moment Ray had not even been sure that she was there.

'I'll talk to you,' she said. She glanced at her mother who was fuming and about to protest.

'I'll get my coat,' Miri said. 'We'll walk, if you don't mind. I think it might be easier.'

They walked in silence for quite some time, their meandering taking them eventually to the street where Damien had lived. Miri paused then, standing opposite his house, gazing up at the bedroom window as if she expected to see him there, looking out and smiling. 'I miss him. Even now.'

'Do you feel guilty about him? As guilty as your mother does?'

'Guilty? Mum? What would she be guilty about?'

'Because deep down she might suspect that you had something to do with Damien taking that stuff. There were rumours at the time, Miri, she would have heard them.' For a moment the careful equilibrium was shaken and Ray glimpsed the frightened child beneath.

'You know that I can't just let this lie?'

'I guess I've always known that sooner or later the truth would . . . Did you mean that, about my mother?'

'I did,' Ray told her. 'Miri, your mother is, I think, a woman who thrives on rumours and gossip. I don't know her, but . . . forgive me . . . I know her type. She'd have heard all the stories about you. Heard them, not wanted to believe them but dredged for more, partly because she would have wanted to defend you, partly because she would have worried that they might be right. I doubt she'd have been able to help herself.'

Miri stared at him, then she said in a small voice, 'Is it true, what she said about Martin Galloway?'

'He didn't kill those men and he wasn't drunk. The rest of it . . .'

'Oh.' She turned away to stare once more at Damien's house. She didn't ask what 'rest' so he figured she must have read the papers for herself and listened to her mother's tirade. He doubted that Joyce Taylor would have been quiet about her disapproval.

'What will you do now?'

'About you? Miri, did you need to earn your drugs that way? I mean, that house, your parents . . .'

'Gave me everything I wanted so long as I kept up the A grades and smiled sweetly at their friends.' She sighed. 'Oh I'm making no excuses, Mr Flowers. In fact, it all sounds so pathetic now, doesn't it? I thought I was being so clever. So worldly wise, putting one over on them like that. And you know the ironic thing? There I was, trying to "show them all" and to "show them" I was doing something I'd never dare to confess to. To show them, I was doing something they'd never even know about.'

He touched her arm, trying to convey his sympathy. Trying to control his feelings of utter frustration. He didn't understand teenagers. Didn't really understand kids, having none of his own and few friends with any either. 'Miri, I need names. I need to know exactly what went on. Who was dealing, who was in the chain and dates as close as you can remember them. Chances are the dealers you worked for are long gone. This business shifts like sand. But I need to know.'

She nodded, her face grim and pale.

'I talked to Michael Morrelli last night,' Ray continued.

'Micky?' She was startled. 'I haven't spoken to him since . . .'

'I know. He told me about the threats. About the letters.'

The pallor of her face increased. White skin framed by very dark hair. Her lips bloodless now beneath the vivid red of her lipstick. It looked as though she had lined them in blue.

'He told you that?' It was little more than a whisper. 'They said, if we told anyone, if we even talked to each other . . . We daren't even talk to each other about it.'

'Micky told Martin Galloway,' he said. 'He told him a long time ago.'

Slowly, as if not believing, Miri shook her head again. She was genuinely frightened, Ray realized. Genuinely distressed.

He took a deep breath before piling on even more. 'What did you take that night? What did you give Damien?'

'I didn't give him anything!'

He waited for a moment to see if she'd retract her vehement denial, but she said nothing. 'Let me tell you what I think happened, Miri. You were off the cocaine, because of Damien, because you'd promised him and he'd helped you kick the habit. But you couldn't give everything up, could you, and the excitement of, what did you call it, "showing them" even if you couldn't tell, was as addictive as anything you'd been shoving up your nose for the past however long it was. True, your parents didn't know, but your friends did. Chances are half the school knew, or suspected, and it gave you a buzz. Wondering if you'd be found out. Wondering if anyone would believe that Miriam Taylor, perfect student, perfect child, was getting herself into deep water. So deep in fact that she was threatening to drown.'

'It wasn't like that. I still kept my grades, I still did everything they wanted.'

'I'm not denying that, Miri. That night though, you had something special. You were celebrating. Not just your birthday but getting back in control. And Miri, I've seen enough people trying to break their habit to know how tough it is. This something you had was something different, Micky said. I don't know if he was right and you were given it. If you were, then that begs all kind of questions. Or if you stole it, which begs a whole other set, but whatever. You brought it to the party and you gave it to Damien.'

'We both did it,' she blurted.

'I don't believe that. The tox results show that whatever muck Damien took was almost unique and I've seen the effects it had on Martin Galloway.'

'Martin? What are you talking about?'

'Someone gave him the drug, or something similar.'

'What? When?' She swallowed nervously. 'The letter. The letter said it could happen any time, anywhere, we'd never know until . . . Oh my God! Oh my God!'

He took her arm, suddenly afraid that she might panic and bolt away from him. 'Do you still have the letter?' he asked, but she didn't seem to hear him.

'We were given five tabs,' she said. 'For my birthday. He said it was like Ecstasy only better. We'd all taken E, it was what you did to have a good time. We'd all been fine after. We didn't think anything—'

'Five? What did you do with the rest?'

'Damien took one, I did another and I didn't get around to offering Micky. We'd had a row and Micky didn't come.'

'Why five?'

She shrugged. 'He said just give them to my friends but be discreet, you know. I wouldn't have dared supply anyone else, Mr Flowers, I wasn't into that. God no!'

'You took one, Damien another. Did they look normal? All the same?'

She was nodding her head. 'Yes, yes, little white pills the size of aspirin. No markers. Sometimes they stamp them. Mr Flowers, it could have been any one of us, couldn't it? It just happened to be Damien.'

'It just happened to be Damien.'

He thought about it for a time. It was obvious that it didn't matter to the supplier which kid took the contaminated pill, which meant it wasn't personal. It wasn't someone getting back at Miri directly because she'd stopped using, stopped being so useful. Whichever. Not because Miri had threatened to expose them either. Had she done that, Ray knew, she'd most likely have ended up in a ditch somewhere with a bullet through her head. Like those two from the warehouse. Something nice and direct, not elaborate and chancy like this. No, there was some other reasoning behind this. 'Miri. What did you do with the rest? Did the police do a search?'

Slowly, Miri nodded. 'They searched pockets and bags, nothing heavy, patted people down. The ambulance took Damien away but the rest of us were all still there. The police arrived when the ambulance did. A friend of my mum's did CPR. She'd dived in and fetched him up from the bottom, but it was too late. She got him breathing again and then the paramedics arrived and they took him away.

'I thought of flushing the things down the toilet but I didn't get the chance. My mum was hanging on to my arm so tightly she left bruises the next day. I don't think she could believe what was going on and I was sure she'd insist on going with me if I said I wanted to use the loo, and then, if they didn't flush . . . I couldn't think straight. They were in my bag and I didn't know what to do. I was scared. Just so scared.'

'So, what *did* you do?'

'I pretended I needed a tissue from my bag and while I was fumbling around I managed to slip the others inside my bra.' She shrugged. 'There were so many adults there and some of Mum and Dad's friends were, you know, local councillors and doctors and that kind of thing. I guess the police didn't want to get too heavy. So they just searched our bags and our pockets and kind of patted us down. But they didn't find the others.'

Ray nodded. He remembered from the newspaper reports the comments about pillars of the community and how if it could happen here, at a party held for the daughter of a celebrated consultant surgeon, it pointed to major moral decline. Ray wondered at the time if the reporter had been aware of just how high up doctors, psychiatrists, police and other 'pillars of the community' were on the scale of likely drug-abusers.

Ray suddenly thought of something else. Something that didn't fit with what he had read or already been told. 'Hold on,' he said. 'I thought at first everyone just thought Damien was drunk. That, as I remember, was the generally held view for a good three or four days. Who called for the search, Miri? Was it Martin?'

Miriam thought about it. 'I'm not sure,' she told him. 'But Martin Galloway wasn't in charge anyway. That was another man. A tall, thin guy with a funny name. He had long hair and a scruffy goatee beard and didn't look like a police officer at all, but everyone treated him as if he were God or something.'

'Funny name?' Ray asked her. From the description it sounded as if the man had been working undercover. Vice or drugs presumably.

Miri was trying to recall.

'Was it Whissendine?' Ray asked her. That might pass as a funny name, he thought, but the description didn't really fit. Whissendine could never be described as thin and Ray could not imagine him any way but clean shaven.

She shook her head. 'Foreign,' she said. 'Foreign sounding. Something like Inverness but not that. Inverni. Inverna. I didn't speak to him and he didn't introduce himself. Martin Galloway did most of the actual talking. I just heard him say something like, "It was up to DCI Inver-whatever it was." My dad figured out he was in charge and tried to talk to him but the man just cut him dead and Martin said we'd have to wait along with everyone else. This man wanted more thorough searches I think. I was really scared he'd get his way.'

'And afterwards, what did you do with the pills?'

She shrugged. 'I dumped them in the nearest bin.'

Ray shook his head. 'I don't think so,' he said. 'If they suspected drugs right from the start and it's obvious they did then the bins would have been searched, Miri.'

'Maybe they were and it just wasn't reported.'

'Maybe.' He turned her around to face him. She had dark blue eyes, he noticed for the first time. Very dark and very frightened. 'What did you do with the other pills?' he asked her again.

She sighed and pulled her gaze away. 'I gave them to Martin Galloway,' she said.

Ray was becoming increasingly aware of what Martin might have meant when he talked about being in deep water. What had he done with the pills? Martin, Ray recalled, had told him that there had been no clue as to who had supplied the drug to Damien. He said that Miri had vowed her innocence and had given no clue that the facts may have been otherwise. Martin had come to Ray and seemed to be telling him the honest truth of what had gone on. But even while he seemed to be giving so much away, it was now clear that he was keeping back knowledge at least equal to that he shared.

Had Martin simply been mindful of the threats that had been made and so not wanted to implicate Miri and the others? If so, then why hadn't he gone to his superiors and had protection put in place for them?

Ray could think of two answers to that. One must have been that Martin knew such protection could not have been long term, that three years on it would have long ceased and left them vulnerable, and Martin, judging by what he didn't tell Ray, must have felt that the threat was still there. The other reason had, Ray felt, far more to do with the timing of events.

A little more than two years ago, Ray had been attacked. At the time it had been accepted that the man who had burned him had mistaken him for another officer, one who was to be key witness in an upcoming court case involving one of the biggest drug busts that had ever happened in the area.

The Pierce brothers had connections that spread out across Europe, and connections that permeated the local police force. Ray had been shocked to find just how deep their influence went. Three years ago the undercover operation that had led to the gang being busted would have still been going on. He calculated quickly. Coming to its end probably, which would account for the man with the odd name that Miri could not recall, coming out from under cover. Which meant also that there had been a perceived link between what had happened to Damien and the bigger picture. Which meant in turn that Miriam's connections, Miriam's ill-conceived adventures, would have been so well documented that if Damien had not suffered his tragic fall it was quite likely the party would have been raided anyway, especially if surveillance had indicated that Miri had been carrying on the night in question.

'Do you remember the Pierce affair?' he asked her.

She looked surprised. 'Sure, I read about it in the papers.'

'That was all? You didn't have any involvement with them?'

She shook her head.

'And the people you worked for? Did they?'

Miri shrugged. 'How should I know?'

'You carried for them, you ran errands. Who *did* you have contact with, Miri? I want their names.'

'I told Martin.' She had calmed down enough now for her earlier reluctance to have returned.

'And Martin's in no fit state to tell me. Names, Miri. Just start with the ones you remember then write me that list.'

Miri hesitated, then said, 'Rick Myers. The person I had most dealings with was Rick.'

Ray nodded. The name was a familiar one. But he was strictly small-time. A middle-man, a distributor. 'Rick was the money man from what I remember,' he said. 'He kept the books. Sent the collectors in if payment wasn't prompt enough.'

'I wouldn't know,' she said sharply. 'He was all right with me.'

'Sure. You never tried to double deal.'

She glanced anxiously in Ray's direction. 'I'm not that stupid.'

'Then you knew he wasn't all sweetness.'

'I heard stories about him, that was all.'

'And who else?'

'I don't remember.'

'Sure you do. Miriam, I'd be willing to bet this is etched upon your brain. Who else?'

'Eldon. Eldon Firth I think his name was. I used to carry messages back and forward, nothing more.'

Ray nodded, recognizing the name. 'And who gave you the tabs the night of your birthday?'

She shrugged again. 'I guess that was Eldon.'

'*You guess.* From what I remember Eldon Firth was a crack dealer. He kept to what he knew. Had a little empire maybe four streets wide that he ran like it was a frontier town. You wanted what he was selling you came and asked to be let in, and if his boys liked the colour of your money you might make it through. He didn't deal in recreational stuff.'

'Yeah. Maybe. Look, the night before I went to see him with a message from Rick. Rick said that he'd heard it was my birthday and as . . . as I'd been such a good girl,' she said the words mockingly. 'As I'd been such a good girl, he'd told Eldon to have a little something ready for me. I asked him what it was and he said it was good stuff. E, but better than usual. When I met Eldon and gave him the message—'

'Just hold up there. Where did you meet Eldon?'

'Where? Oh,' she thought about it for a moment. 'There were a couple of places, it would depend. This night, it was outside the Birch Tree pub on the Main Road. It was a summer evening, there's a garden at the back with a kids' play area. I met him there. He had a Coke waiting for me like always. I sat down and drank the Coke, gave him my message, made like we were friends meeting up, you know. And this night I told him what Rick had said and he gave me the five tabs.'

'Just handed them over?'

'Pretty much. Yes.'

'And was he alone?'

'Not usually. There'd be someone with him. Rick didn't like to be alone and neither did Eldon.'

'I wonder why?' Ray commented mockingly. Their walk had brought them full circle back to Miri's home and they perched on the low wall that separated the driveway from the rest of the world. 'And this night, who was with him this time?'

Miri shifted uncomfortably. 'I didn't know this one,' she said. 'He was a white guy and he seemed, I don't know, different. Jumpy and unsure of himself. Eldon told him to give me the stuff and he took the bag out of his jacket pocket and just sort of shoved it across the table at me. I remember being scared in case anyone saw. Eldon was usually more subtle.'

'And no names?'

She shook her head. 'Eldon just called him "my friend here". I didn't hear his name.'

'And he looked like?'

'It was three years ago, Mr Flowers.'

'Enough time for you to have gone over it a thousand ways, Miri. Look, for what it's worth, I think you cared for Damien. I don't believe you meant for him to get hurt, but you realize just how naive and downright stupid you were. You've been telling yourself that exact same thing ever since the day Damien nearly died.'

'I wish he had, you know. Isn't that a terrible thing to say?'

Ray didn't answer. He didn't think there was one he could give honestly. 'What was he like?' he persisted, gently.

Miriam sighed. 'White, thirty maybe, but no older. Pale blue eyes, ginger hair, freckles. He was dressed in blue jeans and a white T-shirt with a denim shirt over the top. Open like a jacket. It was a really warm night, but he looked sort of pinched and cold. I remember that. It was like, however hot the sun was, he still couldn't get warm.'

'Did he say anything? To you, to Eldon?'

'Not to me and not to Eldon while I was there but as I left I heard him say something though I couldn't catch the words and Eldon laughed and said something like, "that's life, lovely, ain't it?" '

'And you told Martin this. All of it?'

She nodded. 'Yeah. Not at first. I told him bits of it, but Martin was like you, he didn't let things go.'

'And you're ready to tell someone now, aren't you, Miri?'

'I don't know. I'm scared, Mr Flowers . . . Ray. I told him some of it and then we got the warnings. We were told to retract anything we'd already said. To deny everything, say we'd no idea what Damien was into. Not to cooperate with the police at all. I told Martin that what I'd confessed so far was something I'd made up because I felt guilty. After all, Damien was at my party and someone at the party probably supplied him. He didn't believe me, I mean, I'd already given him the pills, and he didn't let up. He talked to all of us again and again and finally, Micky showed him the letter. Martin promised he'd keep it to himself. He promised all of us.'

A promise, Ray guessed, prompted by the suspicion he must already have had that someone in the force was on the take and would transmit anything Martin reported back to their paymasters. Ray's own actions a few months later and the arrests that followed must simply have confirmed to Martin that he'd been right to be silent . . . then. But what about now? Had Martin been having doubts? The nagging question coming back again. Or was Martin simply paranoid?

'You gave him your letter too?'

She nodded.

Ray thought about it some more. 'Did Martin ever mention this other officer to you? The one with the odd name?'

'I don't think so. Sorry, I really don't remember.' She sighed. 'What now?'

'I don't know. I have to think.'

'Will you go to the police?'

He didn't answer her directly. He knew he'd have to, sooner or later, but Ray felt he needed time to assimilate all that he had learned. It wouldn't be tonight, and he'd rather go with something concrete. 'Make the list, add all the detail you can even if it's slight. Write me a statement, Miri, everything you told me tonight. But you know you'll have to come clean about all this, don't you?' And so will I, he thought. He expected her to deny it, to want to back down again and just escape from all the bad memories and all the things that would come out once she had gone to the police with her story. That she'd retreat to her safe little world behind the ornamental wall and retract every single word she'd said to him. But she didn't, she simply nodded slowly, turning her head away so that he could not see the tension in her face or the tears threatening in her eyes.

Her mother had seen them return and she stood on the doorstep now with her arms folded, staring at them both as though she'd like to kill Ray and wasn't so sure about her daughter either.

'I'm sorry,' Ray said, and meant it. Whatever Miriam had done, there had never, he felt, been any malice there. Just stupidity and, he thought, if we all had to spend our lives paying for the stupid things we did when we were just eighteen, then we'd all be for it big time.

'One more thing,' he said to her. 'Then I think you'd better go inside before your mother sets the dogs on us.'

She laughed at that. 'Mum has a Yorkshire terrier,' she said. 'It's called Itsy.'

Ray smiled back. 'Small dogs, big egos,' he said. 'But like I say, there's one more thing. These messages you carried. Were they written down?'

She bit her lip and shook her head.

'So you had to remember them.'

She nodded.

'Help me here, love, you know what I'm going to ask.'

Miriam hesitated. 'I don't know,' she said, then, 'but I guess I've told you everything else. It was like some kind of code, I never knew what it meant. It always started the same though. Always, "Angel says", and then the street names.'

'Street names? What, like an address? Somewhere in Mallingham?'

'I don't know. I mean I don't know what they meant. They were street names yes, but like America. Like it was New York or something.'

'Like . . . Forty-second and Vine,' he asked her, recalling the personal ad Martin had shown him. Miri nodded. 'Yeah, just like that. "Angel says, Forty-second and Vine".' She glanced to where her mother was still standing. 'God knows what she's going to say,' she commented.

Ray took a business card from his pocket and gave it to her. 'If you want to talk or you're scared, call me,' he said. 'And be careful,' he went on. 'I mean it. Be really careful. We're stirring up a hornets' nest here. I don't believe the threat ended three years ago. What was done to Martin is plenty proof of that.'

Chapter Twenty-eight

Winter had fallen asleep on the sofa. Never a good idea. It didn't give him the support his back needed and he always woke stiff and cramped with his muscles in spasm, about as much able to right himself as a turtle turned upon his back.

He'd never broken himself of the habit though. It was a way of touching normality. Making contact with the time before, when it had been an accepted part of coming home, flaking out exhausted in front of the television, his long limbs overhanging the end. Gita had long since given up trying to persuade him that it was a stupid thing to do.

He'd been dreaming. Again. Before, he'd never had such vivid dreams, or if he had, he'd not remembered them. Perhaps, he thought, he'd not had so much to dream about back then. Certainly, the subject of his nightmares had not existed.

'Gita?'

She appeared from the kitchen, standing in the doorway, polishing a glass until it shone.

'You stuck?' she asked him.

'Yeah. Help me will you?'

She set the glass and cloth down on the counter. 'Don't know why I should,' she told him. 'Come here.' She slid an arm beneath his shoulders and braced herself so that he could use her to lever himself upwards. Then she swung his legs down and made sure he was balanced enough to leave while she fetched his chair.

'You OK? You're sweating like a pig.'

'Sorry,' he apologized automatically, realizing abruptly that his shirt was soaked. 'I'd better wash and change, I guess.'

She nodded. 'Same dream?'

'Isn't it always?' He wheeled himself through to the bathroom. It wasn't exactly wheelchair-friendly though the local council had installed handrails for him and the residents' association paid for a shower attachment with a seat across the bath that he could use if Gita helped him transfer from his chair.

Same dream.

Always the same dream. Chasing, being chased. It no longer made sense to try to sort the sequence. He had followed Eldon Firth onto the warehouse roof and Eldon's people had followed him up. Pursuer becoming pursued, the hunter cornered and then driven out onto the asbestos ridges. Either that, or risk a bullet in the back.

It was strange, Winter always thought, but he'd known the outcome from the moment Eldon's men had fired the first shot and the bullet had hit the wall not two inches from Winter's hand. He'd seen the signs warning that no one should come onto the roof without the use of crawl boards. He had known full well that he would fall if he disobeyed those warnings, but he had done it anyway, fleeing from the second shot fired the instant before the brittle roof gave way and sent him plunging.

Winter had not been armed.

In his dreams he saw faces staring down at him through the broken roof, faces framed in jagged grey against a pure blue sky, like something drawn in a comic book, and their voices floating up in speech bubbles, though he knew now that the speech bubbles had appeared much later, morphine-induced as the doctors tried their best to deal with his pain. Drug-induced voices floating in bright spheres up into the cloudless sky.

Winter stripped off his shirt and washed himself in the basin. It wasn't easy. The pedestal was in the way and his chair didn't fit close enough to stop the water slopping into his lap if he wasn't careful. He spread a towel over his knees to catch the drips and used a face cloth wrung out in soapy water to wipe himself down and clean away the sweat. Gita said his sweat always smelt sour after he'd had nightmares and she should know, he thought, grateful for the modicum of response his body was still capable of when she touched him, tasted him, lay beside him, the length of her body pressed tightly against his. He'd been lucky, his spinal cord had not been severed, not completely, and some signals still made the long-haul trip from his lower body up into his brain, though there had been times when the pain had been so bad he'd almost wished that he had broken cleanly in two and the pain receptors that fired so enthusiastically had been blocked off totally.

But that was then. Not now. Now was better, and Winter was grateful.

*

When he emerged from the bathroom feeling a little cleaner and more human, Gita was sitting on the floor by the coffee table with Beck at her side, the dog gently nosing at the papers Gita was reading. Two local evening editions. Gita looked up at him. 'They're talking about Martin,' she said.

Winter wheeled himself over and took the articles from her, reading, as Ray had done not long before, the half-truths and assorted lies.

'I want to see him,' he said, dropping the discarded papers back onto the table.

'Who? Martin or this Ray Flowers man?'

Winter thought about it. 'Both,' he said.

Gita shook her head. 'I told you, I drove by this Redfern place today. It's got one main entrance and that's besieged by journalists now and there's a police cordon not letting anyone through that didn't have their name on a list.'

'Ray Flowers first then. Maybe he can get me in.'

Gita nodded. 'Martin believed that Whissendine was honest,' she said. It was a conversation they had started earlier but which had led nowhere. 'Maybe you *should* go to him now.'

Winter frowned momentarily, but Gita could see he was not as vehement as he had been earlier that afternoon. Maybe the nightmare had unsettled him enough to make him listen to what she knew was good sense. Maybe seeing Martin's name splattered once again over the front pages. Gita waited for him to say something more. She had believed in what Martin was doing as much as Winter had, though she had worried for several months now that a new element had become influential in the residents' association and that Martin's control was wavering.

'We could talk to this other man first,' she offered as a compromise. 'You know he's looking for you from what that boy, Michael, said.'

'Yes, I know.' He seemed to come to a decision. It was often that way with Winter, Gita thought. He'd prevaricate for ever and then suddenly make up his mind and God help anyone who tried to slow him down once he had.

'We'll go now,' he said. 'You've got the address Martin gave us?'

'Sure.'

'Right, you get the car, I'll meet you in the lobby.'

'What about Beck?'

Winter called the dog to his side, stroking the soft freckled muzzle. 'Flowers had just better like dogs,' he said.

Chapter Twenty-nine

He'd had to look it up to find the location of 42nd and Vine. Time was when he knew all the locations by heart, but that was close on three years since and he'd let them slip from his memory.

He'd listed the keys in a little book, an old diary of the kind you could buy cheaply at any garage or stationer's, and the pleasure he had taken in making up the entries so that to the casual glance they might seem like appointments had been quite out of accord with his usual stolid exterior. Max had a very active inner life that few people knew about. Even fewer might care to. And it amused him further that the keys to the locations were all given as though for an American city, giving the impression that Max was a real globetrotter. Max, who hated to fly and liked to be able to sleep in his own bed at night.

Lexington and East 79th Street, for instance, meant the Bear's Head pub out at Thrussington, so he wrote in his diary, Mr Bear, corner of Lexington and East 79th, together with a fictitious time. 42nd and Vine referred to a local country club that Max and his associates liked to frequent. That went down as Barny, 8 p.m., 42nd and Vine.

Max enjoyed his games. Angel took pleasure in them, too, and Max was glad to have his old playmate back out of the obscurity that had swallowed him this last year or two. Not that Angel had gone away, of course. The Angel never went far, and even when he wasn't watching over his business concerns Max knew that he had eyes everywhere. Angel Eyes, Max mused to himself. Cold and blue and fired by an intelligence that Max himself could never hope to match in a thousand years.

Max always arrived first for these meetings. He sat in the usual corner of the plush hotel bar, looking out over the golf course – Max didn't play, but he admired the view – with a G&T in hand, waiting, as the ice melted in his glass, for his employer to appear.

He was late, Max thought. That was unsettling. He liked Max to be early so that he could be on time, conduct their business and be gone. It occurred to Max that this was unusual enough to be a bad omen. That maybe this contact after such long absence was a set-up . . . but for what? Max was in a place he often visited, with friends due to arrive in another half-hour, just to give him a cover story should it be needed.

He need not have worried. Ten minutes after the appointed time a man appeared in the doorway, accompanied by two others. One walked with him to the bench seat by the window where Max waited. The other went to the bar to order drinks that, Max knew from experience, would be barely touched, there just for the look of things.

'Max.' The other man was young. Not tall but he carried himself as though he were six foot plus. Slim, too, making Max all too aware of the paunch he had acquired as he aged.

Max nodded. 'I thought you weren't coming. You're late.'

'I'm sorry,' the other apologized smoothly. 'Traffic coming out of town. You know my associate, I believe?'

Max nodded. Rick Myers, a face he hadn't seen for quite a time.

'So,' he asked, swallowing the rest of his drink and reaching out for the fresh one that had been brought over. 'What gives?'

'The kids that were with Damien Pinsent when he took his late-night swim. It seems we didn't sort it well enough. They think we've lost our grip, Max, just because it's been three years or near enough.'

Max shook his head in what he hoped was a sympathetic manner. Sympathetic, without seeming like he was judging the Angel too harshly. 'I said at the time,' he mumbled. 'We should have done for the lot of them.'

'Yes, Max, we should have had a murdered cop and the bodies of two teenagers on our hands just after their best friend nearly killed himself. Wise move that would have been. No, we acted for the best. Controlled the situation without the excess violence that only draws attention. And, Max, if the pressure had been kept on, as I asked, we wouldn't have this little problem now. Keep people scared, keep them off balance and they keep their mouths tightly shut. You let the pressure off, Max, and pouff, all the steam escapes. All these people ready to spout a lot of hot air, mouths wide open, spilling their souls.'

Max fiddled with his glass, swirling the ice until Rick Myers placed a hand upon his and held it still. He laid a copy of the *Mallingham Guardian* on the tabletop.

'Folded inside the paper you'll find two little commissions,' the blue-eyed man told him quietly. 'The first one must be done tonight. She's already said too much and she knew too much to start with, though she might not have realized it. Time she did, I think. The second, in your own time, but within the week would be good for me.'

Max gripped the paper hard. He could feel something bulky wrapped inside the pages.

The blue-eyed man smiled at him again, that same tight smile that never reached higher than his mouth.

'Have fun, Max,' the Angel said.

Chapter Thirty

When the doorbell rang, Sarah went to answer it. Ray could hear her talking to someone, a woman from the sound of it, with a lightly accented voice that made him think for a moment it was Sonia Dattani.

Then he heard the door close and Sarah came back through. She was not alone. A young Asian woman followed her. She wore jeans and a winter coat and her black hair was cut into a short bob and tucked back behind her ears. She turned to help her companion negotiate the door. The wheelchair was a tight fit in a house built before such things were given much thought. He was a tall man, Ray could see that despite the chair. Tall and rangy with longish hair and a beard that was rather better trimmed.

'My name's Inverno,' he said. 'Enrico Inverno. But Martin called me Winter. I thought it was time we met.'

It was Sarah who made the connection. 'Inverno,' she said. 'Italian for winter. We never thought of anything like that.'

The man laughed. 'Martin's sense of humour,' he said. 'Now most people who know me well call me Winter. I've not been Enrico in years.' He turned back to Ray. 'So,' he said. 'What do you have for me, and more to the point, what are we going to do about it all? And can you get me in to see Martin?'

'To the last, probably. I can talk to his doctor, though she called me this afternoon and said they'd got extra security on the gate. Someone reported which clinic Martin had been taken to and they've been under siege ever since. As to the rest, I'm willing to trade what I know. After that, we'll have to decide, though my feeling is that Whissendine's our best bet.' He saw the young woman, Gita, nod her head, but Winter continued to be noncommittal.

'Maybe,' he said. 'OK. So I'll begin. And I promise you, you'll be surprised at just how often our paths have crossed. That we've not met before was just a question of bad timing.'

He took a deep breath as though preparing to dive deep and then began. 'Three years ago I was working undercover, running with the Pierce mob and right at the heart of their operation. It'd taken me a full two years to get that far inside and just when it looked like we would get a conviction and I could finally come up for air the whole works started to collapse about our ears. There were rumours that some idiot copper had planted evidence just to make sure of things. Evidence that didn't need planting, there was enough of the genuine article around to sink the Pierce brothers without trace, but, of course, it gave their defence team all the ammunition they needed.' He glanced at Ray. 'I don't need to tell you any of this. You came along a few weeks later and blew the whole thing wide open.'

Ray nodded. 'I didn't know Martin had any part in the Pierce case,' he commented. 'He never worked vice or drugs so far as I knew.'

'He didn't. He wasn't. Martin and I go back a long way.' He smiled wryly. 'Martin came very close to blowing my cover one time. A bunch of us were picked up on a possession charge. Martin saw me brought in, damn near spoke to me. Fortunately, Martin Galloway catches on quick and realized what I was into. We met later and for months he fed me info I wouldn't have got any other way. A lot of it about you.'

'Me?'

Winter nodded. 'You were making waves. Martin and I had both suspected for a long time that there were officers on the take. We watched what you were into with great interest, Ray. Trouble was, I found out later, someone saw me talking to Martin one night and when everything blew up in the Pierces' faces I found myself with my cover in pieces and nowhere to run.' He paused and smiled bitterly. 'You know the most ironic thing? I'd broken cover that night Damien jumped off the high board. Thought that was the time to pull out, but no, they said. Just a few more days and I was stupid enough, macho enough, I suppose, not to argue the toss, but I spent those three more days shitting bricks, sure someone would make the connection. Someone would have seen me that night. Turned out it wasn't that at all, it was a casual meeting with Martin Galloway in the Red Lion that did for me.'

Ray nodded. 'That's often the way,' he said.

'I'd been working as a messenger boy,' Winter continued. 'A courier, a general gofer. Nothing too high profile, but it meant I was everywhere and still invisible.

This night, I was sent with a sealed package to a guy called Eldon Firth.'

Ray looked surprised at mention of the name.

'Ah, I see you know our boy Eldon. I'd done the same trip a hundred times before, kept the boy supplied, taken payment home. This time though there was a little extra message in the package. I ended up on the roof of one of those old warehouses down on Riverside being shot at by a couple of Eldon's punks. The roof was asbestos. Rotten. I fell. End of career.'

'But Martin stayed in contact.'

'Martin was my lifeline. Martin and Gita here. When I fell out with one, the other took over and kept me sane. I'd been seeing Gita for a while before my accident. She didn't know who I was, what I was.'

'She thought you were one of Eldon's boys?' Ray asked. 'From what I remember Eldon was active on the Armitage three years ago.'

'He was, yeah, 'til Rick Myers moved in. Eldon shifted ground, Myers took over his old deals.' He shook his head. 'Martin and I could never understand how come Eldon took that one so calmly. We figured Myers had someone bigger backing him up.'

'Someone else? Not Pierce?'

'Definitely not Pierce, though they knew about this other mover and were none too pleased. If Pierce hadn't been taken down when he was we'd have had a full-scale war on our hands.' He fell silent, thinking about it.

'What did you think he was?' Ray asked Gita.

She laughed. 'Oh I thought he was a car mechanic,'

she said. 'He told me he worked across town, even got me a cheap service on my old car. When Martin came and told me about his accident and about everything else I didn't know whether to run all the way to the hospital or leave the country, I was so bloody mad with him.'

'At least now you know where I am nights,' Winter joked, taking her hand.

'Doesn't mean I know what you're up to. I'm serious,' she said to Sarah. 'I think he'd almost forgotten who he was by the time he came out of hospital. He'd had so many different identities, had to remember so many lies that when the nurses called him Enrico he looked around for someone else.'

Ray nodded. He'd seen officers work deep cover for so long that they felt compelled to lie if you so much as asked them the time.

'So afterwards, when you came out of hospital, you went to live on the Armitage with Gita.'

Winter nodded. 'Martin and the residents' association helped us modify the flat. I'd been half living there for a while before. I'd nowhere else to go and there was no one I wanted to be with except Gita.'

Sarah was looking puzzled. 'You must have had a pension,' she said. 'Compensation or something. Couldn't you have both gone away somewhere? Found somewhere more' – she glanced apologetically at Gita – 'well, more salubrious to live. Somewhere safer.'

Gita laughed. 'There was nowhere safer than the Armitage for Winter,' she said. 'The residents' association knew what he'd been doing. They knew all about his association with Martin. They looked after us. No one comes onto the Armitage without them knowing about it.'

'I can believe that,' Ray said.

'And as for pensions and compensation, it's taken a long time to sort out. Winter only started getting his proper payments a few months ago.'

'It can take time,' Ray agreed. 'Especially if you'd been hospitalized for a long time, had to be assessed. It's not always as straightforward as it should be.' He grinned awkwardly at Winter. 'I had blackmail on my side and a superintendent prepared to offer me the world if I'd quietly disappear. Things happened a lot faster for me.' He paused, then, 'Winter, Martin seemed to be saying that you were the only one he confided in.'

'I'm not even sure that's true. Martin believed the less people knew the less they could tell. It wasn't a case of trust, though obviously that came into it. I think Martin was scared. He was on to something, or afraid of something, and he let as few people in on it as he could. Fewer people to get hurt. He needed to be in control. He told me a lot, Ray, but I don't know where he went that day he crashed his car, only that he was excited about something. Someone had come back on the scene who'd been there three years ago. Whoever it was behind Rick Myers is my guess. Only this time, Martin believed he knew names and what they were peddling, and where to find them.'

'I think we can assume that he found them,' Ray agreed. He paused. 'You knew all about Damien?'

'About Damien. About Miriam Taylor and her involvement – as a matter of fact I brought Martin up to speed on that one –and poor little Michael Morrelli.'

Ray looked questioningly at him.

'Martin figured he was in love with Damien. Ray, I came from a family just like Micky's, big, Italian, Catholic and very loving but very conventional.'

Ray thought about it some more. 'Did Martin show you the letters?' he asked.

Winter smiled. It was the wolfish smile of a man who knows he holds the cards and is enjoying the sensation. 'Better than that,' he said.

Gita's coat was hanging on the back of her chair. She reached down and fished in the pocket. 'Here,' she said, handing Ray a brown envelope. The envelope contained two evidence bags, each with an identical letter contained within the thin plastic.

> *Be like the three wise monkeys* [the letter read]. *You heard nothing, you saw nothing and you will say nothing. The third monkey drowned. Worse can happen, any time, any place, no warning and no reprieve. You don't hear, you don't see and you don't say.*
>
> *Remember. I'm like God. My eyes always keeping watch.*

It had been printed, Ray guessed, on an ink jet, judging by the quality, on the kind of plain white paper that could be purchased at any stationer's.

'Envelopes?' he asked.

'Sorry, don't have them. Micky dropped his in a school bin but he said it was one of those white selfseal things so no possible forensics from the saliva on the flap and nothing written on it. Miriam said pretty much the same but she couldn't remember what she'd done with it.'

'You said, in the school bin?' Sarah asked.

'They'd gone in to collect their exam results. Their results were in the school office in alphabetical pigeon-holes. Just plain white envelopes with their names printed on. Micky said the other envelope was paper-clipped to this one. He opened it thinking it was something to do with the exams. Someone was going round with a bin collecting the discarded envelopes and he dumped that in without looking too closely, before he'd even read the letter. Miri had the same.'

'Martin left a cutting from a magazine on the day of his accident. Neither of us was here, so he screwed it up and posted it through the door. It's at the office, so I can't show you, but it was a detail taken from a painting of angels. Just the eyes, torn in a strip from a magazine advert.'

Winter shook his head. 'No,' he said. 'I didn't see that. Do you know what it was about?'

'Not really. Angel Eyes, presumably, same as in the newspaper ad. He showed you that?'

This time Winter nodded. 'We figured it was some kind of contact address but didn't get any further than that. I'd guess you'd need a key to work out what the message meant. Martin got excited about it though, because it was the first that had appeared in a couple of years. I take it it's the recent one you're talking about?'

'He showed me two, very similar. One from two or so years ago. One more recent. A few days before he came to see me, he said.'

Winter nodded. 'He thought it meant that whoever it was that had begun moving in on the Pierces' territory had come back to finish the job.'

'Why wait?'

Winter shrugged. 'I think Martin assumed he'd never really gone away,' he said. 'Just stepped out of the limelight for a while.'

Chapter Thirty-one

Miriam had been up late writing. Her mother had given her the third degree when Ray had gone but Miri had said very little, certainly not enough to satisfy her. She had then retreated to her room and lay for a long time on the bed trying to get things straight in her head before embarking on the list and statement that Ray had requested.

Twice her mother had come and knocked on the bedroom door. The first time she had still been angry, shouting through the door that Miriam had better open up and give her some straight answers. Miri left the door locked and ignored her. Later she heard her parents arguing, an all-too-familiar sound since Damien. Life could be divided into separate parts like that. Almost like AD and BC only in this case it was BD, before Damien and after . . . after.

After Damien everything had changed. Everything.

On the way to bed her mother knocked again. She sounded more conciliatory this time, a state of mind enhanced by large quantities of whatever she had been drinking that night. She didn't ask Miri to open the door, just wished her a good night and threatened they would talk about this again tomorrow. Tomorrow, Miri thought, there would be plenty to say, but she doubted it would be what her mother wanted to hear. It would not be comfortable, not for any of them. More 'after Damien' fallout for their world to absorb.

Miri didn't hear her father come to bed, and when she crept downstairs to fetch herself a drink she saw the light on in the living room and heard the TV chatting to itself, some late-night talk show that she knew her father wouldn't watch. He was sleeping on the sofa again, she guessed, but she didn't open the door to take a look, not wanting to wake him and face the inevitable questions all over again.

He'd slept on the sofa a great many nights lately and even when he hadn't fallen asleep downstairs rarely joined her mother in what was now her bedroom, sleeping most often in the guest room down the hall.

Another result post-Damien, though Miri knew the cracks had been there long before they began to suspect that their daughter had been involved in the near death of one of her closest friends. Miri was still not sure of how much they knew, or guessed, or speculated, but Ray Flowers had been right. Her mother had delved deep into the well of rumour and speculation and been shocked at the water she had drawn there, polluted as it was with all the things that they believed fondly were done by other people's children. Experienced in other people's lives, and not their own.

It was two in the morning by the time Miriam had completed the rough draft of the statement she had promised Ray. It was full of corrections and scribbling in the margins and little notes that said, 'See over the page'. And this was her third attempt. The first two lay in the rubbish basket piled in alongside the empty cosmetic jars and chocolate wrappers and cleanser-soaked cotton wool. Miri made a mental note that she really ought to empty her bin more often.

Finally, half satisfied, she stretched her stiff back and started to get ready for bed, unfastening her shirt and shrugging it from her shoulders, ready to drop into the dirty-clothes hamper beside her bedroom door.

A slight sound attracted her attention. It seemed to be coming from outside on the landing but she couldn't readily identify just what it was. A small metallic click and a tiny scraping sound like metal over metal only not so harsh.

'Mum? Dad?' Her parents usually slept like the dead and if her mother got up in the night she used the en suite bathroom, not the one down the hall. 'Dad?' Miri asked again, the feeling that something or someone was outside the door so reminiscent of childhood nightmares that she felt almost embarrassed to acknowledge it.

The key was in the lock, but when she'd come back up from getting herself a drink Miri had not bothered to lock the door again. She did so now, turning the key swiftly, then standing back and staring at the handle as though willing it to move.

Nothing happened.

Miri stood for several long minutes waiting but nothing happened, no sound, no hint that anything untoward might have occurred.

She forced herself to relax. 'Stupid, stupid. Overworked imagination.' The stuff she'd been writing for Ray Flowers had obviously upset her more than she had thought. Jerked her mind back to that time three years ago when every sound, every stranger, every unknown thing however small had been related to the threat implicit in those letters. Though the truth was, Miri had never really left that time behind. She still jumped at strange noises, kept her windows closed even in the summer, went nowhere alone if she could help it. Three years she had lived with that terror. Miriam admitted finally that she would be so incredibly relieved to let it go.

She sighed, turned her back to the door and continued to get undressed, tossing her clothes into the hamper and slipping into a nightshirt, knowing she should really go and shower but too tired and still too shaken to want to bother with that now. She lay down and tried to sleep, wishing vaguely that her room had an en suite shower room like her mother's did.

Miri slept for perhaps an hour before waking again to find that her bladder was too full to allow her to complete the night. Reluctantly, half asleep, she hauled herself out of bed and unlocked her bedroom door, switching on the landing light, looking carefully up and down the hallway before venturing out. From her mother's room she could hear heavy, sonorous breathing, the half snore of a drink-induced sleep. As she passed the stairway she noted that the light was still on downstairs. She shrugged. Her dad would regret it in the morning, sleeping on the couch all night. Then she went on to the family bathroom at the end of the hall.

Max was waiting for her there.

Chapter Thirty-two

It was nine thirty in the morning by the time Ray learned of Miriam Taylor's death. He'd stayed up late the night before talking to Winter, and first thing he had called Sonia Dattani to arrange for them to visit Martin that afternoon, then rushed into work, arriving late.

Whissendine was only minutes behind. One look at his face told Ray that something was very wrong.

'Six fifteen this morning, Mr Gerald Taylor wakes up on the couch and thinks it's time he took himself to bed. On the way, he stops off at the bathroom and finds his only child gutted like a bloody fish. When he's finished screaming long enough to call us and he's settled down enough for us to get two sensible words out of him it emerges that *Mr* Ray Flowers called round yesterday and had a long talk with his little girl, much against the mother's wishes. Seems this *Mr* Ray Flowers told them there was new evidence concerning Damien Pinsent and seemed to think that their daughter might be able to confirm it. Of course, it never occurred to *Mr* Ray Flowers that the police might have an interest in knowing about this new evidence, neither did it occur to the bastard idiot of an ex-copper that if the girl could confirm this evidence it might put her in any kind of danger. Oh no, that never crossed the mind of clever Mr Frigging Flowers, did it? Did it hell.'

He leaned across Ray's desk, peering at him through eyes that were enraged and bloodshot and filled with images of dead, defiled Miriam Taylor. 'And if I find out that Mr Flowers' little habit of acting alone and keeping back relevant evidence led in even the smallest slightest way to that young woman being butchered I'll take you apart my frigging self and give what's left to Gerald Taylor to feed to his frigging dog.'

Ray was stunned. He closed his eyes and took a firm grip on the wooden top of his desk as though contact with something solid might stop the world from reeling.

'When,' he asked. 'When did it happen?'

'Why?' Whissendine asked sharply. 'You want to make sure you have an alibi? No doubt you were all tucked up with that redhead of yours. All peaceful and cosy while that kid was being killed. God, I've never seen so much blood.'

Rowena had followed him into the office. She'd stood wide-eyed while he had continued his tirade. Now, she pulled a chair away from George's desk and positioned it behind Whissendine. The man glanced her way momentarily, then collapsed into it, leaning his arms on Ray's desk and placing his face in cupped hands, rubbing at his eyes as though to deny what was now imprinted on his vision.

'Her mother went to bed around two,' he said. 'She spoke to Miri. Her dad found her at six fifteen. That's all we know. There wasn't enough left intact to do a temperature comparison. Whoever it was, they'd taped her mouth so she couldn't scream.'

'Oh my God.' Both men had forgotten about Rowena, but she collected herself swiftly. 'I'll . . . I'll make some tea,' she said. 'I'll do it now.'

She disappeared into the outer office. Ray felt he really ought to go to her but he was rooted to the spot, pinned by the force of what he'd heard and by Whissendine's accusations.

'She was making out a statement for me. A statement and a list of names,' he said.

'For you? I don't suppose we were to be included in this little tête-à-tête?'

'We'd agreed. We were going to come to you today, tell you everything we'd put together so far.'

'Generous of you. Pity someone got to her first. It might have been an interesting little chat.'

Ray said nothing. He didn't feel that he deserved to say anything.

'There were pens and paper on her dressing table,' Whissendine told him, not relenting, just wanting more. 'Her room had been entered. Whatever she'd been writing had been taken away. He wore gloves. He left them in the bin in Miri's room, covered in her blood. He must have taken your list.'

'How did he get in?'

'French windows in the dining room. Out the same way. The house was alarmed, but Daddy was sleeping downstairs, so the alarm wasn't set. The French windows were old. One lock, with the key left in. He took out the glass panel and turned the key.'

'So he must have had information. The layout, their habits.'

'If you're trying to offset blame by making out this

was planned long since you can forget it. Anything he needed to know could be learned by climbing over next door's fence and looking through a few windows. And before you try the other tack, nothing was stolen. He wanted Miriam, not her mother's frigging jewellery.'

'I wasn't trying to shift the blame,' Ray told him angrily. He took a deep breath. 'Miri was scared,' he said. 'There'd been threats issued and I was stupid. I should have come straight to you. I should have had Miri sent away, protected any way possible and there's nothing I can say to excuse that.'

'Damn right there's not. You're as guilty in my book as that bastard with the knife.'

'Michael Morrelli,' Ray said, his voice suddenly hoarse. 'Get someone to him now.'

Whissendine listened while Ray gave the address, scribbling it down quickly, then picked up Ray's phone. In the outer office, Ray could hear Rowena speaking to someone. George, he thought, his voice calm and concerned, Rowena's rising in panic and distress.

George came through as Whissendine put down the phone. 'Just pray that he's still all right,' Whissendine said. 'Pray hard. And now,' he grabbed a stack of A4 paper from George's desk, 'I want to know it all. Leave anything out and I swear I'll have your balls.'

Chapter Thirty-three

Ray had experienced many bad events in his life: episodes of near disaster, of physical pain, of despair, but never anything like this. The initial shock followed by a creeping numbness that chilled his body and froze his thoughts. His initial responses to Whissendine's questions were slow and stilted as he tried to come to terms with what had happened to Miriam Taylor. He was grateful that some impulse of Whissendine's had induced the DCI to come to him, approach him directly, questioning him informally here instead of hauling him to Mallingham station to make a formal statement, cautioned and processed according to the letter of the law.

It slowly dawned on Ray that this was nothing to do with his benefit. Whissendine was not in a fit state to behave professionally. Here, privately, he could swear and curse at Ray. Could rail at the stupidity which had led Martin Galloway and now Ray Flowers to act alone, 'Like some damned vigilante. Like Charles Bloody Bronson. Putting yourselves above the law.'

It was not lost on Ray that he had made such comparisons himself only a little time before. Nothing Whissendine accused him of could be refuted. And because of him a girl, a young woman who'd not yet even begun her life, was dead.

Whissendine listened as Ray outlined what Martin had told him that Sunday. Took notes, listened some more, railed again. Eventually, when Whissendine had calmed down a little, George quietly placed a tape recorder on the table between the two men and seated himself close by with a pen and paper in his hand.

'We should get all of this down,' he said softly. 'Others will need to be briefed.'

Whissendine stared at him and then he nodded. 'Go ahead. You're right, we've lost more than enough time already.'

So Ray began again, talking about Martin, telling what he had discovered from Miri and Michael Morrelli. Occasionally Whissendine butted in. He demanded to see the angel picture and sealed it carefully in an evidence bag.

Occasionally his outrage got the better of him. 'You did what?' when Ray told him about his trip to see Gladys at the spiritualist church, and making his own note of Richard Hayes's name, obviously scheduling him next on the list for a visit.

By the time Ray had reached his meeting with Winter and had told Whissendine his real name, the superintendent had calmed enough to comment that he remembered Inverno. 'He used to be a fine officer,' he said, 'which still gives him no damned right to collude with Martin Galloway.'

It emerged that Whissendine was still smarting from the criticism in the local media that there were no further leads on the shooting of the two men from the warehouse. What did Ray know of that?

'Nothing,' Ray told him honestly.

'Nothing. That's about what we've got.' He glared at Ray and then appeared to decide something. 'There was a card left at the scene,' he said. 'A business card.'

Ray sighed. 'Let me guess. Compliments of the residents' association.' He shook his head. 'It could have come from anywhere. And I don't believe that Martin had anything to do with that.'

Whissendine didn't look so sure. 'He broke every other frigging rule.'

'He didn't kill. I'm certain of that.'

'Not like you?'

Ray flinched. He didn't need Whissendine to turn the knife. His gut was doing that all on its own.

'Not very professional,' George remarked quietly. He reached out and rewound the tape, editing out Whissendine's last comments, cueing it carefully so that the edit would go unnoticed to all but a professional analyst. Whissendine glowered, but he made no move to stop him. Instead, as the tape spooled on again, he carried on. 'It's possible you were on to something, of course, when you talked about someone intent on discrediting Galloway. Everything points to them wanting him and his little group to take the rap.'

'He's hardly in a position to defend himself now, is he?' Ray commented.

'No. No, he's not,' Whissendine agreed. He got up and stopped the tape, removing the cassette and putting out his hand for the account George had been writing. George tore off the sheets and handed them to him.

'I'll be talking to you later,' Whissendine said to Ray. 'Meantime, just butt out. And I want to know where you are. From the moment you get up in the morning to the time you go to sleep at night. Though if you *can* sleep, I bloody want to know how.'

Ray watched him leave through the outer office and let the glass doors slam behind him. He didn't know what to say, what to do.

'Clear out for a few days,' George told him. 'There's room at my place for the both of you and you're not likely to be disturbed there.'

Ray nodded gratefully. George had bought a house locally the year before. It was set in its own garden, back from the road and behind a high wall with a Flowers-Mahoney security system ensuring privacy. George was like that, Ray thought, so protective of his own space that it almost verged on the paranoid. He still did the routine checks on his car he'd learnt from his stint in Ireland and the Balkans and he was the only person Ray knew who automatically checked for anyone hiding in the back seat before he got into his car.

'Thanks,' he said. 'I think that might be a good idea.' He paused, a thought striking him. Something he really did not want to deal with. 'What shall I tell Sarah?'

George was not a man big on physical contact but now he reached out and touched Ray's arm. It was the equivalent of a hug from anyone else and Ray was startled. 'I'll tell Sarah,' George said. 'Go and pack some things now before the press get wind of it, or some enterprising neighbour decides to act in the public interest or whatever it is they excuse themselves by doing.'

Ray nodded, unable to speak.

There was no one outside the cottage at Peatling Magna. Ray packed quickly, hoping that he'd put in the right things for Sarah, snatching shampoos and cosmetics from the bathroom shelf that he thought she used most regularly. Locking the door after setting the alarm he felt as though he were a refugee being driven from his home.

As he loaded the bags into the back of his car their neighbour came scurrying out. 'Ray, there was a man here looking for you. A young man with sandy blond hair, about your height. I told him you'd be at work by now and he said did I know if you'd heard the news.'

Ray closed the car door. 'Did he leave his name?'

'He said he was called Richard Hayes and to ask you to give him a ring.' She peered through the car window at the bags on the back seat. 'Going away, are you?'

'Sarah needed some things,' he told her, knowing that it was a poor excuse. She nodded wisely.

'I listened to the mid-morning bulletin on the radio,' she told him. 'Oh that poor girl. Did you know her?'

'It's bad,' Ray said, not replying to her question. 'It's really bad, Mrs Evans.'

'And in her own home too,' she clucked her tongue, despairing at the state of the world.

'I have to go, Mrs Evans. I'm sorry, I've got an appointment.'

She nodded. 'Always so busy, you two,' she remarked. 'I'll tell that nice young man that he just missed you, if he comes back.'

Ray didn't bother to pursue the conversation, he just nodded and then returned her wave as he drove away.

The night before, Ray had promised to take Winter out to Redfern. He made a major detour to drop the bags at George's house, letting himself in with the key George had given him and unsetting the alarm, hoping he'd remembered the numbers right. He was half an hour late getting to the Armitage. Winter and Beck were waiting for him in the lobby.

'I didn't know if you'd still come,' Winter told him, 'not with all that's been going on. Micky called me just after ten, said they had a police guard now. His mum's giving him hell and there was someone called Whissendine wanting a statement. I told him to be as honest as he could without implicating himself in the warehouse business.'

'He might have to come clean about that. You had a visit yet?'

'Not yet. No doubt my time will come. Whissendine come down hard on you? Micky said you'd been to see the girl last night.'

'I'd say he was my number one fan, if you're voting for relegation. Oh, and from their point of view I can't blame them. It'd been me in their shoes I'd have arrested me as an accessory.'

'That would never stick and you know it.'

'No, maybe not, but trying to make it would have made me feel a whole lot better.'

'Would it? I doubt that.'

'No, maybe not. Anyway, it wasn't that way round, was it?' Not that way around, and the guilt that left him with was eating a hole through his insides.

His hands were shaking as he rested them on the steering wheel, Winter in the front seat, his chair in the estate's boot. Beck lying sprawled on the back seat.

'Are you going to be all right?' Winter asked, looking at Ray's shaking hands and grey features.

His gentleness somehow made it worse. Anger, Ray could deal with, but he wasn't ready yet for sympathy. It undermined him.

'I've never felt this bad,' he said and his voice was hoarse and parched. 'Never. And I don't know how I'll ever make it stop.'

They arrived at Redfern and gave their names to the security man at the gate while the police on duty kept the surge of journalists at bay, long lenses poked right into the car. Or so it felt. It was an unnerving situation, one Ray, as a serving police officer, had faced many times and dealt with easily enough. This time was different though. Did they know yet, he kept asking himself. Did they know who he was? That he had talked to Miriam? That he had failed to protect? For all he knew, their looks and shouted questions were simply speculative. That the photographers would be snapping anyone who came within range. He felt that it was already personal. That they must be looking at him and seeing his guilt and Miri's blood on his hands.

In the back of the car Beck whimpered uncertainly. Ray knew just how she felt.

Richard Hayes was close to the back of the pack as it surged forward, but that was deliberate. He had recognized the car even before he had seen the face of the occupant within. Detaching himself from the others, Hayes made his way back towards his car.

'Hey!' Someone noticed him and grabbed his arm. 'You're local, aren't you? You know who that was?'

Hayes just laughed. It wouldn't take much to find out, he knew. Ray's face had appeared many times both in the local and national press and on the television news. But he wasn't going to tell them that ex-DI Ray Flowers had come to visit his friend, or that Superintendent Whissendine had spent two hours questioning him that morning at the Flowers-Mahoney office and had come out, so Hayes had been told, with a face like thunder.

Sonia Dattani was scared. Ray could see that in her face from the first moment, even though she greeted them both cordially and bent down to fuss Beck who nuzzled her hand approvingly.

'I'm staying here tonight,' she said when Ray asked her how she was. 'Sunil's joining me, then I'm due some leave, I think we might go away for a little while.' She found it hard to meet his eyes, he noted, whereas before she had been so open.

'You'd better talk to Whissendine,' Winter commented.

'I already did . . . he . . . er . . . he said he thought it would be a good idea.'

Ray didn't ask her where she might be going. He didn't want to be responsible for her having to lie.

The news on Martin was a little better. Psycotrex had given permission for a newly tested antipsychotic to be used and Martin at last seemed to be responding, though there was still a long way to go and no way of knowing what long-term effects there might be. Ray stood beside the door as Winter wheeled himself across to Martin's bed. Beck's paws skidded on the linoleum floor and her claws skittered on the smooth surface. Ray almost thought that he saw Martin turn his head towards the sound, though he could not be sure.

'Martin, it's Winter. Can you hear me?' He glanced back at Ray, his expression shocked as Ray knew his own must have been the first time he saw his old colleague lying there.

Beck sniffed at the bed and Martin and then licked his hand, her rough tongue cleaning and grooming the palm and then between each unmoving finger. As Ray watched, Martin slowly but deliberately turned his hand.

Martin dreamed.

The nightmares that had tormented him had diminished just a little. Enough to leave room for sleep and other dreams.

In his dream Martin walked with Damien, the young man pacing out so boldly that Martin almost had to run to keep pace with him. Martin saw, felt, touched, not the Damien he had first seen – white-faced, eyes staring, unmoving, lying beside the pool – or the Damien of the hospital – machines monitoring and controlling the ebb and flow of life pumping in his chest. No, this Damien was young and strong and moved purposefully towards his destination.

'She'll be scared, you see,' this other Damien explained. 'They often are. It's the shock. Oh Lord, do I remember the shock. But I try and help them while they're passing through, until they know which way they want to go or someone comes to meet them properly.'

Martin nodded, the conversation making perfect sense. 'Am I dead then?' he asked Damien.

The young man shook his head. 'No, you're not dead,' he said gently. 'Dead is something different. You'll know it when it happens. It's not quite like anything else, you see.'

They had reached a narrow path now, leading through a wood, though Martin could glimpse a small clearing not far along. The ground was dusty as though it had not rained in quite a while and the sun was warm where it filtered down between the branches of great dark trees. Martin thought he could hear birds singing.

'Lovely place for a picnic,' he commented.

Damien agreed. 'Beautiful,' he said. 'You'll have to come back one day.'

'Yes, I'll do that. I certainly shall.' Martin could not remember a time when he had felt more at home with anyone or in any place. 'Is this like dying?' he asked. 'Just a little bit?'

The young man smiled. 'Oh, that all depends on what your expectations are,' he said. 'She didn't have time to form any, you see, so all the fear will still be there. That's all that will be there. Come on, it isn't far.'

They had approached the clearing now, an open sunny space between the trees, a beautiful spot, though too warm with the unfiltered sun streaming down from a crystal blue sky.

The young man knelt down now and Martin, moving around to see, noticed the crumpled figure of a woman kneeling on the thick green grass, her black hair falling forward and all but hiding her face. He watched as Damien carefully and gently folded her in his arms and drew her close to him, though her body shook so much that his own vibrated in response, his image shivering like a reflection in a wind-disturbed pool. And then, as she raised her head, Martin knew her.

'Miriam?' Martin said.

I dreamed, Martin whispered, but no one heard him, though Beck might have tasted his dreams as he clasped them tight, turning his hand to catch them as they fell.

Chapter Thirty-four

On the way back to the Armitage, Ray called the office and spoke to George. Sarah had been shocked by the news and was in agreement that they should spend some time at George's house, though reading between the lines Ray suspected that she had taken some persuading. Sarah would not take kindly to being driven from her home and probably only the memory of the last year's events, when Ray had featured heavily in the media coverage of the Eyes of God, would have convinced her.

She would drive straight there from work, she told George, and had expressed grave doubts that Ray would have included half the things she classed as essential when he had packed her case.

'She's probably right,' Ray agreed. 'Anything else?'

'Fortunately, no one seems to have made the connection yet, but I've no doubt that it will come. I've told Rowena to take the day off tomorrow. I have appointments all day and Phil can work from home. It seems easiest. You had one more call though, from Gladys Wright; wanted to know if you still wanted to keep the appointment you had with her for this evening. After all that's happened she wasn't sure you'd still be available.'

'Damn. I'd forgotten all about her. I wanted her to talk to Emily Pinsent.' He hesitated. 'Tell her yes,' he said to George. 'I'll pick her up as planned. Seven thirty from the church.' He put down the phone.

'Church?' Winter sitting beside him questioned. 'I take it this is your spiritualist lady.'

Ray nodded.

'You believe in that stuff?'

'I didn't.'

'And now?'

'Now, I don't know. Let's just say I'm prepared to keep an open mind. Anyway, Gladys is something else. I think she might be good for Emily. I'm not so sure this Frida Appleton is.'

'You think she's a fraud? I mean, if we're assuming that what she does is possible anyway?'

Ray shrugged. 'I think there's something odd about her. Something not quite kosher. Look, I don't know if either of them can do what they say they can but something tells me Frida Appleton had another agenda. It might be as simple as self-delusion. Might not.'

'Is self-delusion simple? Seems we've all been guilty of that one. You, me, Martin – deluding ourselves that we were acting for the best. I don't recall it feeling that simple then and it bloody isn't now.'

He had a point, Ray thought, but he didn't bother saying so. It wasn't an area he wanted to debate just now. Instead, he switched on the car radio. It was a local station he kept tuned to one of the presets so he could get the traffic reports. He hadn't noticed the time but the news bulletin was just about to start. Angrily, Ray reached out to switch it off again but Winter leaned forward and covered his hand.

'Leave it, Ray. You have to know what's being said and if you hide from it now it'll only catch you worse later.'

Ray swore at him but knew he was right.

'The murder of Miriam Taylor has shocked this quiet neighbourhood,' the reporter said. 'She was found by her father at just after six o'clock this morning, though police have given no details as yet of how she died. They say they are awaiting postmortem results but death is thought to have resulted from multiple stab wounds. No one from Miriam's family has been available for comment and it is believed that the parents of 20-year-old Miss Taylor, who was studying to become a music therapist, are being cared for by relatives. A statement issued by the college she attended speaks of their shock that such a lively, popular and bright young woman should have her life ended in such a brutal way.'

Ray had heard enough. He reached out again and this time Winter did not stop him as he turned it off.

'Stab wounds,' he said. 'God!'

'What do you expect?' Winter asked him. 'The public doesn't want or need to know how bad it was. Not now. It'll come out later, no doubt, courtesy of the tabloid press or some true-crime reconstruction. You think her parents want to turn on the TV and have someone tell them publicly that their kid was killed by some mad butcher who enjoyed his job too much? Someone turned him loose on the girl and said, go on, use your imagination. Make a bloody mess of it, as if death isn't enough on its own. As if losing someone isn't bad enough.'

Ray glanced at him and then back at the road. 'You talking about Miriam or someone else?'

'Does it matter?'

Ray didn't reply. They had arrived at the Armitage. Ray coaxed a sleepy Beck from the car and took Winter's chair from the boot, glad he'd kept his tank of a car despite Sarah's dislike of it. He helped Winter to slide back into his chair and watched as he wheeled himself up the slight incline and into the tower block, Beck trotting contentedly at his side.

Chapter Thirty-five

Ray and Gladys spoke little on the way to the hospital that night. Ray had gone back to George's house long enough to shower and change, half hoping that Sarah would have come home early and he could see her before he went out again.

She had not. He had made himself a sandwich in George's immaculate kitchen and gone out again to meet Gladys Wright.

The silence between them was not uncomfortable. The woman understood silence, Ray thought, and he was grateful not to have to make small talk.

The car-park entrance was blocked by a small knot of people talking to the attendant. One held a film camera and another a fluff-covered boom mike, but neither was in use. Oddly, they seemed to be asking directions, and as Ray pulled up to the barrier he heard the attendant tell them again that any questions they had should be put to the hospital administrator and that she wouldn't be in until the morning.

Ray pressed the button for a ticket and the barrier was raised. Unnoticed, Ray and Gladys drove on through.

'From the local cable company,' Gladys commented as they passed the camerawoman.

'I didn't notice.'

Gladys smiled at him. 'Community television,' she said. 'They came and did a piece on us not long ago. It wasn't bad and they're too unsure of themselves yet to be pushy. The poor dear who interviewed me was fresh out of college. I kept having to prompt him.'

Ray laughed harshly. 'That will soon change,' he said.

'You don't like our friends in the media?'

Ray thought about it. Like most police officers he had a love–hate relationship with the press. With journalists in general. He guessed it must be like the relationship between celebrities and the paparazzi. Keen at first until they made it big, then just as keen to disappear and cry privacy from the attention they had courted not so long before. 'I find them difficult,' he said at last. 'I know they have to be there, doing their thing, but I'm happier if I'm not in the same place.'

Gladys laughed at him and Ray felt himself relax, then tense his shoulders again, almost indignant at the sound. Today was not a day for laughter. She touched his arm, patting it gently as she might a child who was being sulky. 'You keep on punishing yourself like this, my friend, and you'll be joining Martin Galloway.'

Ray scowled at her but she merely smiled. 'I know, it's too soon to expect you to ease up on the guilt trip – I believe that's the "in" expression.'

'Don't trivialize it! A girl died.'

'I know. And you're partly to blame. You'll have to live with that, Ray, and I mean *live* with it. You've got a lot of years ahead of you in which to scourge yourself.

Take my advice and learn to pace yourself. Guilt is a hard master.'

'You don't understand,' he told her, his tone far harsher than he'd intended. But Gladys merely smiled at him. Just for an instant Ray felt an unexpected rage rising from his belly. He'd have done anything to wipe that self-satisfied, knowing smile from the woman's face, but the impulse faded almost as quickly as it began. He felt ashamed of it. Quietly, he folded the shame away and added it to the stored-up guilt.

The hospital was busier at this time of night. The visiting hours in the main ward finished at eight but here, in what he'd discovered was called the Montgomery wing, visiting was open. Every patient here was chronic in some way or another, he had discovered from talking to the nursing staff. Most were terminal. 'We hope one day to build a proper hospice,' the sister had told him when he and Sonia had chatted to her after seeing Damien. 'But we don't have the funding yet. We try and make this wing as peaceful and stress-free for the families as we can. If they can't sleep and want to visit their loved one at two in the morning, we let them do it, so long as they sign in first.'

Ray wondered how many visits Emily Pinsent made at 2 a.m. He wondered sometimes if she ever managed to go home.

She was there, talking to Damien, and so, as Ray had been told she would be when he had asked Emily if he could bring Gladys, was Frida Appleton.

Emily glanced up as Ray entered the room. This time she seemed to remember him straight away. 'Ah, Martin's friend,' she said. 'And the lady you told me about. The one that might help Damien.'

This was not the way that Ray had explained Gladys to her and he glanced at the grey-haired lady standing at his side, intending to apologize. Gladys though was way ahead of him. 'I can't promise anything, my dear,' she said, pulling up a chair and taking Emily's hands as naturally as though they had known each other for ever. 'You look so tired, my love,' she added sympathetically. 'When did you last manage to get any sleep?'

Emily shook her head. 'I can't sleep,' she said. 'I wake up thinking that maybe he won't be there. He's getting worse, you know. All of these machines . . .' She nodded towards the monitors behind Frida Appleton. To Ray's unpractised eye it looked as though they had increased in number since he'd last been here.

'Would that be such a terrible thing?' Gladys asked her gently. 'If you woke and it was all peaceful, for you and for Damien? Sometimes the right thing, the only thing, to do is to let things go.'

Ray held his breath, momentarily appalled that Gladys should come out with such a direct question. Frida Appleton must have shared his feelings. She looked sharply at the older woman, her mouth dropping open in shock.

Emily Pinsent stiffened. She began to draw her hands away from Gladys's gentle grasp, and then she relaxed again, shaking her head sadly, her blonde hair, streaked with grey and long uncombed, falling forward onto her pale face. 'I think that sometimes, too,' she whispered. She looked into her son's face and Ray understood that she was unwilling to speak of it because of the thought that he might hear. That even to voice such a thought in his presence was tantamount to a betrayal.

'He knows you love him,' Gladys told her gently. 'Spirit always knows love, is drawn to it like a moth to a bright light. While you love Damien, he'll never truly be gone.' She changed her focus then, peering at the thin woman with the tight perm on the other side of the bed. 'I never got on with automatic writing,' she said. 'Always thought it was so hard to maintain focus. I'd love to see you give a demonstration.'

She let the question hang between them and Ray winced at the thought of how it must feel to face someone like Gladys across the bed as a fellow professional. It must feel like being told to take the witness stand in a particularly unpleasant trial.

'It doesn't always work like that,' Frida told her, a trifle defensively.

'No, dear. I know it doesn't. I remember well the first time I went up onto the platform to give a demonstration. I wasn't on my own, of course. The teacher in my development circle was the main attraction. She liked to give her students the chance to show their mettle though. But I do remember, I couldn't think of a thing to say and it was only when I stopped thinking – fear, I believe has that effect – that I gave room in my mind for the other voices to be heard. Spirit never fails to amaze, you know, even after all these years. Perhaps,' she added, looking back at Emily. 'Perhaps if we all linked together, put our thoughts towards the same end, then that might help.'

Clever, Ray applauded, though he wasn't sure about becoming part of the action. He'd heard strange things about seances and such. Did they all have to hold hands or something?

Emily nodded eagerly. 'Please, Frida.'

'I'll try,' she said. 'I will try, Emily, but I can't promise. Sometimes it just doesn't happen.'

Gladys nodded her approval and then closed her eyes and Emily did the same. 'Try not to think too much, Ray,' she told him quietly. 'Think how annoying it is when you're listening to a badly tuned radio.'

Ray smiled in spite of himself and, like the others, he closed his eyes.

For a while there was only the silence of the room broken by the hiss and buzz and bleep of the monitors and the ventilator and then the added sound of the scratch of Frida's pen upon the pad. Five minutes, maybe a little longer. Stop–start scratch, hesitation, scratch. Ray concentrated almost in spite of himself on the broken rhythm of Frida's writing. The anticipation that charged the tiny room was tangible. It filled it, overlying the clinical and the functional and the ordinary with a sense of what might be, if the world were a righteous place.

Finally, the writing stopped, and Frida's voice broke through the concentrated silence. 'That's all. He's gone now. That's all I could get.' She sounded so mournful that Ray was shocked into genuine sympathy.

'Let me see.' Emily was reaching out for the paper. With some reluctance, Frida handed it over. She looked puzzled and unsure.

Emily read and then passed the sheet to Gladys; Ray leaned to read over her shoulder.

> *Tall trees. Light filtered through the leaves like daytime stars. We walked into the wood and I said to him that it would be a lovely place for a picnic. He said he thought so too and I asked him if I were dead, being here like this, I wasn't sure. And Damien told me no, that I'd know it when it happened because it was quite unlike anything else.*
>
> *Miriam?*

Ray took the paper from Gladys and stared hard at it. Some idea he didn't want was shaping itself in his mind.

'Was the other message from Damien?' Gladys asked her softly. 'Or was that from this other person too?'

'I don't know.' There was a catch in her voice and a look on her face that spoke of great inner distress and confusion. 'I thought, with the other one, that it truly was. I asked to speak to Damien and that arrived. Came through to me so strongly. The same this time, so strong. I've never known anything to be so clear.'

Gladys turned her attention back to Ray. 'You know who it is, don't you? Come on, don't be silly and deny it just because it hurts your sense of reality. We're all friends here, and I, for one, don't believe that this comes from Damien.'

Ray found himself laughing at her tone then immediately resenting her for it. For this ability to cut through his grief and remind him that the world held other emotions and that some of them were good. The resentment, though, was not nearly so strong this time.

'It's Martin,' he said at last. 'I don't know why. I mean I can't explain it to you, but I'm certain that it's Martin.'

Chapter Thirty-six

On the edge of the Armitage Estate, the Morrelli household was guarded. The police, a sergeant called Field, and then a big man called Whissendine, who'd reminded Micky of Ray Flowers, had come too to ask more questions. And Micky's family had added to the interrogation. In fact, there had been moments when this man, Whissendine, just sat back and watched the show while Micky's mother dragged every scrap of truth from him kicking and screaming into the world, like a red-faced baby drawing its first breath. That's what it felt like, Micky thought. That he was giving birth to thoughts and feelings and things he didn't even recognize he knew for the first time since Damien drowned. On balance, he felt better for it. He didn't know what the consequences would be, but Winter and then his mother told him to be as honest as he could and Micky had been, reminding himself of everything Miri had told him or that Damien had suspected about her involvement with the likes of Rick Myers and Eldon Firth and others, and Max something who'd not been above taking a baseball bat to late payers, and Maria Whittering who'd also gone to their school and who dealt herself, small-time, and sometimes slept with Rick to get a better price – or so she told Micky. Micky didn't believe that Rick Myers would give anything away. And Andy Spears who was so stoned in class he could barely sit on his chair, and the kid, Toby something, who'd driven while high on coke and sliced his car straight into the back of a flatbed truck. And all the other casual users who had populated Micky's world. Kids like him who tried stuff and either gave it up after a couple of times or used on the odd weekend just to have more fun. Like alcohol, he said, only cheaper than booze a lot of the time and easier to get if you knew who to go to.

And the man in the suit Miri said was there the day before her birthday when she'd scored some E for all of them. Someone she didn't know. Anything. Everything until his fund of knowledge had run dry and he'd been reduced to speculating.

Whissendine had taken over by then and he had stopped him in his tracks. 'Facts, Micky, that's what we want here. Don't muddy the waters with things that might have been.'

'I don't know any more,' Micky told him truthfully. He felt as though he had been sucked dry. They hadn't asked him anything about the warehouse yet, so Micky hadn't felt so bad about not mentioning it. After all, Winter had said not to if he didn't have to tell. He was glad he didn't have the gun in the house. He'd chucked that in the river the day after the two men had been killed. The excitement he had felt knowing that he had it safe in his bedroom was diminished by that event, though a part of him wished that he still had it now.

The man who came for Miri would come for him, he

had no doubt about that, and Micky determined he would fight. Go down fighting, no matter what.

Max had followed Ray from the hospital. He'd figured Ray would show up there sooner or later, his contacts having told him that Ray had visited several times lately. The hospital was a good place to wait unnoticed, with its constant flow of visitors and its area by the main doors where people congregated to smoke and drink coffee. And if Ray hadn't turned up there, other places suggested themselves to Max as being excellent points of contact. His office, for example, though Max guessed he'd be steering clear of there once he'd seen the evening papers. Hayes had found his niche, complete with by-line: the exclusive revelation that ex-DI Ray Flowers, who had been consultant to the Mallingham force the year before during the Eyes of God episode, had been visiting Martin Galloway in hospital, had been seen visiting the dead girl the evening before her murder and was believed to be assisting the police with their inquiries. 'Assisting the police.' Max liked the wording. Liked the ambiguity of it. The little tip-off about his visit to Miriam had come from Max himself and the journalist had been careful to word this as a 'reported' visit and not a fact, but his write-up made Ray look very suspect and Max fully enjoyed the irony.

He watched as Ray dropped a grey-haired lady off close by a block of low-rise flats on the Evington Road. He noted the woman go in but then lost interest. Max rarely bothered with anyone who was not a contracted target. It wasted his energy, to say nothing of it being unprofitable, and he preferred to save his treats. To restrict himself rather than to gorge. It made it so much better in the long run.

Chapter Thirty-seven

When the phone rang George and Sarah assumed it would be Ray, calling to say he'd be a bit longer than he thought. But it was Phil and he had news, sounded excited about it.

George listened and then told him to come straight round, that Ray was due home any time and he could show all of them what he'd discovered.

'Well?' Sarah asked when he had replaced the receiver.

'Phil has found our angel,' George told her. 'He'll be here in about an hour.'

When Ray still had not returned by the time Phil arrived, Sarah was really concerned. His phone was switched off, not that unusual in itself, but it was strange for him not to have called them when it was nearly an hour and a half after they expected him home.

George recalled Gladys Wright's name and tried the phone book, hoping that she was not ex-directory. He found the right person on his second attempt – 'Is that the Gladys Wright who had an appointment with Ray Flowers this evening?' – and listened as the woman told him that Ray had dropped her home long ago.

'He said he was going straight back,' George said,

turning back to Phil and Sarah. 'That was around nine. She saw him drive away from the flat window when she'd let herself in.'

'Puncture?' Phil suggested.

'He'd have phoned us and called out the recovery people.'

'So. What then?' Sarah looked scared.

'I don't know.' George picked up the telephone again and fished in his pocket for his address book, finding Whissendine's number.

'You're calling the police?' Sarah asked. 'George? What do you think—'

George signed her to wait. Whissendine had answered and George filled him in quickly on Ray's lateness and their anxiety about it.

Sarah, watching his face closely, half expected him to be told that Ray was a grown man and would no doubt turn up soon enough. To report him in the morning if he still had not arrived. She would have felt better if he had said that. It would have told her, despite her doubts, that Ray would be all right, even if her instincts screamed that he was not. But when George finished listening and said, 'Right, I'll expect you then,' Sarah gasped, horrified.

'He thinks something might have happened, doesn't he? Doesn't he?'

George sat her down and poured a large measure of brandy from the decanter on the sideboard. Stood over her while she drank it. 'He thinks we should be cautious. He's putting out an obs call for Ray's car,' George told her gently. 'But Ray's a sensible man and an experienced officer. He'll be all right, Sarah. Believe that.'

'Do you believe that?' Sarah demanded.

'Yes. I do,' George told her firmly. 'And, Sarah, you have to believe it too.'

Martin dreamed again. Sometimes he surfaced close enough to the real world to break through the film of water that lay so thickly upon his senses, and he heard voices, footsteps, other sounds distorted through the fluid world that surrounded him and flooded his eyes and insinuated itself into his ears. But he could make out oddly familiar sounds and oddly coherent passages within the chaos.

Mostly though, Martin slipped back beneath the surface. A surface clear enough for his eyes to see the strange faces that dipped towards his, their movement rippling the surface of the pool. Yet when Martin let go and allowed himself to float downwards into dreaming, there was only stillness. No tide, no movement, only the sunlight dropping down like rain through the heaviness of trees.

They sat in the clearing. The three of them together, though this time the girl did not cry and her body no longer shook with the fear of dying.

Damien sat beside her, stroking the black hair, though to Martin's eyes it seemed that he passed his slender hands through the slight figure of the girl as often as he brushed the surface of her skin.

'She'll move on soon,' Damien told him, and Martin could not decide if there was sadness in his voice or merely resignation.

'Do you want to go?'

Damien seemed puzzled by the question, as though the context was lost on him.

'I don't know,' he said. 'How can I know? But often,' he added softly, 'I *am* tired of being alone.'

Whissendine had not driven to the speed limit, George reckoned, when his car pulled up in front of the gates some twenty minutes later and George buzzed him through. He hoped that Sarah did not note the time and draw her own conclusions about the superintendent's haste.

'Like Fort Knox, this place,' Whissendine commented.

'I like my privacy.' George led them through to the smaller of the two front rooms. Both had bay windows looking out onto the drive and small lawn. A computer was set up on a walnut desk, the matching half of which pair George had installed close by the window, angled so that he could see out through the bay but not be seen, a lifetime of caution ensuring that he liked to see the exits from whatever room he found himself in.

Tonight the heavy curtains were drawn and the dark wood of the library shelves closed in what on a sunny day was an open, light-filled space. George had sent Sarah to help Phil make tea – coffee for Phil – and they followed Whissendine into the room carrying trays and setting them down upon the small table set beside the open fire.

Whissendine looked about him with an interest not unmixed with awe.

'You didn't earn this place from Flowers-Mahoney,' he said.

'No,' George agreed. 'I did not. But we're not here to audit my accounts. I have that done yearly by the Inland Revenue. Phil, if you'll do the honours?' he indicated the computer. 'We've tracked down that picture of the angel,' he told Whissendine. 'I thought you ought to see.'

'Any news of Ray?' Sarah burst in. 'Look, George, I'm sorry, but I'm not interested in anything else right now.'

'Nothing yet,' Whissendine told her. 'Miss Gordon. Sarah . . . I've got every officer alerted to look for his car and a description out. They'll find him.'

'And if they don't? If—'

George held up his hand to silence her. It took a brave man to try to silence Sarah Gordon, but tonight she was too distracted to argue.

'Sarah, everything is being done and what we all want is to find Ray. But all of this is connected and what Phil has found may well give us something.'

Sarah sat down in one of the wing chairs set either side of the fireplace and stared into the fire. 'And if they don't,' she said. 'I mean, I know I'm being stupid. I know he's a grown man, not a little kid. I know he's been late before, so why do I feel so . . . so frightened for him?'

No one answered her. Across the room Phil's fingers played the keys and an image appeared upon the screen.

'The Adoration of the Angels,' George told Whissendine. 'It's an altarpiece. Artist unknown, painted some time late in the eleventh century. There are at least two hundred and fifty sites that we've found so far that feature this image or a part of it, which considering it's not all that well known is quite a number. Phil's been checking them detail by tiny detail. Now watch.'

Phil manipulated the image so that the detail of the angel's eyes filled the screen, then enlarged it again, the image fragmenting into an uninterpretable mass of tone and colour.

'Someone's lifted the original pixels,' Phil said, 'and replaced them with other images that are so small they're unnoticeable unless you blow the original apart. Look.' He expanded the image again and suddenly a tiny section of it clarified, coalesced into another picture, clearly distinguishable now. Eyes, less than a pixel across, enclosing other eyes on into infinity.

Phil positioned the cursor and clicked on the eyes. The screen image faded, each section of the picture falling away and running, dripping towards the bottom of the screen.

'First time it did that I thought I'd picked up a virus,' Phil said cheerfully. 'And with all the virus-protection stuff I run on my machine anything that could get through would have to be worth a look. But it isn't.' He sounded almost disappointed. 'It's just a back door.'

They watched as the image changed again, now like water rippling across the screen, flowing outward from several points at once as though rain dripped into a pool and broke the surface, the ripples crossing and creating still others in their wake. It was a mesmerizing effect in its own right but then when it cleared and a man's face filled the screen in place of the water and spoke, there was no one in the room who did not jump.

'Welcome, gentlemen, oh, and the fairer sex of course.'

'He can see us?' Whissendine was glancing suspiciously about the room.

'No,' Phil assured him. 'It's just a recording. Plays the same every time. Clever though.'

'Welcome to my world,' the voice continued. The man in the recording had a way of looking about him as though he addressed an audience. Sometimes, by the merest chance, he would catch the eye of one or other in the room. It gave the disturbing effect that he addressed them personally. An impression difficult to shake.

'I'd like to demonstrate my product to you all in good time, but first a little background information on the history of Chimera.'

'What the hell is this?' Whissendine demanded.

Phil was on the keyboard again. 'I've run this three times on different machines,' he said. 'Each time it's crashed out on me. I'm hoping this time it'll hold a little longer. Your set-up isn't as clean as mine.'

Whissendine was looking confused.

The image on the screen now split into two. The man talking on the one side and what looked like a promotional video running on the other.

'Welcome to Psycotrex,' the man was saying. 'Makers of Chimera, though they didn't know it then. No, what they called it then was simply Test Substance B1436. Imaginative?'

'Psycotrex?' Sarah questioned.

'You know the name?'

'I'm not sure. I think I heard Ray mention it but I can't think what the context was.'

The commentary continued, overplaying what had originally been a presentation by the company on the other screen.

'B1436 was set to become the next miracle. An antipsychotic of a new generation that would reform the treatment of severe psychosis in much the same way that drugs like Prozac reformed the treatment of depression.

'And it worked. Like a charm, until you tried to wean the patients off. Then did your troubles really begin.'

The image shuddered and began to drift like a bad television picture. Phil swore and played with the keyboard again, sending signals to the processor to reinforce and stabilize the image. For a moment it held steady and then crashed. The screen went blue and an error message appeared warning of an illegal operation.

'What happened?' Whissendine said.

'Sorry,' Phil apologized. 'I warned you that might happen. It must have recognized that we were not a legitimate user.'

'How?'

Phil chewed his bottom lip, a habit he had formed when he was thinking of a way to explain computers to the nonliterate. 'Well,' he said slowly, 'as near as I can tell, whoever set the program up set it to run only for machines that carried certain . . . tags . . . recognizable names, if you like. Whenever you log on you leave a trail behind you. Where you've been, what you've looked at, even how many skips you made between different networks. Sometimes your download, for instance, will go halfway round the world to get to your machine when the machine you're loading from might be only up the street. It all depends on how it's routed. Everything you do is registered on your machine, stored on the history file and in the cookies.'

'In the what? Never mind.' Whissendine looked about as happy as Ray usually did when they got onto the subject of the Internet.

'Even if you click on one of those big banner adverts, it's recorded,' George told him. He'd had this conversation before.

'Pop-ups,' Phil said. 'Yeah, that's right. You click on one to take a look, then that company will register when you're next online and send out pop-ups for similar products, together with a little bit of code that implants itself on your machine waiting for the next search you do.'

'You're joking. It's like being bugged.'

'It's exactly like being bugged. I use software that cleans my system down every time it's used. George here is not quite so careful, and Ray – you tell him to clean out his history files and he'll think you mean one of Sarah's archives.'

There was silence for a moment, the mention of Ray reinforcing the tension already present in the room.

'As near as I can guess,' Phil said, 'anyone logging onto that site through our back door would have been told first to visit other sites, maybe a selection of them in some sort of sequence, so that when they came in through our friend's hidden door, their machine would be scanned to see if they were wanted there. Legitimate users would have stuff in their history that the server running the site would recognize and it would let them see the whole review. I didn't know till now if it was simply that my system looked too clean or if they were looking at something specific. I guess we've got our answer.'

Whissendine nodded thoughtfully. 'My brother's into all this stuff,' he said. 'He set my Internet access up with this automatic cleaner on it. Every time I fire up Windows I get this big squeegee thing come across the screen just so I know it's working. The kids love it.'

'But what does this have to do with Ray and Martin Galloway?' Sarah asked. Then she frowned. 'That's where I heard the name. The pharmaceutical company that made that drug, B1 whatever it was. Sonia Dattani told Ray that someone had found a match for what Martin had been given and was trying to persuade their company to treat him in some trial or other. That was the company. I'm sure of it.'

'Do you have her home number?' George grabbed the phone.

'Back at the cottage. Maybe in the office as well. I don't know.'

'I have it,' Whissendine said, 'but she won't be there. When I spoke to her today she'd made arrangements to spend the night at the clinic. She felt it would be safer there. She's scared after what happened to the Taylor girl.'

'Understandable,' George said. 'Should we call her now?' He glanced at the wall clock. 'I suppose it's late. First thing tomorrow then. You'll be going out there?'

Whissendine looked thoughtfully at George as though trying to make him out. 'You can come with me,' he said. 'Make yourself useful.'

George smiled wryly. 'In other words you want to make sure that anything I find out gets straight back to you.'

'Got it in one.'

George shook his head. 'I think we're past that, don't you? My concern is finding Ray. The rest is yours, but I think it might be useful if we could bring some pressure to bear on this Psycotrex . . .'

Whissendine nodded. 'I'll leave that to you,' he said. He glanced about him once again, taking in the book-lined walls and the Turkish carpet on the wooden floor. 'Good job, was it, before you got into your present game? Putting pressure on people something you did a lot of?'

George ignored him. 'What time?' he asked. 'If you collect me around eight?'

Whissendine nodded. 'Did you manage to get print-outs or anything?' he asked Phil. 'I mean that man, if we could get a picture, he might have a record.'

'I did a frame grab,' Phil confirmed. He found his bag where he'd left it beneath the desk and riffled through, emerging with a bundle of paper and a disk. He lay the pictures down on the coffee table. 'The quality's a bit iffy,' he apologized, 'but I can probably clean it up.'

'Good enough for a start,' Whissendine said. Sarah

stared at him as though ready to challenge him. Tell him he should be staying, or out there helping to find Ray, but she said nothing, just turned her head back towards the fire.

'I'll see you out,' George said and Whissendine nodded. He closed the library door after them when they left and guided George to the point furthest from it across the hall, producing a piece of folded paper from his pocket. 'I didn't want to say anything in there,' he said, 'but I think we know who killed Miriam Taylor and probably who's gone for Ray.'

'Oh? How?'

Whissendine handed him the paper. It was a photocopy of a list of names and it looked as though the original had been screwed up and thrown away. There were stains along one edge, darkening the words, but it was still readable.

'As you know, Ray asked her to make a statement and write a list,' Whissendine explained. 'We know the final version was taken. It'd been torn from the pad in the girl's room but we've sent the pad to documents for an ESDA test to see if there are impressions from what she wrote before. She had a couple of goes before the final one though, and screwed them up, threw them in the paper basket. The bin was full of those cosmetic pads women use and old wrappers and the like. Whoever killed probably didn't look too far. But one name. One name stands out. This one.'

'Max O'Brien? You know him?' George asked.

Whissendine nodded and he didn't look happy. 'A dozen aliases, but his trademark's just the same. Only works for contract and we know he was in Mallingham three years ago. Michael Morrelli mentioned him, though he didn't know his full name, only what he looked like and that he was violent.'

'A contract killer. In Mallingham?'

'So, maybe he was slumming it. He'd been out on parole. Skipped off. Who'd think of looking for anyone in Mallingham?'

'Parole? What exactly had he done?'

'What everyone knew he'd done couldn't be proven, at least not to the satisfaction of the CPS. They had to settle for a lesser charge of GBH, but word was that at least three drug-related killings had his name on them. They weren't pretty.'

'Drug-related? I take it you mean over territory?'

Whissendine nodded. 'He's a knife man, for preference. Likes to get in close. But, George, rumour is he only ever kills on contract.'

Whissendine left after that and George pocketed the piece of paper. He went through to the other room and prepared another drink for Sarah, finding some sleeping pills the doctor had prescribed for him some months before when he'd been suffering from yet another episode of insomnia. He crushed one and dissolved it in the brandy. Not advisable, he knew, but Sarah would never make it through the night sane unless she got some sleep. And he thought about Ray and what he had told Sarah earlier about Ray being sensible. A man able to take care of himself. He hoped that it was true.

Chapter Thirty-eight

How to blackmail a multinational?

George was a past practitioner in the art of misinformation and possessed of all the patience that usually went with such activities. This time, though, he needed to move fast.

'Can you devise something?' he asked Phil. 'A package of information, a rumour backed up with just enough fact that could be released onto as many news groups as possible. Can you arrange it so that it can be activated at a moment's notice, but held back until . . . or if . . . I choose to use it?'

'Simple,' Phil told him. 'What do you have in mind?'

'How fast could a piece of information be spread?'

'How fast do you want it? Look, if I put something out on, say, ten of the news groups, most will have links to maybe a dozen more. They'll link to maybe another dozen each . . . exponential, you see. So, what do you want to spread?'

'A rumour. I'll make a bet that Psycotrex is a subsidiary of one of the big multinationals. The parent company won't like to be linked with an organization that's producing dangerous street drugs and we need the pressure as high as we can get it.'

'Easy,' Phil said again. 'I'll make a start.'

'Good. Meantime, I'll pull down a few favours and find out about our friend Max.'

George had been busy. He'd contacted various old colleagues he had in the Home Office, getting one out of bed and catching another as he came from a late party. He'd filled them in quickly on the situation, and reminded Dignan, his previous employer, that in effect he and Ray were still on the payroll, having done a little freelance work for him from time to time. By five in the morning everything known about Max O'Brien, and half a dozen aliases, had been faxed to him, with a second copy waiting for Whissendine when he arrived at the office that morning.

George's second line had been to run a background check on Psycotrex. Who the directors were, what other interests they held, what dirt he could pull from the various corporate watchdogs, both legitimate and otherwise, that routinely monitored the activities of such companies and their parent groups. Psycotrex, as he already guessed, was merely one branch of a much bigger corporation, the parent group having holdings in the pharmaceutical industry and an interest in genetic patenting which had recently brought it into conflict with those attempting to protect the interest of Third World farming.

As a corporate profile it was hardly unusual, but it gave George a good idea of where he could place the lever to get the information he wanted.

When at 11.30 p.m., United States East Coast standard time, the CEO of Psycotrex's parent company got a call from the FDA regarding rumours about the activities of one of its junior partners, then he was bound to listen, and soon the MD of Psycotrex was woken by a call from his US boss demanding action. All information on the abortive test substance B1436 was to be released to the relevant authorities.

'B1436?' The MD, half awake, is confused, but not so confused that he does not recall the serial number or the effort his company had to go to cleaning up after it. He tried to bluff. 'Offhand I'm not sure I can remember—'

'Then remember this. Your recall should be up to a certain employee by the name of Wilson taking samples of this substance B1436, a test material, already shown to be unstable and scheduled for termination, and modifying them for street use. Apparently, the right dosage of the drug gave a high comparable to pharmaceutical-grade heroin, or so I'm told, and I've got that from your own damned records. The wrong dose resulted in severe psychosis. This Wilson was dismissed and no one's seen hide or hair of him since. I'm being threatened with publicity over this, Carl, I suggest you cooperate with this Dr Dattani or whoever it is your Dr Oliver's been in contact with. Full cooperation with them and with the police, Carl. We must be seen to be intolerant of any abuse of our products. Is that clear?'

Carl Emerson didn't know what he was talking about but it didn't seem a good idea to say so. What Dr Dattani? What Dr Oliver? But he agreed that they must be seen to be doing everything.

An hour later, he'd been on to personnel, dragged them in early to sort out which doctor, if either, they actually employed. He'd pulled the records on B1436 and taken his first drink of the day several long hours early to steady the fit of shaking that had been instilled in him. And he had Dr Oliver into his office, explaining that Dr Dattani had put a request out on the forum, wanting information on something that happened to coincide with a set of results they had in their records. He knew nothing about the scandal associated with it, just that it was a discontinued test, one of many they kept on record to ensure that they weren't duplicated.

'And you say this B1436 was given to a police officer?' Carl Emerson was incredulous.

'Apparently. One of the victims from when this unmodified version hit the streets a few years ago was a young kid who almost died. This policeman was still after the supplier. Dr Dattani is of the opinion that he found him, so are the local police. I've been on to R&D to include him in our next round of tests. The poor man's got nothing to lose. Dr Dattani's doing everything she can with the resources they've got but . . .'

Emerson made up his mind. Damage limitation. That was it. It might well come out that they'd had some problems and no doubt the press would have a field day but if they could be seen to be doing their best to recover the situation . . . to have been merely innocent parties, who since that incident had increased their security levels and their screening procedures . . . A thought struck him. Presumably, they had done both of those things . . .

'Pull every bit of information we have on record,' he

said. 'Go down today to see this Dr Dattani and offer every cooperation that Psycotrex can give. Speak to this Superintendent Whissendine who's apparently in charge of operations down there. Make this good, Dr Oliver. Make this very good indeed.'

Chapter Thirty-nine

George left early, collected by Whissendine, and they were out at Redfern by eight fifteen, running the gauntlet of the press corps, now confined behind improvised barriers of wooden planks laid out across plastic chairs, with a couple of uniformed officers on duty to ensure that this creaking Berlin Wall was maintained.

George's BMW attracted less interest than Whissendine expected. 'They'll assume I'm a consultant,' George joked. 'Ray's old Volvo has suspicious-person-who-might-know-something plastered all over it.'

Whissendine made a sound in his throat that might have been a laugh. 'You think he's still alive?' he asked abruptly. He'd avoided the subject of Ray so far that morning.

George shook his head. 'I wouldn't say so to Sarah, but from what I've been reading about Max O'Brien, aka Milo Grey, Sam Hines and a dozen more, I don't give a lot for his chances.'

'Reading? Reading what?'

'I had his records faxed over to me last night.'

'You did what? We've not had everything yet. How come you—'

'I have contacts at the Home Office and you'll have got your copies by now so don't get upset about me pulling no-longer-existent rank.'

'No longer?' Whissendine gave up. 'He's a nasty piece of work,' he said feelingly.

George nodded. 'That he is.'

Sonia Dattani was just about to go on her ward rounds. Not having to travel in from home and not having been able to sleep much meant she was getting an early start. They filled her in on the Psycotrex connection so far as they knew it and showed her the printouts from the website that Phil had managed to capture.

Sonia was looking puzzled. 'Dr Oliver has just emailed me,' she said. 'He's coming over and they've agreed to release all the documentation on this B1436 and on the trials they're doing on the next generation. I couldn't figure out why. I emailed him back and he said it was on the direct instruction of their CEO. Their parent company in America got on to them some time early this morning and said they'd heard rumours that one of their products had . . . what did he call it, something silly . . . "gone wild", I believe. Apparently that means someone's manufactured a version of one of their drugs for street sale and he thinks that's what was given to Martin.'

George nodded. 'That's good then. We might be getting somewhere.'

Phil was watching the morning news programmes on the television when Sarah came down. She looked sick, he thought, but more together than the night before.

'George has gone already,' he told her. 'You should eat something.'

'What did he give me last night?'

Phil shrugged.

'I'm going to kill him when he comes back here.'

'Guess that's why he went early.'

Sarah glowered but, Phil noted, her eyes were hard and full of purpose and had lost the anxious, frightened look.

She sat down and peered at the television.

'Anything?'

'Not yet. Next bulletin's in a few minutes. There'll be something on that, I dare say. There's tea in the pot,' Phil told her. 'It's fresh. I made it for you a few minutes ago when I heard you moving about upstairs. You should just have time to pour yourself some.'

'Thanks.' She wandered through to the kitchen and came back a minute later with a mug of hot, rather too strong tea, Phil applying the same logic to his tea making as he did to coffee, that the more caffeine the better. She arrived just in time to hear the announcer giving the headlines. She watched in silence with Phil as the events surrounding Miriam's death were reported, DCI Whissendine standing in front of the Taylor house and giving a brief statement to the press that this was a horrific crime, one of particular brutality. The statement had been made the night before, Sarah noted. It was dark and the streetlight cast an odd glow all around him as he stood in its spotlight.

In the absence of further news about Miriam, the gap had been filled with background information about the girl and her family. Damien was mentioned. '. . . not the first time tragedy has hit the Taylors' circle. Just under three years ago, at Miriam's eighteenth birthday party, her then boyfriend was critically injured in a fall from a high diving board.' Sarah listened woodenly as they recounted the rumour, not proven they said, that the boy had been high on Ecstasy at the time, a rumour that his family had always been at pains to deny. Library footage was shown of the front view of the leisure centre and the photograph of the friends celebrating the end of exams flashed up on screen as a 'memory of happier times'.

Much speculation surrounded why Miri had been killed and the police had 'refused to comment' either on the theory that this was a break-in gone horribly wrong or on the tentatively held view that Miriam's death might in some way be linked to Damien's fall.

'Hayes,' Phil said as a sandy-haired man was seen being interviewed.

'Who?'

'Local journalist. Works for the *Mallingham Guardian*. He came to see Ray a couple of days ago wanting the crack on Martin Galloway. Ray sent him off with a flea in his ear.'

'Tactful as ever,' Sarah commented.

Phil smiled at her and reached out to take her hand, a very un-Phil-like gesture, which left her ready to cry again. Instead, she swallowed hard and tried to concentrate on what this man Hayes was saying.

'I've been trying to talk to ex-DI Ray Flowers,' Hayes was telling the reporter. 'I spoke to him this week about the rumours that Inspector Galloway had reopened the

Damien Pinsent case and had in fact been working on it the day he crashed his car.' Cutaway to library footage of the accident scene, voiceover of Hayes telling them that Ray had not been able to confirm this, but that he had been talking to Miri about Damien the day before she was killed. He cited 'sources close to the family' as providing him with this information.

'The police have not commented on this aspect of these tragic events,' the woman reporter said, turning back to the camera and speaking direct to the anchor in the studio, 'but undoubtedly there are questions to be answered here.'

'Talk about stating the obvious,' Phil commented.

Sarah nodded. Irritation and frustration were slowly replacing despair as her motivating emotions. She let the feelings build, knowing she'd be far more use to everyone if she could stoke her anger than if she gave in to her despair. It came home to her strongly just how much Ray had come to mean in her life. Their relationship was such a comfortable and in some ways such a low-key affair that it was a shock to consider just how much this big ugly man had insinuated himself into her life and into her heart. She had never in her life felt as easy with anyone as she felt with Ray.

There followed a brief resumé of the careers of both Martin Galloway and Ray Flowers, outlining their excellent records, their courage, both under fire – both having been involved in firearms incidents that Sarah didn't even know about – and their moral courage in confronting authority when they felt that it had overstepped the mark. The Pierce affair was reprised, and Ray's consultancy in the Eyes of God, and then the unspoken but tacit question: had the two overstepped the line themselves this time?

Hayes again, hinting that Galloway's superiors had no notion of what he was up to. The much-vaunted inquiry into Martin's affairs that was supposed to be going on but which no one in the force would confirm or deny. The fact that he had been going to see Ray Flowers on the day of his crash. The rumours, gleaned from eyewitness statements, that he had appeared to be drunk . . .

Sarah got up in disgust and went to fetch more tea. Her head felt clearer now. Maybe Phil had a point about the caffeine. Much to her surprise, she felt hungry too.

'Where am I likely to find this Hayes person?' she called through to Phil.

'You're not going to see him, surely?'

He followed her into the kitchen, watching as she sliced bread.

'I have to do something.'

'Sure, but that's maybe not the best option.'

'You have others? What have you and George been doing while I was sleeping?'

Phil grinned. 'I showed George the best way to blackmail a corporate CEO,' he said.

Sarah raised her eyebrows. 'Oh?'

'Publicity,' Phil added. 'You put a rumour out on the web, it's halfway round the world a few minutes later and it spreads exponentially. Especially if you post to a news group you know is linked to others. Helps if the rumour's true, of course. Last I heard, Psycotrex were bending over backwards to help.' He shrugged. 'We got lucky. Their parent company's in the middle of a Senate hearing on malpractice in some genetic patent scandal. You know the sort of thing, we buy your local variety of wheat, patent it, sell it back to you and make it illegal for you to save your own seed corn.'

'I thought that had been banned.'

'When you have an office block stuffed with dedicated legal eagles all set to find loopholes, they'll find them, especially in an area of international law as new and complicated as this. Psycotrex has promised full cooperation, which has to be good news for Martin.'

Sarah nodded, looking down at the bread she had just sliced and wondering what had possessed her to cut up an entire loaf. Good for Martin, she thought. But what about Ray? Suddenly, she didn't feel that hungry any more.

Whissendine and George joined Field at the junction of a little road called Shady Lane where it joined the road between Stoughton and Oadby.

It was a narrow, winding throughway but one which saw a surprising amount of traffic and on which an abandoned car was a serious hazard.

The Ford Orion had been reported the previous evening by a member of the public who'd had to take avoiding action to miss it, parked as it was half on the verge, half in the carriageway. He admitted he'd been coming up to the junction a bit too fast, but it was late, dark and not the easiest of roads to drive even if you kept to the limit. A routine check recorded the car as stolen, reported as missing at around five that evening. The owner was contacted, told the car was driveable – remarkably, the keys were still in the ignition, though there seemed to be a fresh bump on the nearside wing. The owner knew nothing about that, but was glad to have his car back at all. He'd stupidly left the car outside his house with the engine running for a few minutes while he went to hurry up his kids who were due at their dance class. He knew it was daft, but he liked to let the engine warm up before he drove off. His wife was never home to take the girls and if he didn't rush them they never got ready on time. He'd done this so many times, he said, left the car with the engine running parked on his drive, that he'd never thought . . .

He counted himself lucky, so many stolen vehicles ending up as burned-out wrecks, and he said he'd arrange for a friend to come and drive it home on account of the fact he'd had a drink or two and wasn't sure if he was still under the limit.

The officer who found it pushed the car further off the road, warned the owner that he couldn't guarantee its security, locked it and took the keys with him, having been assured that the owner had a spare. That might well have been that if it hadn't been that the car was still there the following morning. The reason for its continued presence was quite innocent, the friend having been unable to help out the night before. But daylight showed details that had been missed in the dark. The owner called the number he'd been given the previous evening and caught PC Deals going off duty.

'My car, the Ford Orion on Shady Lane, I think it might have been involved in an accident.'

'Yes, sir, I mentioned to you last night that there seemed to be a fresh dent in the wing.'

'Yes, well, you probably didn't see it the night before, but there's half a number plate lying on the road just in front of it. I wonder if that's from the car the thief hit.'

Deals thanked him, noted down the number and told him to drive safely and did he mind taking the piece of wreckage with him, since if it flipped up and hit another car there was just the chance of it causing damage. The owner agreed and, again, it might have finished there. But PC Deals thought it odd and the more he thought about it the odder it sounded. If a stolen car had rammed into the back of another, say at a junction like that on Shady Lane, then although it might be no surprise for the joyriders to leg it, it was surprising that the driver of the other car hadn't reported the incident. Deals would have been mad as hell, had someone done that to his vehicle.

So he checked for any reports of no-stop RTAs the night before, anyone who'd called in to complain about being rammed in the backside by kids driving a Ford Orion.

There was nothing of that kind, but a routine PNC check on what they had of the plate gave them a list of possible cars and owners. Deals would have had to be living on Mars not to have recognized it when he saw the name of Raymond Flowers, ex-DI.

'The owner's already taken his car,' George confirmed as they were filled in on events.

Whissendine nodded. 'We've tracked him down at work and I've someone explaining to him that we've got to impound his car for the lab boys to take apart and also take samples of his clothing, fingerprints, hair, the usual for elimination, and from his family. I'll bet this is the last time he plays good citizen.'

George grimaced. 'And if you do turn up anything useful it'll only be circumstantial,' he commented. 'The chain of evidence has already been compromised. A half-decent lawyer would have a field day.'

'Still got to go through the motions.'

George nodded, making a note to himself to arrange a hire car to be made available to the owner of the Ford Orion. It seemed only appropriate that Flowers-Mahoney take on that expense.

He watched as a uniformed officer placed a sign at the roadside asking for witnesses to an accident which happened the night before at approximately nine fifteen, a guess based upon when Ray had left Gladys and how long it might take to get to here. This had to be where Max had accosted him and it gave them a lead at least. Ray must have been driving his own car, presumably with Max threatening him.

'I've put out a nationwide notice for Ray's car,' Whissendine told him as though reading his thoughts. 'And it's likely to stand out now, missing the rear plate.'

George nodded. 'He could have killed him here,' he said, 'but he didn't.'

'It's something though, to know Max kept him alive then. That they drove off somewhere.'

'Somewhere he wouldn't be disturbed,' George said.

Chapter Forty

They were back at Redfern by three ready to meet Dr Oliver. George had called home to bring Phil and Sarah up to date on the finding of the car. He had at first been alarmed when neither answered the home phone. He finally caught up with them on Phil's mobile. Sarah answered, from which George deduced that Phil must be driving. A sensible move. Sarah's driving style was more suited to the rally circuit at the best of times and he doubted that this was the best of times.

'Don't you pull a stunt like that again,' she told him, referring to the drug and alcohol cocktail he had given her the night before.

'I doubt I'd get away with it a second time. I know my limitations, Sarah. Where are you two anyway?'

'Driving,' she told him. 'George, you couldn't expect me to just sit at home waiting.'

'No, I suppose I couldn't do that. Driving where?'

She sighed. 'Oh Lord, we've been all over. We got a map this morning and divided it up as best we could. We worked outward from where Ray was last seen, street by street, just on the off chance we might see his car, and we've stopped off at every garage, every corner shop that looked like it opened late last night, and we've asked about a big man in a scruffy old Volvo. George, I know it was a stupid thing to do, but at least it was doing something.'

'And you found?'

'Bugger all.'

'Did your excursion take you to a place called Shady Lane?'

'Well, yes, one of our first routes. It's the most direct route Ray could have taken, or one of them. Why?'

George filled her in quickly about the Ford Orion and the theory they had built on the basis of the number plate.

'Damn it, George, we drove past that. Dark green thing on the side of the road, looked as if *I'd* parked it.'

'That's the one,' George smiled. Sarah was famed for her ability to make it look as though she'd simply abandoned her car even in a completely empty car park. 'Sarah, get Phil to drive out to Redfern,' he glanced at Whissendine for confirmation.

Whissendine merely shrugged.

'OK, get Phil to come out. This Dr Oliver is supposed to be arriving this afternoon. Like you say, it's better than sitting around. And, Sarah.'

'What? If you're going to apologize, George, there's no need. When we get Ray back, I'll get even with you. Until then, just don't even think about doing anything like that again or I swear, George, you'll be celibate for the rest of your life and it won't be through choice.'

Dr Oliver was a small man with a nervous manner and heavy glasses that cast him in the role of Woody Allen clone. The size of his audience, Dr Dattani, George, Whissendine and now Phil and Sarah, seemed to put him off his stroke and he stumbled awkwardly through his explanations, beginning with the history of B1436.

'Um, it began as . . . um, legitimate test substance for the, um, treatment of certain types of psychosis. The . . . the model we used included subjects suffering mild but recurrent, um, schizophrenic tendencies to, um, the more serious forms of reactive depression. Um, it wasn't considered that it could be of use for bipolar conditions. Um, the swings were too difficult to treat adaptively.'

'You mean because in illnesses like manic depression the dosage has to be monitored so closely that this drug wasn't suitable? From what I've seen of its effect in Martin—'

Dr Oliver interrupted Dr Dattani. 'Oh, no, I've been . . . asked to point out very clearly that this isn't B1436. It's modified, its—'

'OK. From what I've seen of the modified version and its effects they are polycrest in action, far too uncontrollable when you might need to change the chemical balance fairly quickly as in patients with a pronounced manic phase.'

'Um, right,' Dr Oliver told her. 'Yes, right.'

Sarah wanted to hit someone or failing that to stamp her feet and scream. 'What's that got to do with anything?' she said. 'We don't want a history lesson, just a solution.'

'Some background *would* help,' Sonia Dattani told her gently. 'Truly, Sarah, it would be useful.'

'Yes, I'm sure. Sorry. I'm behaving badly, aren't I?'

Sonia Dattani smiled at her. 'I'd be more concerned if you weren't,' she said. 'She turned her smile back to Dr Oliver. 'Please go on, Ian,' she said.

Sarah could almost hear the collective sigh of irritation in the room and Ian Oliver began again.

'Um, so, at first, everything went well . . .'

Slowly over the next hour they pieced together the history of B1436, or Chimera as the street version had come to be known, a name used by the man who created the Angel Eyes website and was unconcerned enough to show his face to whoever was clever enough to see.

At first, Ian Oliver told them, haltingly, B1436 had proved remarkably successful first in computer models then in animal testing, and finally in limited clinical trials. At low dosages it encouraged a feeling of well-being and contentment similar to the effects of many modern antidepressants. At higher dosages and in susceptible patients it appeared to cause anxiety and on occasion uncontrollable highs, akin to mania in bipolar patients. But get the dosage right and the psychosis became controllable and eventually eliminated. The patients in the test group were those who had already proved resistant to standard treatments and had been referred by a group of doctors who had been approached by Psycotrex.

'And no doubt paid well for their recommendations,' Sonia Dattani said coldly.

'Dr Dattani, we're . . . we're . . . all adults here. No money changed . . . changed hands.'

'No membership of the local country club? No luxury weekends for the doctors and their partners?'

'Please,' Sarah butted in. 'I'm sure it matters and I'm

sure you two can get to grips later with the morality of it all, but can we just get on?'

Ian Oliver seemed almost reluctant to take her suggestion. 'There were problems,' he finally admitted. 'B1436 was fine while the patients received treatment. The big difficulty was when time came to wean them off. Withdrawal from B1436 proved to be impossible.'

'Impossible!' Sonia Dattani stared at him. 'Permanent change? You mean it brought about permanent change in the chemistry?'

Reluctantly, Ian Oliver nodded.

'My God! Surely your computer models would have suggested this? Surely the animal results? No, don't tell me, standard clinical practice in places like yours, isn't it? You destroy the test animals as soon as you have the results you want. You wouldn't have known if there was an ongoing effect because your test subjects wouldn't have been around long enough to tell you.'

'You, you're being very harsh, Dr Dattani. Regulations . . . regulations say that animals should not be used for successive testing.'

'And when they've done their bit, they're not worth the cost of feeding.' She held up her hands to prevent the seething of protest she could feel. 'OK, OK, we'll fight later. Please go on.'

'The high from B1436 was intense. Concomitant with the effects of pharmaceutical-grade heroin or crack cocaine and just as addictive. And a version of the drug hit the streets just over three years ago, about six months before Damien. Three people died, and five suffered severe psychotic reactions when they could no longer get the supply.'

'Who supplied it?' Whissendine wanted to know. 'Presumably it was one of your lot.'

Ian Oliver nodded uncomfortably. 'An employee by the name of Joseph Wilson had been dismissed from the company after being caught stealing supplies. He'd worked on B1436 and seen its potential, but not its downside. It took him a while to get the production right and so far as the company could tell, Wilson had produced several different batches and sold them as Ecstasy, then monitored the results.'

'And you reported this, of course. As soon as your company got wind of it?'

'I, er, I wouldn't know,' Ian Oliver admitted. 'I . . . didn't know until this morning. I read the . . . reports coming down here on the train.'

Whissendine didn't look impressed.

'Too concerned with what your shareholders might think if they took a pay cut I suppose,' Sonia Dattani said scornfully.

'You said it was impossible to withdraw from,' Sarah asked him, 'so what happened to the poor buggers who'd been given it?'

'Well, they were compensated, of course, and given maintenance doses of the substance, and Psycotrex has been working hard on a safe alternative. We're very close.'

'How close?' Sonia wanted to know. 'Close enough to help Martin Galloway?'

'Well, we think so. Yes.'

'And presumably the families have been kept quiet because they're scared you'll withdraw support if they create a stink,' George said thoughtfully.

'This sort of stuff happens often?' Whissendine wanted to know.

'Often enough,' Sonia told him.

'Our test subjects are being closely monitored and supported. I . . . I can assure you of that.'

'Psycotrex must be pig sick it can't just get rid of them like it can its monkeys.'

'I can assure you, we don't use primates. Psycotrex does not subscribe to the use of higher animals as test subjects. And, Dr Dattani . . . you're a scientist yourself. You, um, must at some time have been involved with animal testing? I'm not sure you can take the moral high ground here.'

'Oh, I'm pretty sure I can. But what about your patients. How many are still alive? How big was your original test group? What condition are they in now?'

There had been twelve. Nine were still alive and variously stable, but dependent. Two killed themselves during the attempted initial withdrawal – 'That's what made us realize we had a problem.' One died of other causes unrelated to the drug. Three of the remaining nine were severely affected, withdrawal having been attempted and worsened their psychosis. They now lived in a dream world where reality impinges only occasionally and their lives pay out against a backdrop of ever shifting fantasy.

'The other six have been able to return to something

like their normal lives provided the drug is administered regularly, and their progress is being monitored very closely indeed.'

'I'll bet it is,' from Sonia Dattani.

After the Wilson fiasco, Chimera slid underground but they didn't believe it had ever gone away. There was evidence that Wilson had been taken on by someone with the money to set him up properly. That something or someone that used the logo and tag Angel Eyes traded in the drug he referred to as Chimera, a reference to its now hybrid character, and tested each new batch on unsuspecting buyers out to have a good time, dealers getting to know their customers, building a relationship personal enough that anything unusual could be monitored. There had been instances where Wilson had evidently got it wrong. Two deaths, one episode – one that had been recognized as due to Chimera, that was – of acute paranoia in a 22-year-old man called Samuel Tompkins, who was now in a high-security unit. Others had been damaged but were still functional. And most recently, there had been a new alternative to E hitting the clubs big time, so new it had as yet received only fragmented coverage in the press. An intense high and rapid addiction. A manufacturer's dream.

'There's, um, always room for something new,' Ian Oliver said non-committally.

'You sound as though you admire this man, Wilson.'

'Admire, him? No, no. But he's skilled. No mistake. It's a big loss to a company like Psycotrex to have someone, er, someone go overboard like that. Big loss to research, you know.'

They looked about to start round three when Whissendine's phone rang and the message he received put everything else out of their minds.

'They've found Ray's car,' he said. 'I'm going out there now.'

Chapter Forty-one

Emily Pinsent had been trying to reach Ray all day. Had she asked any of the nursing staff they could well have told her that this was futile. They watched the news, saw the reports, but only those directly involved with Emily and Damien recognized the man as one who had visited in the past week and they thought it best to say nothing for fear of upsetting her. And, anyway, Emily rarely took in what was said to her so there seemed little point.

And Emily had other things on her mind. Damien's condition was deteriorating and Emily was afraid for the first time that her battle was a lost one.

In truth, Damien had been getting worse for the last few months. There had been a time when at least he had breathed unaided. As time flowed on, that had finished and Damien been put upon a ventilator. Now it was clear even to Emily that the machines that kept Damien technically in the land of the living were failing in their task. There was a new urgency to their rhythm, an intensity to their song that Emily knew was different.

The doctors admitted to her that Damien was failing. That organs that had previously seemed to be at least intact for all that they could not function without help were now unresponsive even to the artificial stimulation. That her son was not 'there' even in the limited sense she had perceived him to be only a week ago.

And she turned to Ray, someone who'd tried to understand. Who'd been there for her, she felt. Some memory of what he had told her about Martin being ill permeated deeply enough into her consciousness that she knew Martin was not available in her time of crisis, and now, Ray had gone too. Fallen from Emily's world as surely as if he had never been.

Finally, late in the afternoon, when her efforts had foundered yet again and when her attempts to obtain advice from Frida Appleton had also met with failure, Emily remembered the older woman Ray had brought with him and how she had scribbled her name and number on the A4 pad Frida had been using for communication with Damien.

She called her, looking for Ray. Told her about Damien. 'I think he's leaving me,' she said and she sounded so bewildered by it all that even the hardest of hearts would have melted for her. And Gladys was never possessed of a hard heart, even when she knew that sometimes she ought to cultivate the appearance of one.

Gladys arrived at the hospital just after six to find Emily sitting by the bed and holding Damien's hand. She was singing to him, the songs of childhood she had hummed to get him off to sleep. Snatches of half-remembered rhymes and little bits of childish poetry she delved from those places in her memory where everything was warm and glowing with sunlight and Damien was whole and small and under her care and nothing in the world could do wrong by him.

And Gladys knew that there was nothing *she* could

do but sit by and hold the mother's hand and wait quietly as the doctors suggested Emily call Damien's father and that they switch off the electronic noise that sustained the boy and just let him die.

'I don't believe he's still in there,' she told Emily gently. 'I didn't believe that, not from the first time I saw him lying there.'

'Where then,' Emily whispered. 'Where is my son?'

Gladys took her hands and held them tightly in her own. 'I can feel him,' she said. 'I can feel him, so close to you. He's never very far away but he's not yet passed over into spirit either, so I don't know how to reach him for you.'

Emily gazed at the older woman with her eyes full of tears. 'And when he does?' she asked. 'When he does pass over? Will you be able to talk to him? Will I?'

'I don't know,' Gladys told her. 'We can never know. But Damien loves you and he'll want you to know that, so I believe, yes. I believe you'll be able to talk to him, that you'll feel him with you every step of the way until you're ready to go on again.'

Emily bowed her head and wept. 'It's been so long,' she whispered. 'I've felt like I'd be betraying him if I let them . . .' She jerked her head towards the machines. 'But now, somehow, I know you're right. My son is gone and I can't sit here waiting for him to come back to me. Not any more.'

Even if Phil and Sarah had driven all day they would not have found Ray's car. It was eighty miles away on the

East Anglian fens, parked in a lay-by close to Whittlesey and Flag fen.

It had been spotted by a routine police patrol early in the day. When it had been noted again that afternoon, with, on closer inspection, the rear number plates missing, they'd run a check to see if it was stolen and had discovered that it had been flagged for immediate notification.

What the car was doing out in the middle of nowhere was at first a mystery, until George, who'd had longest to study Max's notes, remembered that Max had lived out that way for a couple of years before his last prison sentence and even held down a job for a while at a fruit nursery of all places. The location of Ray's abandoned car was not fifteen miles from Max's last known address.

Max had indeed been looking for a quiet place. One where he was unlikely to be disturbed.

So, where were they now?

As calmly as he could and with as little drama, George told Sarah what they knew about the man that they believed had taken Ray. Sarah sat in silence and absorbed it all, sitting quite still and gazing straight ahead until George found himself willing her to speak.

'He didn't kill him last night,' George said finally. 'There's still every chance, Sarah,' but he knew better than to lie to Sarah Gordon. A chance was all there was, and the truth lay between them like some solid block of fear while Whissendine drove and said not a word.

The car had first been noted at eight that morning but had almost certainly been there for hours longer. At night the roads would have been almost empty and, with no traffic to slow them down, even at ordinary speed they could have reached the spot by, say, midnight or a little after.

Would Max have had another car waiting? Or would they have left on foot? George was betting on the second. If the first option were true then Ray could be anywhere by now and their chances of finding him, already slim, were almost non-existent.

If they had left on foot where would they have gone? There'd have been little traffic and few pedestrians to take note, even if they'd kept to the roads. Cross-country in that area would not have been an easy option. It appeared from the map to be mostly farmland, but George and Sarah, who both knew the area fairly well, knew that the drainage which maintained the fields in usable condition meant the maintenance of deep dykes or fleets which criss-crossed the landscape and made travel by night dangerous and unpredictable unless you knew where you were going.

There were various villages marked on the map but the scale wasn't large enough for either of them to gain a real perspective, sitting in the back of Whissendine's car with it stretched out between them.

'At least we have a starting point,' George said.

In Redfern, Martin dreamed, and this time Ray was with him, sitting beside a shallow stream in the centre of the wood. He had his shoes and socks removed and his trousers rolled to mid-calf and his feet dangling in the clear cold water.

'It's nice to have you here,' Martin told him. 'You know, I saw a trout in a pool upstream of here. Beautiful thing. It broke surface to take a fly and the colours on its scales rippled in the sun. I swear to you, Ray, it was like a rainbow arcing from its back and flaring right the way across the water. I wish I had my rods with me.'

'You fish? I didn't know that. I never had the patience for it. My idea of fishing is sitting on the bank with a glass of beer and a good book and watching someone else not catch anything.'

Martin laughed. 'You've got yourself a deal,' he said. 'I fish. You read and we'll share the beer.' He frowned. 'I should have asked Damien,' he said softly. 'I can't imagine there wouldn't be a tackle shop in a place like this and a library. And there's bound to be a pub. Can you imagine, somewhere as pretty as this and no pub?'

'No. Wouldn't be right. A nice old pub and a game of cricket somewhere in the background.'

'You like cricket? I'd have had you down as a rugby man.'

'I didn't say I *liked* cricket,' Ray objected. 'But I like the sound of it. Distant calls of not out or whatever it is. Willow on leather. Church bells chiming the hour.' He sat back, leaning against a tree whose roots grew right down into the water. 'Bound to be a pub round here,' he confirmed. 'We'll look in a little while.'

And Martin nodded. Later. There was plenty of time here where the afternoon was always blue and the sun shone the way you thought it did when you were just a kid and it was the middle of July and the holidays stretched for ever into time.

Chapter Forty-two

At six that evening Sonia Dattani made her evening rounds. Sunil had come over to meet her and to decide whether they would spend another night in the safety of Redfern or go home. Sonia knew that Sunil would like to sleep in their own bed that night but she was inclined towards the former. The new therapy had begun for Martin and she really wanted to stay and monitor him, an option she told herself was simply professional curiosity and not because she disliked Dr Oliver so intensely that she couldn't bear the thought of him succeeding in Martin's treatment where she had failed. She explained this in a rather shamefaced way to Sunil.

'You know you're being stupid about this, so what do you want me to say? There's nothing more you could have done for your patient. You didn't have the medication, so of course this Dr Oliver stands more chance than you did. As to not liking him, well, no one can like everyone.'

Sonia had laughed then, releasing some of the tension that had been twisting her gut all afternoon. 'You're probably right,' she said and they compromised on their arrangements. They would sleep that night at Redfern so that Sonia would feel safer and also be close to Martin, but they'd sneak out for an hour or two to eat at one of the local pubs.

When Sonia went down to her office a little after six

she was surprised to find Ian Oliver there using her computer. The modem winked at her from the desk.

'Um, you said I could send an email,' he said.

'Oh, sure. I'll just grab what I need and leave you to it.' She had forgotten her earlier invitation to him to use the facilities of her office, a courtesy she felt obliged to extend despite her aversion to the man.

She went around her desk to fetch the files she needed from the cabinet. When she turned back towards him, Ian Oliver was standing up, blocking her view of his message on the monitor.

'I'll be up in a minute,' he said. 'To see Martin.'

'OK, no rush.' She shrugged and headed for the door, thinking his behaviour a little odd. But then people did get a bit protective of their privacy, she reminded herself. Sonia wasn't too keen on being overlooked when she was online, though in her case it was worry that someone would see her get something wrong. Technology of the medical kind she could master easily. But something that she was convinced could lose a day's work just because she pressed the wrong key – that she was still very wary of.

He was an uncomfortable man though, she thought. Uncomfortable both to be around and, she felt, with himself.

She put Dr Oliver out of her mind and finished the evening ward round, calling last to see Martin. Steve was chatting to him as he often did.

'He's looking better, you know. I'll swear he turned his head towards me when I touched his hand. You think this will work?'

Sonia nodded. 'I hope so. There are a lot of people waiting to talk to Martin if and when he finally wakes up.'

'I'll bet there are.' He patted Martin's hand gently. 'You're a key witness, my friend. A very important man, isn't that right, Dr Oliver?'

Sonia looked up, confused, and saw Ian Oliver standing in the doorway, a strange look on his face.

Chapter Forty-three

Phil had not gone with the others to East Anglia, instead he had been dispatched to talk to Winter, taking with him the new evidence from the website and an overview of what Dr Oliver had told them that afternoon. Winter listened as much as he talked. He didn't recognize the man who fronted the website but he suggested that his appearance may well have been altered anyway.

Winter was fascinated by the back door through the Angel picture. 'Want to give it another try?' he asked.

'What? From here?'

'Why not?'

Phil nodded. 'Look,' he said, 'I've been thinking about the history files and about them acting like a key to unlock this site, or like a password to keep you logged on.'

'Yes?' Winter nodded encouragingly.

'How about the Psycotrex website? If we visited that first? Angel Eyes made such a big thing of using their material, it seems it might make sense.'

Winter nodded eagerly. 'You might have something. Anyway, there's nothing to lose.'

The official Psycotrex site was slick and glossy. Phil recognized the images from the video he had seen on the Angel site, though the building had expanded, with a new lab block added and an enlarged front entrance since the other video had been made.

From there, they logged on to the Angel site. The man's face appeared first, filling the screen and giving his smiling welcome, then the split screen and the earlier promotional shots of the Psycotrex building began to roll. This time, they got further and it looked as though Phil had been right in his guess. The dialogue voiced by the site's talking head, the blond man with unnaturally blue eyes, in no way matched the scenes running on the other side of the split screen. They had been made, Winter guessed, by Psycotrex to interest new investors in their product, though he was at first mystified as to why it should be used on this site, unless as a snide attack upon previous employers. Slowly, though, he realized that this was a promotional video intended for use with B1436, the drug being prepared for marketing before the tragedy it caused had begun to emerge. Twice the test number appeared in the frame, as one or other lab-coated participant in the promotion directed the viewers' attention to the test result.

'Of course,' the added voice told this new audience, 'they didn't have what we have. The faith and vision it took to grasp the seeds of victory from the fields of defeat.'

'Look,' Winter said. 'There's our front man.' The blond man with the blue eyes appeared in the original film, shaking hands with two white-coated men. 'That's Wilson, the empoyee they kicked off the team,' Winter commented, recognizing him from pictures Phil had shown him.

But Phil was staring at the man standing beside him.

'Ian Oliver,' he said.

'What? The doctor advising at Redfern?'

Stunned by what he saw, Phil nodded, already reaching for his mobile phone. 'But he told us he never worked with Wilson. That he knew nothing about B1436 until this morning, when he was told to assemble the notes. That he recognized it from Dr Dattani's query just because he ran a check against filed records. If I'm reading this right, Dr bloody Oliver was co-creator of B1436.'

Chapter Forty-four

Ray Flowers lay on his side with his arms tied tightly behind his back. His fingers were numb. He tried to get the blood flowing back into their frozen joints but they didn't seem to want to respond and the rest of his arms weren't doing much better. He'd woken up like this some time ago, but drifted in and out of consciousness for quite some time longer, struggling back to some sense of reality. It had been the pain in his arms and shoulders that had finally helped him to complete his journey, that and the feeling that his entire body had been worked on by someone with a baseball bat and a finely tuned grudge.

Dimly he recalled, or thought he recalled, being thrown down a flight of steps and hitting his head on something at the bottom, but the memory was so transient and so dream-like that he wasn't sure he had it right. It would account for the pain though, he supposed. For the all-over bruised feeling and for the greater feeling of agony in his right shoulder when he tried to move. Dislocated, he guessed. The thought that it might be broken crossed his mind, but he tried to drive it away. A broken shoulder would reduce his chances of fighting even further.

Ray struggled to sit up. He'd tried it before but the pain had made him pass out again. He tried now, rolling over onto his back and pushing with his feet until his head came up against the solid wall, then pushing again and twisting his head and body side to side to wriggle himself into a sitting position. It all took a very long time and the agony in his shoulder caused him to halt many times before he finally succeeded. But the screaming pain only increased with his change of posture. Sitting with his back on the wall seemed to drag down upon his injured arm and pull it even further out of position.

Ray was familiar with pain. Burning of your own flesh, he reckoned, had to be the worst kind of torture. But this was coming close and he half wished that the numbness in his fingers and forearms would spread upwards to his shoulders and upper back. It might at least make his breathing easier.

As he sat there, trying to see through the thick blackness that filled what he guessed must be a cellar, he analysed his various hurts, trying to identify them, to separate them out from the general blur of discomfort that confused his senses. In addition to the shoulder, he guessed he'd bust a couple of ribs. It hurt to breathe, stabbing into his side. He'd broken ribs before, falling off a wall when he'd been fooling about with his teenage friends, but that had been a long time ago and even in his most vivid memories it hadn't hurt like this. The straightjacket of his bound arms didn't help, restricting his lungs and forcing him to take breath more often, and his nose felt swollen as though he'd been thumped. And the breath coming in through his mouth was damp and chilled and burned in his lungs.

What burned even hotter was his anger at himself for

being caught by Max. His mind had been elsewhere driving home, the dark road commanding a good portion of his attention and what was left back with Emily Pinsent and Damien. He'd seen the lights of the other car on his rear view, losing them as he rounded the bend, then appearing once more as the car followed. It seemed to Ray that the driver was going too fast for the road, twisting and awkward even in daylight with three or four blind bends. He pulled up at the junction and began to look for traffic, taking his eyes off the lights behind, then becoming fully aware of them again as they filled his rear view, dazzling him just before the car rammed into his rear.

More irritated than anything else, Ray got out, planning on giving the fool of a driver a piece of his mind. The lights from the other car were still full beam when he got out and Ray added that fact to the list of failings he was about to deliver. The other driver was in turn hauling himself out onto the road.

'Turn your bloody lights off,' Ray told him, trying to shield his eyes from their glare. Then the other driver stepped in closer. Max might be a knife man by preference, but he knew how to threaten with a gun.

There had been times when Ray had thought about running, but he knew he couldn't outrun a bullet and he had to assume that this man was a decent shot. So he got back into his car, Max climbing in behind him, and he drove, aware that the gun pointed all the time at the back of his seat.

Eventually Max had told him to stop the car, get out and then turn around. He had a pair of quick cuffs in his hand, the sort with a solid bar rather than a chain between. Now standard police issue, they had been chosen because even with only one wrist cuffed it was possible to control a prisoner. A twist of the cuffs and the wrist bones separated, causing intense pain.

Max captured one wrist, then demanded the other hand, cuffing Ray tightly behind his back. They had walked for, Ray guessed, about twenty minutes and arrived at a building that Ray could not make sense of in the dark. Max opened a door and pushed him through, then slipped a loop of rope around his forearms and proceeded to tie him just below the elbows, dragging his arms as tightly as they could be made to go. Then he'd opened another door and pushed Ray through. Ray had tumbled down the stairs, unable to reach out and break his fall, hitting his head on something at the bottom. He remembered nothing more.

And in all the time of driving, walking, everything, Max had barely said a word.

Chapter Forty-five

Phil had driven to Redfern as quickly as he could with two carloads of uniformed officers sent to join him there. Whissendine had called ahead, warning the gate to let them straight through. No sirens, nothing to alert Dr Oliver, nothing to cause him to run. He tried to get hold of Sonia Dattani but she was not answering her phone, and at that time of night there were few others about to take her call for her.

Sonia Dattani was worried. Unable to shake off her unease, for the next hour or two she had kept watch on Dr Oliver. When she had seen him go back up the stairs to Martin's floor, she had followed, and now stood watching him on the monitors from the nurses' station as he went into Martin's room.

'What are we watching for?' Steve asked her.

'I hope nothing. I hope we can just slip away and you can think what a fool I am. But . . .'

They watched Ian Oliver check the patient notes at the foot of the bed and note down Martin's obs, just as Sonia or a member of the nursing staff would have done. Then he moved around so that his back was to the camera, blocking the bed from view.

'Damn,' Sonia muttered. 'Come on.' She gestured to Sunil to follow and they moved softly down the hospital corridor, drawing almost level with the room. If nothing untoward was happening, they could simply say they had come to say goodnight to Martin on their way out. But if something else was going on . . . Sonia wasn't sure what they would do but they would have to do something. Not certain enough of her worries to have notified the clinic security, she knew that they were on their own. She looked back towards Steve who signalled that he still couldn't see anything on the monitors. She moved into the doorway. Ian Oliver stood beside the bed still blocking the view of the camera. In his hand was a syringe.

'What are you doing?'

He looked up, startled, but recovered himself quickly for a man who always seemed such a bag of nerves.

'Just administering the evening dose of his medication.'

'He's had enough for today. You told me that yourself earlier.'

'I've reconsidered. I think I'm the expert here, Dr Dattani.'

'And it's clinic policy that no medication is administered without a pharmacy nurse or senior member of staff being present. In case of audit, you see. Everything is always double-checked.'

'I'm sorry. I didn't know that. I don't work here, do I?'

Sonia could feel Sunil and now Steve close behind her. She could sense their unease, matching her own now.

'How many ccs, doctor?' She took the notes from the foot of the bed and flipped to the right page as though to note it down.

Steve had followed her into the room and now shifted to the other side of the bed.

'And what do you want?' Ian Oliver asked him irritably.

Steve smiled at him innocently. 'Dr Dattani thought that someone should stay with Martin tonight,' he said. 'Monitor him more closely. Experimental drugs carry a risk, Dr Oliver. I'm sure you'll agree. It would be tragic to get this far and then have something go wrong.'

'Now,' Sonia repeated. 'How many ccs was it, Dr Oliver?'

Ian Oliver lost his nerve. He lunged at Martin with the syringe, but Steve grabbed his arm. Sonia dived in with the clipboard she was holding, hitting his hand sharply with the edge of it. Surprise as much as pain made him let go and the syringe dropped to the floor.

Oliver hit out, catching Sonia on the temple, a glancing blow with his fist that sent her spinning, but Steve still had a tight hold on his other arm and Sunil had joined the fray, grabbing him on the other side and wrestling him to the ground. The sound of feet thudding along the corridor told them all that someone had witnessed the whole fracas from the monitors at the nurses' station along the hall, and a few seconds later Phil and two uniformed police thundered into the room.

'You got him?' Phil was astounded. 'How did you know? Whissendine said he couldn't reach you.'

'Whissendine?' Sonia asked breathlessly. 'I don't understand.'

'Then what?' The two uniforms had Oliver now, though Sunil seemed a little reluctant to let go.

'I was worried about him,' Sonia Dattani explained. 'Something didn't feel quite right and so we watched him come up here. He was going to inject Martin, even though I knew he'd had his full allocation for today. I challenged him.' She shrugged and grinned at Phil, high on the adrenalin of the moment. 'His behaviour was, I thought, a little unprofessional.'

'This is standard practice for dealing with unprofessional conduct, is it?' Phil asked, regarding a dishevelled Ian Oliver who had acquired a bruised jaw and a rapidly purpling eye somewhere along the way.

'It was really quite invigorating,' Sonia Dattani told him.

Chapter Forty-six

Ray's eyes slowly adapted to the dark. A tiny amount of light filtered in under the door at the top of the steps but it was barely enough for him to even define the location of the stone walls that surrounded him. The air felt damp against his skin and he was very cold. He tried hard to get the circulation going in his body. His exertions earlier when he had managed to sit up had revived him a little. Enough to shiver at any rate, not enough to generate any lasting warmth. The effort he had put into moving earlier had made him sweat, the perspiration cooling rapidly and lowering his temperature once again. Ray knew he must have been lying unconscious for a long time and he knew that, chilled as he was, he was at risk of hypothermia. He tried to remember if he'd ever been given any advice on how best to survive the cold and was reminded of some television programme he had once watched which tested a stunt man's reactions to cold, both keeping still and moving about. Trouble was, he couldn't for the life of him remember which had been the best thing to do and, truthfully, the thought of forcing his body into an upright position was not one that filled him with joy.

Why was he still alive? That was a conundrum in itself. He could only assume that Max wanted to do whatever he planned somewhere undisturbed, although, he was reminded forcibly, that didn't seem to be one of

Max's primary concerns. He had, after all, killed Miriam with her parents sleeping only yards away in the family home.

He thought about what he knew of Miri's death and Whissendine's graphic descriptions. It didn't fill him with confidence about his own survival. Almost, he wished, he had hit his head harder when Max had thrown him down the stairs. Staved in his head or broken his neck, saved Max the trouble he would take over the killing of him. Generally Ray was no coward, but now he was afraid. Terribly, blood-chillingly afraid.

When Phil called Whissendine to tell him that they had Ian Oliver in custody he was poring over a detailed map of the area with the detective in charge of the night's operations.

'That's good news,' he said. 'Very good news.' But as he signed off he knew that it was little help to them in finding Ray Flowers. There was no telling that Ian Oliver even knew about Max, and even if he did would volunteer the information.

They were counting on Max having walked Ray away from the car. On Max not knowing they had found it. On Max not even considering that they would have been looking for Ray anywhere but the Leicester area, if they were looking for him at all.

Where he might have taken him was another problem even in an area as sparsely populated as this. If Ray was still alive then there was a good chance Max had him stashed away in a barn or one of the deserted buildings that dotted the landscape, homes for farm workers in those days long gone now when farming in East Anglia had been labour intensive instead of simply intensive.

If Ray is still alive, Whissendine thought. If he wasn't, there were quite literally thousands of acres to search and mile upon mile of deep-cut wide canals or fleets that drained the land and kept it workable. He thought George and Sarah had been exaggerating earlier when they had talked about the depth and extent of these waterways, but now, looking at the local map, he realized that their estimates had probably been conservative and some of these informal waterways were deep enough to have been navigable in earlier times.

If Max had killed Ray and dumped the body there was no telling when he would resurface. Probably quite literally resurface, as the water level dropped in the summer. Whissendine tried not to think of him being found, bloated and unrecognizable, in one of the waterways at the height of summer, though the possibility kept infiltrating his mind and, looking about him at the busy, hastily improvised incident room set up at a local garden centre close to where Ray's car had been found, he knew he wasn't the only one thinking that way. The one thing in their favour was that Max seemed to like to take his time over killing whenever possible. He was not usually a bullet-in-the-brain sort of man. He liked to keep things long and slow and that . . . that might buy them a little time.

There were still half a dozen different locations in a five-mile radius that might hide Ray and his would-be killer. They had already checked out two farms and the garden centre they had borrowed for their incident room. It was bizarre, Whissendine thought, this scene laid out in front of him, with maps spread out across sacks of potting compost and weighted down with river-washed pebbles usually sold by the bag. To see the clematis stacked against the far wall forming a floral screen for the young woman acting as collator with a laptop balanced on display shelves. But they'd done well in the few short hours they'd had, Whissendine acknowledged, and the longest part of that time had been spent seconding every officer, every beat bobby, every armed response unit they could beg, borrow or steal from surrounding divisions, and bringing them here as quietly and unobtrusively as possible.

For that, Whissendine was thankful of the dark.

Word came in that three of the locations checked out as empty. These were Dutch barns used for winter storage and no one had really expected Max to choose them. They were too exposed and too often visited for that. Two locations left then, and Ray might be at neither of them. Whissendine listened to the briefing. Both locations to be hit at the same time. Hostage negotiators at the ready. Helicopter back-up with its searchlight bringing daytime to any locations where dragon lights could not be used, and to track anyone who might decide to run. There was, of course, no guarantee that Max would be alone.

All things in readiness.

At nine fifteen word came that everyone was in position. Both buildings, a disused cottage and what remained of a mill surrounded by armed officers crouching in the cold.

And it was cold, Whissendine noted as he went outside. Cold as March in England could be, the threat of a frost hanging in the air and the flat landscape of the fens stretching out on every side.

Max had decided that he had waited long enough. The excitement he had felt at the killing of the girl had worn off, and his anticipation at this new prey was growing. It was rare for Max to act out his pleasures again in so short a space of time. Usually it was months between, longer even, and it seemed almost decadent for these two to have come to him so close together.

Max went down the cellar steps, a small torch in his hand, which cast a thin beam of light. He carried two larger lights in his other hand, ready to position as needed down below.

'Ah, you're awake,' Max said. 'Good.' He shone the light into Ray's eyes, dazzling him, and when he could see again Max was on the opposite side of the room, placing the lamps so as best to illuminate the space in which Ray sat. Ray watched him, feeling his heart race in anticipation, his breathing shallow and tight.

Lights positioned as he wanted them, Max drew a tool roll from his pocket and extracted from it two slender knives, laying them in front of the lamps so that the steel shone against the dark of the flagstones. Then he took a reel of tape from the same pack and tore off a long strip. He was smiling as he drew closer to Ray.

It was now or never, Ray knew. Now to find out if the attempts he had made to work his muscles had paid off. Max bent close and pressed the tape across Ray's mouth, pushing him back against the wall and leaning in close enough for Ray to feel his breath upon his face. Ray drew up his knees. His plan, such as it was, had been to wait till his assailant got in close and then throw everything he had into an upward swing of his legs, hope to catch the man off guard, and maybe, just maybe, gain himself enough time to get up the stairs and break free.

But it all happened too fast for Ray's fuddled brain and pain-wracked body to cope. His legs just wouldn't move . . . Max drew a third knife from his pocket and slowly, deliberately, began to slice his way into Ray's shoulder down onto his chest, cutting through the flesh like butcher's meat.

Overwhelmed by the pain, Ray, gagged though he was, was astonished by how much sound he could make as he tried to cry out. His nose swollen with bruises, his mouth covered with tape, he could not breathe. He felt his lungs bursting with the effort of getting oxygen into them and all thought he had of putting up a fight as soon as Max got close enough faded in the sheer effort it took to deal with pain and lack of air.

And then he saw it, something moving behind Max. A figure that he recognized but could not believe was real. Something in his eyes must have alerted Max because he turned, moved his body aside to look behind and that instant was all that Ray needed. He knew he couldn't win, but he wasn't about to go down without a fight. As Max shifted his weight, seeing for the fleeting instant, or thinking he could see, what Ray had seen, Ray kicked out with both legs and all the force that he could muster, sweeping at Max's legs and rolling himself sideways and onto his knees.

Breath hissed angrily from between his assailant's lips, but Ray had pushed himself onto his feet and he kicked out again, this time making contact with the man's side. Legs threatening to give way beneath him, the room swaying because of lack of air, Ray struggled to climb the stairs, knowing that Max was right behind, reaching out for his legs and grabbing at his feet, trying to pull Ray down.

And then the unmistakable sound. The helicopter overhead and the voice over the bull horn shouting for Max to show himself.

Ray kicked back again, making contact with something he hoped was Max. His vision was going now and the searing pain in his shoulder clawing at him like a giant cat. And he was bleeding heavily, he could feel it seeping from him, pouring down into the waistband of his trousers and soaking his shirt. Ray willed those outside just to storm the building. Get on with it and damn procedure and negotiation.

He felt the pain as Max sank a knife deep into his calf and pulled down. Then as he passed out, half heard the thud and hiss as the gas canister hit the floor of the room above and thick, smothering smoke billowed down through the open door.

*

'Ray, oh dear God, Ray!' Sarah's voice filtered through the network of pain and confusion. Something over his face. He remembered the tape and tried to pull it free, surprised for an instant that he could move his arms. Alarmed at the thought that Max had Sarah now.

Hands over his, easing his fingers away from the oxygen mask. Silence.

He surfaced in a hospital room, one that sounded like Damien's, and for a moment he thought that he was like the boy, in that limbo land between the living and the dead. It was a thought he could not bear. He called out, trying to tell them that he was alive, that he could hear, that he would rather die than live like that . . . no longer knowing if that were true.

'It's all right.' Sarah again. 'It's all right now. All over.'

'How did you find me?' His voice was slurred but she made out the words.

'We found your car. The local police pulled out every stop. There were two places we thought he might have taken you and then, there was this man, Ray, he went inside the mill and he called Max by name. He disappeared, but he won't get far. They're still looking for him.'

Ray tried to smile but it was just too hard. 'Won't find him,' he whispered. 'Won't find him, Sarah. I saw him in the cellar. It was Martin Galloway.'

Chapter Forty-seven

Ray was not well enough to attend Damien's funeral but Sarah went on his behalf, accompanying Gladys and Frida Appleton. It was a cold day, drizzling with rain and no one felt able to say very much. Micky arrived, together with two plain-clothed officers in tow, and told Sarah that he planned to go away, to stay with family in Italy for a while.

Micky brought white roses, placing them upon the coffin in the crematorium. A sad little bouquet and, Sarah could not help thinking as he arranged them, of the wrong colour.

She was glad when it was over and she could discreetly slide away. Whissendine stood by the crematorium gates and Sarah stopped her car to talk to him.

'Give you a lift?'

'If you promise not to frighten me. I've heard about you.'

Sarah smiled, something she still found hard. In the days when Ray had first been in hospital, they had worried for his sanity as much as for his physical well-being. He talked constantly about Martin, insisting that he had been there, in the cellar, distracting Max for just long enough for Ray to fight back. No amount of reasoning could persuade him otherwise and eventually Sarah had decided it was better not to try.

'How's Ray?'

'Improving. He seems . . . quiet though. He talks a lot about Miriam. I don't think he'll ever forgive himself.'

Whissendine said nothing. He wasn't sure that he would ever forgive Ray either. He was certain now that Miri was killed because she talked to Ray. Because, if Max's evidence was to be believed, Miri could identify Ian Oliver as the man who had supplied her with the drug that had ultimately killed Damien. Miriam had seen him that day, and his face was not one she would have forgotten. Oliver's name was on the list she had made for Ray. The complete one which they had recovered from Max's flat. She had called him Oliver and put a question mark beside it, but her statement told the full story, that their version of B1436 had come from him.

'If Ray had only come to me sooner,' he couldn't help but say it, even though it hurt Sarah, herself innocent of any blame.

'You think he doesn't know that?' she told him sharply. 'He's talking about resigning from Flowers-Mahoney. I think he might.'

'I wanted to tell you,' Whissendine said, changing tack. 'Wilson was arrested late last night. One of Oliver's leads finally got us somewhere.'

'That's good. And his backer? This Angel person?'

Whissendine shook his head. 'Nothing so far. We know now who he was when he worked for Psycotrex, but that means sweet F.A.'

She let him out of the car outside the police station and drove away feeling oddly lonely. Somehow bereaved. When she glanced back through her rear view, Whissendine was watching her and she knew that he was feeling much the same.

Ray visited Martin Galloway at Redfern about a month after. It was late April and the air filled with the promise of spring, the leaves greening in the weak sunshine.

Martin was sitting beside the window looking out towards the wood that surrounded the clinic. Ray pulled up a chair and sat down beside him. It was some minutes before Martin noticed him, but Ray had been warned of this. Martin's trip back to reality was likely to be one long delayed.

'Ray,' Martin smiled. 'It's good to see you. How have you been?'

How had he been? It was a good question but not one that could be debated with Martin yet. 'I'm fine,' he said, 'and you, you're looking well.'

'I am well, yes. It's lovely here. I never thought I'd be spending my retirement in a hotel with such good fishing.'

'Fishing?' Ray was a little surprised. Hotel? He smiled, feeling the scars stretching at the side of his mouth. 'What have you caught?'

'Oh nothing much yet,' he said. 'But yesterday I saw the most beautiful trout in a little pool not far upstream.'

They chatted for a little longer, but Martin's attention drifted easily and his gaze was drawn time and again towards the woods. Ray left after half an hour. He glanced back at Martin through the open door, wondering what it was he saw.

Martin watched them as they walked back beneath the canopy of trees, pausing to wave as they slipped back out of sight. Damien and Miri.

Martin Galloway waved back, and smiled.